FRAGILE
scars

A FRAGILE HEARTS STANDALONE

LILIAN HARRIS

Editor: Pretty Little Book Promotion

Proofreader: Horus Proofreading

Interior Formatting: CPR Editing

Cover: Jennifer Watson

AUTHOR'S NOTE

Below is a trigger warning for those who may need it. Please stop reading now if you don't want one.

This story contains graphic violence and sexual assault, which may not be suitable for some readers.

FOR EVERYONE WHO'S
WITH AN ASH BUT
DESERVES A DAMIAN.

It's never too late.

Damian
AGE 10

PROLOGUE

"**S**top!" Her blood-curdling scream pierces through my hearing. My pulse races violently, and my heart threatens to escape from within my chest. Covering my ears, I will myself to another place, another time, where neither of us are being hurt. If only it was that simple.

I hide in my closet as he hurts her. Again. Something heavy shatters in the living room, maybe a plate or a vase. I'm not sure what it is, but it causes my body to jerk, goosebumps prickling my face and arms.

"You fucking bitch, when I tell you to do something, you do it! Who the fuck do you think you are talking back to me? You did this to yourself, you cunt!"

"You're hurting me Kevin, please get off me. I'll do better, just please don't hurt me!" There's a loud crack, like skin on skin, which makes my mom cry louder. My heart hammers in my chest as cold drops of dread enter the pit of my stomach.

Whenever my father has fits of rage, Mom tells me to hide in my closet and not come out until it's over. So, the main reason I'm in here is because she asked. At least that's what I say to convince myself anyway. The real truth is, I'm a wimp. I can't even protect my own mother.

My father's an angry man who hurts her every chance he gets. He doesn't even need a reason; he just creates one. I don't know why she hasn't left him yet. Maybe she's afraid to walk away because he can find us, or maybe she's not strong enough. I think it's a little of both. I wish I had a lot of money, so I could take her away from this misery. We can go to another country and pretend to be other people. I always daydream of another life, but I always wake up here.

I don't remember a time when he hasn't made my mother bleed, whether with words or actions. He's evil and I wish he were dead more often than is probably normal. But I'm not brave enough to kill him. I'm not brave enough to do anything. I do know one thing though; I don't ever want to become a soulless monster like him, and a monster is exactly what he is. A son shouldn't hate his father with the amount of disdain I have for him. But how can I not? He may never hit me, but he hurts her practically every night. He's got a psycho switch, and once it's been flipped there's no stopping him.

"Get up and fight me, bitch," he yells.

"No, please enough." A sob strangles in her throat. My lips quiver, and I swallow the nausea that has now made a home in my throat. I can't imagine hurting someone I love like that.

I wonder if anyone will call the police this time. We live in a six-floor apartment building in Brooklyn, New York. There are many neighbors who are aware of my father's temper, but they don't get involved, they'd rather stay away from us. They only involve themselves if they believe someone's dying. Isn't it sad when people care so little about each other?

Last month, when the police were called, my father had bashed her head into a wall. That warranted calling the police, I guess. Yet, my mother howling like an injured animal? I guess not. I'm sure they're sitting on their comfortable couches watching The Sopranos or some shit. Their TVs blaring, blocking out the sound of my mother's screams as she begs for her life.

The last time, the police had left without an arrest. My mom told the officers she fell and refused to go to the hospital to get checked out. But at least he stopped hitting her. That night though, he made her sleep in the bedroom with him, even though she wanted to sleep on the couch. As I look back on that day, a painful realization hits me. She'll never leave him. All the times I've begged her to pack our stuff and go has been for nothing.

Suddenly, the door to my room opens and the floorboards creak under a light thud of footsteps as someone approaches the closet. My heart beats like thunder and my throat muscles tighten. I shut my eyes as tightly as I can as though that'll keep the monster away.

"Damian…" My mom appears through a large crack in the closet door and I release the breath I didn't realize I was holding. She makes her way to me and stops short in front of the door. "Whatever you hear..." she pauses, catching her breath, "don't come out. Please baby, just stay here." My eyes well with unshed tears and I nod, unsure whether she can see me or not. "I love you my boy."

I love you too, Mommy.

Seeing her this broken hurts me every time. She's not the same mom who smiles while making breakfast, or the one who asks me about my day at school. I notice her hands trembling as she places her open palms against her chest. I take in her appearance, from the blood trickling out of the cut on her cheek, to the bruises in the shape of his fingers forming around her throat. Please, let him stop.

My father follows her in, his footsteps stomping heavily on the wood floor, his face as red as the blood spilling from her cheek. *Leave her alone!*

"Where the fuck do you think you're going, bitch?" he asks, approaching her. "We weren't done talking!" I watch helplessly as he yanks her by the hair and drags her out of the room. Her whimpers grow distant. I hug my knees to my chest and silently cry for the both of us. I wish I was bigger. I bet I could've stopped him then. Why do I have to be so weak?

"You're going to learn your fucking lesson about who's in charge here. It sure as fuck isn't you."

"Please, Kevin," she begs, her voice splintering with tears.

"Shut up!" There's a loud thump on the ground like he just threw her down. *Mommy.* "You're fucking garbage, and it's time I dumped you in the trash." His tone lashes out at her, as another crack lands across her skin. "You're a good for nothing, lazy sack of shit. I can do so much better than you. You know that, right? You're not even pretty to look at anymore. Do you hear me, bitch? I'm talkin' to you!"

An eerie, unnatural silence follows for a few minutes. *Maybe he stopped hurting her?* Suddenly, my thoughts are interrupted by the loud boom of the front door slamming closed. I rub at the goosebumps pricking my skin, my knee bouncing rapidly. *What the hell is going on? Did he leave?*

Maybe she's just in the bathroom cleaning her face. I'm sure that's it. Yet, dread fills the pit of my stomach as I stand on shaky legs.

My feet take slow, hesitant steps out of my closet. "Mom? Mom are you there? I'm coming out, please answer me."

She doesn't respond. No one does.

I edge toward my bedroom door and gradually open it. Slowly walking out toward the small hallway, I pass the bathroom on my right. She isn't inside. Fear swallows me whole, but I continue my path into the living room.

I look around, my gaze hazy and unfocused. "Mom, where are you?" My lips tremble and I feel warm liquid trickle down my legs. I spot her feet behind the sofa. My knees lock in place, and I take reluctant steps toward her. "Mommy?" There's no answer. I've never hated silence so much.

I move to the back of the sofa and find her there, eyes looking up. She doesn't blink. She doesn't move. She just lays there. So still. A pool of blood has formed around her head and a thick shard of glass partially sticks out of her neck. The blood flows like a slow stream. Uninterrupted.

I'm paralyzed, but my body is shaking in place. *She can't be dead. Not her, no! Please, not her.* My mind races with thoughts of what to do.

I can't stop crying. *Mommy.* I run to her, ignoring the blood, and shake her. "Mom, Mom wake up, wake up now, please!" I continue to shout, but she doesn't answer. I pull at my hair and scream, "help," as loud as I can. But no one comes.

I get up, overlooking the blood dripping from my knees, and rush toward the phone on the end table, instantly dialing the police.

"9-1-1, what is your emergency?"

"My name is—Damian Prescott and my father just killed my mom."

Damian
20 YEARS LATER

ONE

I sit in front of her gravestone with a bouquet of lilies in my hand. Their smell reminds me of her perfume, the one she always wore. I trace the rough outline of her name, MARY PRESCOTT, and clench my hand into a tight fist until a dull pain rushes into my palm. The wound may be faint now, but it's still there, lying dormant like a sleeping beast. My mother was the best person I knew, and her loss still hurts even after all this time.

Once the police found my father, the case was easy to make. The judge gave him life in prison without the chance of parole and I hope he rots in there. I've never visited him, and I never will.

After Mom died, I lived with her mother. My grandmother and I did our best to heal each other. The first few years were the hardest. I blamed myself every day, but she wanted none of it. Grandma told me there was nothing I could've done. Had I tried, she said, he probably would've killed me too. I know she's right, but that realization doesn't diminish the hurt I still feel.

Grandma died last year, and I still miss her. But if there's a chance she's with Mom, I know she's happy.

I visit my mother every month to let her know I remember. Every hug, every kiss, and every lesson she taught me are all still there, etched into my heart like tattoos.

Closing my eyes, I try to hide the grief in my voice. "Hey Mama, I hope Heaven's treating you well today. I'm sure if there's a kitchen, you're making those blueberry muffins I used to love."

I rub at my chest and take a few deep breaths before I continue. "I'm doing well too. The business is still doing great. You would be proud of it. And no, there's no wife or kids," I chuckle. "Yeah, yeah, you're giving me shit, I bet."

I place my hands in my jeans pockets and look down onto the immaculately trimmed grass. "You know I can't risk turning into him. It's safer this way. Don't hate me, Ma," I whisper, looking up at her name. My throat closes painfully tight. I have to get out of here before I lose my tenuous grip on my emotions. "I love you. I'll be back soon." I lay the flowers down, look at her gravestone for one more second, and make my way back to the car.

As soon as I get inside, my cell phone vibrates with a text from Jax, my business partner and friend. Jax, Gabriel, and I started JDG Global Security four years ago when we retired from Delta Force. Our workdays are spent catering to high profile individuals and companies who need private security detail, or the ever so popular bomb sweep. Other times, wealthy people need us to travel with them to offer protection to and from their destination. The guys and I don't do it ourselves though, we have over twenty male and female employees for that. So unless a client specifically asks for one of us and pays the big bucks, we assign our crew the task. They're all ex-armed forces or law enforcement and very capable at what they do.

> **Jax:** Hey D, you coming out tonight or what? The bar is laid back. Not like I'm taking you clubbing. C'mon man! Plus, you need to get laid. It's been so long, I mean does your dick still work? Oh and don't forget, you gotta go see that apartment tomorrow.

Jax wants me to come out with him and Gabe to some place called Whiskey, but I hate going out. Because they're both single, they're always out pretty much every weekend, unless they have work to do. I'm more of a loner I guess. The bar and club scene just aren't for me, so I rarely join them. But I decide to throw them a bone this once. I could use the distraction from the painful memory of my mother's death, which always hits me harder whenever I visit her grave.

> **Damian:** Fine, jackass, I'll come. Stop worrying so much about my dick. If you want some, just ask. And yeah, I remember.

> **Jax:** Ha! You wish D. You're not my type. See ya tonight.

We arrive at the bar around eight, and order Heinekens and some wings. Jax was right, this is more of a pub than a club. I don't mind the vibe.

The guys are watching some game on one of the TVs sitting high around the bar area, while I look around. The door keeps opening and closing as more people pour inside. Music and loud conversations fill the room and I rotate in the swivel chair taking in the crowd.

My eyes drift away from the rest of the people to the two women sitting on the other end of the bar. The wide-eyed brunette looks at her blonde friend while tugging her full, red lip between her teeth and twisting the end of her ponytail around her finger. Wrinkling her brows, she nods her head and looks down at her drink.

I tighten my fingers around the cold bottle of beer and lift it to my mouth just as she looks up, her eyes burning into mine. I slowly turn back around and place the bottle down, all the while maintaining her unrelenting stare. Her lips part slightly, and she gazes intently as if searching for something she'd lost. Neither one of us looks away, our eyes fighting a battle for what feels like minutes but was probably mere seconds. I tell myself to turn around, but I can't find the strength. I'm not sure what's happening.

Her brows knit together, as if we're both thinking the same thing. Then she blinks, and just like that, the connection is broken. Looking back at her friend, they continue their conversation.

I take a big gulp of my beer, needing the cool liquid to douse the fire burning inside me. I have no idea what the hell that was about, but I know she felt it too. I continue to observe her from the corner of my eye, curious about what's making her so upset. Her gaze strays back to me, head tilting to the side as she looks at me with intense focus. I turn back to her, but she quickly turns away.

Thankfully, my two buddies are oblivious to what's going on, too busy complaining about a bad call an umpire just made. Before I can stop myself, I motion for the bartender and tell him to send both ladies another of whatever they're drinking. I grab a napkin and reach for a pen in my pocket. After writing something down, I fold the napkin and give it to the bartender, with instructions to hand it to the brunette.

I don't know what's making you look so sad, but whatever it is, it's not worth it. Hope tomorrow is a better day.
Damian

I sip my beer, watching her as she leans in, listening to the bartender who points in my direction. She looks over at me, her brow arching up, and quickly scans the note. Once she's done, she shoots me an intense glare. Her hand lifts, and for a second I think she's about to say hello, but instead she gives me the finger. *Well that escalated rather quickly.* Her friend reads the note and stifles a laugh.

"Why did that girl just flip you off?" Gabe asks as I turn toward him.

Jax chuckles, looking around for the girl. "Dude, you just got here, and you've already pissed a girl off? That may be a record even for you. How do you expect to get some?"

"Remind me again not to send women drinks."

Gabe studies me with a narrowed gaze. "Why would she flip you off for that? What else did you do, D?"

"Nothing serious. I only sent her a note telling her whatever's upsetting her wasn't worth it," I mutter. "Can we move on now? This is why I don't go out."

"Which girl was it?" Jax asks as he looks around the bar again. "Oh wait, never mind. I'm assuming it's the hot one throwing daggers at you. Well, guess you're not getting *her* number."

"Great, because I wasn't looking for it." I continue drinking my beer trying to ignore him.

"C'mon Damian," Gabe says. "In all seriousness you should try to get out there. I know you want to. You're not him, man."

He's always trying to convince me I won't turn out like my father. He wasn't there. He doesn't know how I lived. I wouldn't put my woman or our kids through that kind of life.

Funny thing is, he refuses to get serious with anyone himself. Suffering more than his share of damage from our days in Delta Force, along with being dumped by the only woman he ever loved once he returned, made him closed off. So now he refuses any real intimacy. I actually want it, but I won't let myself have it.

"Don't start. Not today. Let's just forget it and enjoy the game." They finally leave me alone after that, and I stop watching the mystery woman.

I'm almost ready to head out, when I hear a soft voice behind us. "Hey, sorry about my friend, Lilah." I rotate around to face the blond friend as she continues to speak. "She's had a tough day. Her boyfriend's a big-time jerk. Your note was sweet. I know she'll feel like shit later about giving you the finger, so I wanted to apologize for her."

"It's okay. Don't worry about it. But tell her she deserves better." Why would she be with someone who treats her like that?

"Yeah, tell her to dump his ass. Life's too short," Jax says. "Plus, we're all single here. What about you? Are you single?" he asks, wagging his brows. I glare at him, shaking my head. This guy gets more women than anyone I know and he's still constantly on the hunt, looking for more.

She bites her lip. Her hazel eyes sparkle as if asking when they can fuck, while she absently twirls her long hair with her finger. "I am, yes."

Jax has women hungry for him like puppies clamoring for their favorite snack. And he knows it too. The blond hair and ice-blue eyes will do that. I've yet to see a woman turn him down.

"My name is Lexi." He reaches his hand toward her and they

shake. "I'm Jax. Nice to meet you. This here is Damian and Gabriel." We both offer a tight-lipped smile.

"How about we exchange numbers and hang out another day?" Jax pulls out his cell phone before she even answers.

"Yeah sure, give me your phone." She takes it from his outstretched hand and programs her number into it. "Well, I should go before Lilah gets out of the bathroom and bites my head off for speaking with you guys." She waves goodbye and walks back to her seat.

Just then Lilah steps out of the restroom and scans the bar until her eyes land on mine. She struts toward her friend without taking her eyes off me, but suddenly, she loses her footing and falls hard onto the floor. Her knees hit the ground as I fly out of my chair and rush over.

"Are you okay?" I offer her my hand and she takes it. But just as quickly she withdraws, as if my touch burns her tanned skin.

Finally upright, her cheeks go pink while she plays with the hem of her tight, black tank top. Now that we're mere inches away, her eyes evade mine.

"Yeah, I'm just clumsy. Umm, thanks for that and the drink too."

Warmth spreads across my chest. "No need to thank me." I glimpse at her again but she's too busy fiddling with her shirt.

"Well, I have to go. See ya." Her voice is a tentative whisper in a crowded room. She turns and walks away, leaving me smirking in her wake.

I let my eyes wander a little. She's so beautiful. Her brown hair is up in a high ponytail, the ends curling in waves. She's a tiny little thing with a small waist and full hips. And those eyes? Glistening sapphires. It feels like I've seen them before, but I can't place them. Nah, not possible. A man doesn't forget a woman who looks like her.

I make it back to the guys just as she's heading out the door. She looks back at me, opening her mouth as if to say something, but walks out instead.

"You know D, since I have Lexi's number, I can put in a good word for you with Lilah. We all know I have way more game than you."

"I'm good. And even if I were dating, the girl has a boyfriend." I rub my brow, feeling a headache brewing. "You guys have to stop trying to hook me up. If I need some, I have no problem getting it."

"Okay, if you don't want her, then I do. She's hot as hell. Did you see that ass?" Of course I saw that ass, but I don't like that he saw it.

I clench my jaw, the anger mounting, its swirling vortex ready to swallow me whole. "Stop talking about her ass. But more importantly, keep your hands off of her. I'm not joking, Jax." I spit out the words through gritted teeth. "Don't even look at her. Her boyfriend's clearly an asshole. She doesn't need someone else messing with her."

Jax starts laughing his head off. "Damn! I knew you liked her!" He continues pestering me. "Listen man, I'm just glad you finally showed some real interest. Maybe she was the kick in the balls you needed. See what happens when you come out with us?" He punches me on the shoulder. "So many prospects you've been missing out on, D."

They've only seen me talk to two women and I barely had an interest then. It was just sex a few times. That's all. I never gave a shit about who they've slept with either, so seeing me this pissed at the thought of Jax touching her, well that's new territory for all of us.

I've had enough of tonight. I need to go home before Jax starts finding me more women. "Well, this has been a lot of fun. But I have to get out of here."

"Ignore him. Stay and hang out some more. He won't bother you again," Gabe says, glaring at Jax.

"Nah man, I'm good. I gotta go see that apartment tomorrow morning anyway." Jax's friend owns the building, so he set up an appointment for me. He's good for something after all.

All kidding aside, Jax is a good friend and the most loyal guy I know. He'd do anything for the people he loves. But that doesn't mean he isn't a royal pain in my ass sometimes. Okay, a lot of the time. But there's nothing I wouldn't do for him, for both of them.

The three of us have been through a lot together since we met in Delta training. We lost friends during our missions and that loss affected us all differently. Jax stopped taking life seriously, and aside from us and his family, he doesn't get close to anyone. His focus became random hookups, work, and partying. He hasn't changed much.

We say our goodbyes and I Uber it home.

I'm still thinking about Lilah on the drive back. What did her friend mean when she said her boyfriend was an asshole? Why was she looking at me so intently? I lean my head against the backseat, replaying the entire night. She's so my type. Girl next door with a little sass. I let out a heavy sigh. I gotta forget her though. This constant obsession will do me no good.

After I make it home, I jump in the shower. I hope this whole apartment deal works out. My current one bedroom is getting too small for me. I want to get some home-gym equipment, so I need the extra space. I have enough money in the bank to buy a house, but I have no desire for the suburban life. I don't want the things I can't have constantly glaring me in the face.

The hot stream of water beats over my head before crawling down my body. The steam fills the room while my thoughts once again drift to Lilah. The way she flipped me off was so hot. If she only knew what I wanted to do to her for that. Just picturing all those tight curves in the shower, pressed up against me... "Fuck."

I reach down and turn the cold water on, icing my dangerous thoughts. Then I quickly get out, throw on some clothes, and go to bed, hoping to drown out the thoughts of her. It's too bad that my dreams have a mind of their own.

Lilah

TWO

When people look at me, they probably see an ordinary woman with an equally ordinary life, and in some regards that's true. I've lived in Brooklyn since I was born, twenty-seven years ago. I did what many people do. I went to college, got my degree, and chose a career path. I wanted to go to law school, but I didn't want the debt associated with it. I decided becoming a paralegal was the next best thing. I got my paralegal's certificate and have been working for a small personal injury law firm in Manhattan for two years now. So, if you've been hurt and want to sue for monetary compensation, you know who to call.

My boyfriend and I've been together since our freshman year in college. We sat next to each other during our freshman orientation and the rest was history. He was the most handsome boy I've ever seen with the rarest colored eyes. Looking into his blue-green eyes felt as though I was drowning in the ocean and I welcomed the waves. But now, I'm fighting the current, swimming for all I'm worth to escape the riptide.

We weren't shy about our desires for one another. Being young and infatuated will do that. Our eyes danced with flirtation as we stole glances, not caring if we were caught. He's been embedded in my mind since the day we met, even when I wanted him gone.

I remember when he saw me looking at his full lips. He smirked in the sexiest way and I felt the warmth creep into my cheeks causing me to look away. I thought he'd hear my heart beat from where he sat; like it was frantically trying to leap out of my chest and bond with his. Being around him felt electrifying and I devoured the feeling.

After orientation, he introduced himself and asked if I wanted to go grab some coffee. I immediately agreed. I was a new student and already had a date. Life couldn't be better.

Our conversation was easy and playful. We talked about our plans after college and discussed our families. I learned he had an older brother and that his parents are both still together, unlike mine who divorced when I was ten. I haven't seen my father since. I was envious, yet happy he still had his dad in his life.

He liked touching me, our comfort growing as the conversation flowed for hours. I truly don't know what he saw in me. I never felt adequate or beautiful enough growing up, so to have an attractive guy pay attention to me felt amazing.

We spent almost every day together and our relationship blossomed into love quickly after that. Ash was my rock and study partner throughout my years in college. Even though we majored in different things, we still helped each other succeed. I don't know what I would've done without him. He's currently a successful accountant with a large firm in Manhattan.

He lives in Brooklyn too, in one of the homes his family owns. He's been wanting me to move in with him and has brought up marriage several times in the past, but it's not something I can picture myself doing. Not with him. Never with him.

I haven't been in love with him for years because his version of love hurts. It's a chronic disease with many painful side effects for which there's no cure. So I suffer in silence, aching everywhere. But it's my mind which hurts the most. That's where it all stays. It never leaves. Whoever said time heals all wounds, is a liar. Time doesn't heal shit.

Yeah, my life seems ordinary and probably picture perfect to everyone else. But no matter how normal someone's life may appear to be on the outside, it's probably not. Their beautiful façade may have ugliness trapped underneath. Sometimes faking it is the only way to survive.

Even though it's Saturday, Ash is stuck at work doing who knows what. Don't ask me about accounting because I know next to nothing about the subject, and I'd like to keep it that way. Ash says not to bother figuring it out because I'm too stupid to understand it anyway.

I grab my black yoga pants and a ribbed red tank top, and then get dressed to go get some iced coffee. I leave my hair cascading down my back and tousle it a bit for volume. I put on some BB cream and a touch of gloss, and am ready to head out the door, when out of nowhere, I hear male voices echoing in the hallway.

Inching toward the sound, I look through the peephole and find my super, Erwin talking to a tall man with dark brown hair with his back to me.

It's probably a potential new tenant. We've had an empty apartment across the hall from mine for a week now. The previous tenant, Pearl had passed away, so the building management is probably eager to fill it.

Pearl was a sweet, older woman. She had one daughter who lived in New Jersey, who came to visit as much as she could. Pearl had a home attendant during the day, but she was so lonely. I did what I could and visited her when I was home. We'd become close over the years, and she was even teaching me how to knit. I'm terrible by the way. Utterly hopeless. When her daughter had informed me of her death, I was so heartbroken. It's still sad to see her place so empty and devoid of life.

I unlock my door and walk out into the narrow, white hallway. The two men have just stepped inside the apartment, and I'm ready to head toward the elevator when I hear Erwin's rumbling voice. "Hey Miss Lilah, how are you?" he asks in greeting.

"Hey Erwin, I'm doing well. Going to get some coffee. Do you want anything?" He's a sweet, older man, who's been taking care of this building for twenty years now and continually does a great job. He always fixes a problem right away, instead of ignoring it like many other supers do.

"Nah, Miss I'm okay. I'm showing Pearl's apartment to a young man. He's probably taking it, so I wanted to give him a few minutes to look around."

"Oh, that's great. Let me know if you change your mind about the coffee. I really don't mind. You have my number."

I begin heading for the elevator, when all of a sudden, I hear the gruff voice that's been invading my mind ever since I heard it last night.

"Everything looks great, Mr. Jones. I definitely want it. When may I move in?" And just like that, I'm breathless. I let out an audible gasp and quickly cover my mouth. It can't be. Every nerve ending on my skin hums like it's playing a song I don't recognize.

His massive height and build is the first thing I notice as he makes his way out. He stops short, brows raised in disbelief. My mouth goes slack and I swallow the tight lump in my throat. We both stare, completely overwhelmed by what we're seeing.

Once the shock melts away, his lopsided grin appears on his lips. "Are you stalking me, Lilah?"

My eyes narrow, and just like that the spell was broken. "I highly doubt that's how stalking works, you know considering I live right here," I inform him, pointing toward my apartment. "And wait, how do you know my name? Are *you* some sort of stalker, *Damian*?"

He smiles brightly, revealing his perfect, white teeth, the corners of his eyes crinkling. "I don't think I'm supposed to tell you."

Hand on my hip, I glare at him. "Well now you have me curious."

"Tell Lexi I'm sorry." The smile never leaves his face.

"What did that girl do now?" I roll my eyes.

He tries to hide his amusement by covering his mouth with his large hand. "While you were in the bathroom last night, she told me how sorry you'd be about your very rude behavior and apologized on your behalf."

"Did she now? Well, can't say I'm *that* sorry."

He places his hands against his chest, pretending to be wounded. "Ouch!"

"So, I take it you two know each other?" I completely forgot Erwin was here.

"Oh, umm…" Heat creeps up my chest. I don't want him to misunderstand our playful banter and assume there's something going on.

Damian replies, saving me. "No, we don't. We just so happened to meet last night, completely by chance."

He glances from me to Damian. "Well, isn't that something."

The scrutiny is making me extremely uncomfortable. "It was nice chatting but…I gotta go. Bye." I turn around and hightail out of there.

He can't be my neighbor. I never thought I'd lay eyes on him again. What the hell are the chances? I couldn't get him out of my mind and now I may have to see him all the time.

When he helped me up yesterday, the contact was too much. I couldn't handle the nervous reaction he brought out in me. It felt like I was a fangirl meeting her favorite celebrity.

What's even worse is, he looks so familiar. But I can't figure out how I know him. I must be imagining it. There's no way we've met before. I would've remembered him.

As I'm walking away, I hear his deep, hypnotizing voice. "Bye, neighbor. I guess I'll be seeing you around." The laughter in it is so genuine. Ash and I haven't laughed together in years. I forgot how much I've missed it.

With my right arm high in the air, I do what I did when we first met. I give him the finger. I can't hide the wide smile that appears on my lips even if I tried.

Damian

What are the chances she'd be my new neighbor? Of all the people in the city and of all the buildings, she's the one. I thought my mind was playing tricks on me, but once I locked in on those blue eyes again, I knew she was real. She's even more beautiful in the daylight, if that's even possible.

I have to stop myself from thinking of her that way. She's my neighbor and completely off limits in every way possible. I grip the back of my neck and try to rub the tension away.

Erwin chuckles and shakes his head. He walks further into the apartment as I follow him in. "You like her." It's not a question, but rather a blunt statement. Am I that obvious?

Clearing my throat, I try to find the right words. "Oh no, it's not like that. I don't even know her."

"You can't kid an old man. I've been around the block a time or two." A flicker of a smile passes his lips. "She's a nice woman, Mr. Prescott, but she has a boyfriend. I can't say I like him very much though. He seems like a prick. A real smug you know what. Barely even says hello. When she's around him, her smile never reaches her eyes. That tells me everything I need to know." My jaw clenches as he continues. "I don't know what a sweet woman like that sees in a man like him, but it's not my place to judge."

An unsettling feeling washes over me. "I see." So far that makes two people who've mentioned her boyfriend is a cocksucker. The anger churns in my chest and I take a deep breath. He isn't my father and she's not my mother, I have to keep telling myself. This isn't the same situation.

Finally, a little calmer, I continue looking through the apartment, but it's her whom I think about. Now that I've seen her again, there's no doubt my heart recognizes her, even though my mind forgets. The first time I saw her I felt it too, but I put off those thoughts, too blinded by her beauty to see anything else, to feel anything other than how painfully hard she made me.

But now, there's no denying I know this beautiful woman. You know how sometimes you meet a complete stranger and feel as though you've known them all your life? Yeah, that's what happened when I saw Lilah for the second time.

THREE

A week passes before I see him again. I'm waiting in a long line, about to get my caffeine fix, when I catch a glimpse of him a few people behind me. Hoping he hasn't noticed my frantic gaze, I spin back around, facing the front. The café is loud and busy, so hopefully he hasn't noticed me. I hear footsteps approach. *Please don't be him.*

"Ignoring me?" His warm breath feathers my neck and my lips part instinctively. The proximity of his body, mere inches from mine, sends a shiver of pleasure to my core I haven't felt in forever. I whip my head around toward him, the movement sends a twinge of pain down my neck.

"Oh hey, I didn't see ya there," I mutter. I take a passing glance as he crosses his arms and can't help but notice how the fabric of his turquoise V-neck stretches over his bulging muscles or how the color makes his brown eyes pop. And those distressed jeans accentuate powerful legs too well. He's just so unapologetically masculine and sexy. I do my best not to stare and fail miserably.

"Promise I wasn't stalking you," he says. The corners of his mouth curl upward into a wide grin just as his hands rise in defeat.

"Uh-huh, sure you weren't." A nervous smile plays on my lips. "So, ah, did you get the apartment?" *Please say no. Please say no.*

He gazes at my mouth like it's his favorite meal but quickly looks up, trying to recover. His brows knit together like he's shaking off the lust-induced fog.

"Yeah, I did. That's why I'm here. The guys who were with me at the bar are helping me move in, so I popped out to grab us some coffee. I still have all the furniture and a crap-load of boxes to unpack." *Damn it.* I bite the inside of my lower lip. How am I supposed to live next door to that man?

The line finally moves some more, and I notice there are only a few people before us. "That sounds fun. Oh, and welcome to the neighborhood."

"Thanks." He taps his foot as he brushes a hand over his brown hair while we wait to be served. We're frozen in an awkward silence, the tension so evident we may as well have a neon sign blazing above our heads announcing it to the world. I can't be around him for long periods of time. He brings out feelings in me that have been long since bottled up and locked away. And from the way he just looked at my lips, I know I affect him too.

We finally order our drinks, and as I reach for my wallet, he places his hand over mine, causing every cell in my body to spark to life.

"My treat." The mischievous twinkle is back in his eyes.

"Well, thank you," I blurt out, still feeling a tingle where his skin touched mine. Silently, we grab our drinks and make our way outside. He looks like he's about to say something but stops himself.

And cue the awkward silence, the tension is so thick around us, it has me swaying side to side uncomfortably. I'm saved by the ringing of my cell phone. "I'm sorry, I have to take this."

"Yeah, of course. It was really good seeing you again. I'm sure I'll see you around." A ghost of a smile flashes on his lips, and then he walks away.

I turn around and rush down the street, increasing the distance between us. A huge part of me wants to run after him, grab his arm, and pretend I want to help unpack, all the while just wanting to spend more time with him.

The other part worries about the tumultuous emotions he brings out. *I have a boyfriend.* But do I really? Sometimes I don't know what I have anymore. Ash claims he loves me, but I know what we have isn't love. It's more of a life sentence without the possibility of parole. The bars on my cage tighten even more as each day goes by. I take a deep breath, trying to staunch the tears that are burning my eyes.

I look down at my phone. The missed call from Ash glares at me accusingly. I immediately call him back. He has very little patience, especially when he feels ignored. He answers on the first ring. No surprise there.

"Hey babe, where were you?" His tone cracking like a fire ready to ignite, the anger in his voice is clearly evident.

"Sorry. I was getting coffee and I couldn't get to my phone with the cup in my hand."

"Okay." He sounds suspicious. *Oh no.* "Make sure you're ready by seven-thirty tonight. We have reservations. And wear that red, lace dress I like. You know, the one with the open back?"

"Sure, no problem. I'm looking forward to our date." I hear the tremble in my voice. My blood is laced with utter dread, thrumming throughout my entire body, flooding it with apprehension. I'm hoping I sound more believable to him than I do to myself.

"Is everything okay? You sound upset." *Damn it*. His voice is colored by a touch of barely concealed venom.

"Yeah, sorry. I'm just nervous. I have this big case I'm assisting with on Monday and I have to do some research for it, but the coffee shop was so slow this morning it's really put me behind. I can't wait to see you." Every word is forged on a lie. "How's work going?" I ask, hoping to distract him.

"It's fine, just dealing with some bullshit paperwork. You had me worried for a second," he laughs nervously. "I thought you were still mad about what happened last night. I overreacted. I know that."

My body itches, like I just broke out in hives. *Overreacted? Ha! Is that what he calls it?* I brush off his so-called apology because there's no excuse for his actions. "I wasn't ignoring you. I promise. It's just this case that has me worried. I'm not ending things. What would I do without you?"

Live. I would live.

"I'll even put on those black heels you love so much." Maintaining his happiness is the only tool I have to keep the devil at bay. Most days I feel like a fraud and a pathetic failure. On the really bad days, I want to end it all. No more pain, or bruises, or lies built upon lies just to survive. Only peace.

"Mmm, be careful. We may never leave then," he says in a sultry voice. "Okay babe, I have to get back to work. See you tonight. Love you."

"Okay, see ya tonight. Love you too." I don't waste a second hanging up. The bile rolls in my stomach. My appetite now gone, I toss my coffee away in a nearby trashcan.

Damian

"So, let me get this straight. The hot girl from the bar is your neighbor?" Jax asks, laughing uncontrollably.

"I'm glad my life is so comical to you."

"Come on man, even you have to admit it's pretty crazy. Did you tell her you're in love with her yet?" he asks.

I threaten to throw the box I'm holding at him and he jumps back laughing his ass off.

"Are you going to help us unpack this shit Jax, or are you just going to sit there and gossip like an old woman?" Gabe asks. He's our referee, always sticking up for me whenever Jax teases me for not sleeping around or dating anyone. Gabe knows I can be a little sensitive about my lack of a love life.

Sometimes, I wonder what it'd be like to just say fuck it and find someone to settle down with. I want kids, the white picket fence, and maybe even a dog in the yard. I want everything. I think about that life a lot more than a man of thirty probably should.

I see my kids jumping on me as I throw them on the bed, their laughter filling my veins with sweet contentment. I picture holding my wife tightly in my arms as we sway in a hammock, watching our kids run around in a large yard. I imagine what it would feel like to have her body wrapped around mine after making love and how good she'd feel in my arms as we fall asleep. What would it feel like to have her warm hands cradling my face telling me I'm the only one she needs?

I'll never know.

That life will never be mine. Meaningless sex is what I have grown to accept. I don't even have much of that because it holds very little appeal. I rub the back of my head to ward off the headache I feel approaching.

We finish assembling the gray bedroom furniture and move on to the dining room. I wanted to upgrade what I previously had. I'm not much of a designer, so I chose whatever the salesperson recommended. She said something about glass being a modern upscale look, so I went with a glass table and white, upholstered leather chairs.

We move on to unpacking all my crap and as I open one of the boxes, I come to the sudden realization that in each scenario of the future I had just pictured, the woman I envisioned next to me was Lilah.

Lilah

FOUR

After a shopping trip and a quick run to the bookstore, I make it back home by six and start getting ready for tonight. Exiting the shower, I wrap myself in a towel and straighten my hair into a sleek style. My makeup is sultry, with black eyeliner on both my top and bottom lids. Some nude lipstick topped with lip-gloss completes my look.

I slip into the dress he requested. It has a heart-shaped open back that slides all the way down to my lower back, and a boat cut top that shows off my shoulders. It accentuates my narrow waist and larger hips to my liking, but I would've preferred to wear something else tonight. It's too bad he doesn't care what I want. Just a few more finishing touches to my makeup, and I should be done.

The loud tapping on my door interrupts my preparations. It's only seven. I hate when he's early. I slam my makeup brush down on the vanity a little harder than I should've, then push my chair back and head toward the unwavering sound. He taps again.

"I'm coming Ash, just give me a second." I unlock the door with mild trepidation expecting to see my boyfriend. Instead, I find Damian towering over the doorframe and my body grows hot all over.

"Wow!" His gaze drifts up and down my body without any hesitation. I feel so exposed. His heated gaze has stripped me bare. I swallow an achy lump, forgetting to ask why he's here.

"Your boyfriend's a very lucky man."

"I know," says a voice I didn't expect to hear. My eyes go wide and I freeze in place. Ash appears out of nowhere, acid dripping from each word. He arches a brow at me as he approaches us, lips forming a narrow line.

"You didn't tell me about your new friend, babe." He plasters a fake smile, but I can see the storm brewing in his eyes. A cold shudder drowns out the heat I felt only a minute before.

He eyes Damian with a brutal stare while draping his arm possessively over my shoulders. Damian doesn't so much as flinch. He matches his stare through a clenched jaw, I can see an angry vein pulsating in his neck.

This could end very badly. I need to get him the hell out of here before there's a fight. If the fear growing inside me is any indication, my body knows it too. I have to fix this.

"We aren't friends. He just moved in across the hall." They continue to stare at one another with such pure contempt. I don't know what to do, so I just continue talking. "I met him once, a week ago, when Erwin showed him the place. Can we go? I'm hungry." I wrap my arm around him and try to pull him away, but he's cemented in place.

He turns to me, a snake-like smile on his lips. "Sure, baby. Let's go. Bye, neighbor," he says condescendingly. "Say bye, Lilah. Don't be rude." He sounds so cold and menacing, it sends a chill down my back.

"Bye." My voice comes out small. Damian doesn't even look at me. Instead, he glares at him, not blinking once. His kind eyes have been taken over by darkness, threatening to devour Ash whole.

We turn around making our way for the elevator and it's then I realize I forgot my handbag with my cell phone in it. I don't care; it's not worth going back for, not unless I want a guaranteed fight between the two of them. As we wait for the door to open, Damian stands in the hallway still glaring, his arms folded over his chest. *Come on already, open up!* I'm so afraid they're going to come to blows if this stupid thing doesn't hurry up.

Ash chuckles and looks back at him with disdain. The elevator doors finally open and we step inside. Once they close, he stalks toward me. "Why was he at your door? Are you fucking him?"

"What?! Are you insane? First of all, I'd never cheat on you and second, I just met the man. I don't know why he knocked on my door because he never got a chance to get a word out!" I almost scream. "But wow, Ash, is that how little you think of me? We've been together for how long? And you think I what? Do nothing but sleep around in my spare time?" I turn away from him, breathing heavily. The elevator door opens, and I quickly walk out, not caring if he's following me or not.

He grabs my arm tightly, stopping me. "You're right. He just got under my skin with the way he was looking at you. Not that I blame him. I mean look at you, you're gorgeous." His eyes travel down my body.

"Come here, baby." He pulls me close. My eyes drill holes right through his. Fuck him. He had no right to pull something like that, but then again it's no surprise, nothing is anymore, not with the way our relationship has deteriorated.

He slides his hand up and down my open back, and slowly drifts lower to squeeze my ass. "Come on, let's go babe. Let's forget this ever happened." That's what he always says.

He takes me to a very fancy Italian restaurant on the Upper West Side. The decor's elegant from its black marbled flooring, to its large crystal chandelier in the center of the dining area. We're seated at a corner table, lined with a crisp white tablecloth and three votive candles in the middle. The waiter pulls the red upholstered chair out for me and I sit down after thanking him. He hands us our menus then returns with the drinks we ordered.

Ash hasn't said a word since we've arrived, which troubles me. His gaze flows down to his menu and I glance at him from above mine. "What are you getting?" I ask to lighten the mood.

He won't look at me. He keeps his eyes trained on his menu. "Steak, probably. You?" He finally casts a glance up at me. His neutral expression is completely unreadable.

"I'm not sure. Everything sounds good. Maybe I'll ask for a recommendation." The waiter returns promptly, and Ash orders a steak with a baked potato. "What do you recommend for a seafood lover? I'm having such a difficult time deciding." I smile politely at the young waiter who looks to be about my age.

"Well, I personally love the risotto with squid ink. It's delicious," he says enthusiastically.

"Oh, that sounds amazing. I never had squid ink before," a full smile spreads across my face, "but I can be adventurous."

"Coming right up guys." The waiter walks away with our menus and we're alone again.

"Have you ever had squid ink?" He looks up, dark and dangerous. The thunder's rolling inside those blue-green eyes. I can feel it like a storm on the horizon just threatening to break loose. He picks up the bourbon he ordered and downs it in one shot.

I gulp.

He grits his teeth menacingly.

What did I do now? He must still be mad about what happened with Damian.

Not having my phone, I have nothing to distract me from his glare, so I look down onto my hands. Our food arrives fifteen minutes later and even though it's delicious, I can barely eat. All I could think about is why he's so mad and how I can fix it.

He orders another bourbon, then another, and drinks them just as quickly as the first. "Babe, should you be drinking all that? Will you be okay to drive? We can call an Uber."

"Are you fucking telling me I can't handle my liquor?" His voice hovers right above a whisper. He clenches his right hand into a fist and places it on the table in front of him. His nostrils flare, and his eyes turn cold with scorn. "We're leaving."

He motions for the check, gives the waiter a few bills, and we're on our way out the door. He walks rapidly ahead of me. The car's conveniently parked right across the street.

I rush after him, hoping I don't fall in my high heels, but fear he'll leave without me. I enter the car just as he starts the engine.

"What's wrong, Ash? You've barely spoken to me the entire time. Did I do something to upset you?" My voice is hitched in nervousness. I straighten the lace of my dress just as he guns the engine.

Tightening his grip on the steering wheel, his knuckles turn white.

The car picks up more speed and he sends it erratically from lane to lane, flipping off the drivers honking at him. "We'll talk about it when we get back to your place." The words are said in a raised tone. My body is in panic mode, tingles spreading down my arms. I stare out the window, while my fingers massage my scalp and neck, trying to release the tension.

Once we arrive home, he gets out of the car, slamming the door. "Let's go." His voice shakes with barely controlled fury while my pulse hammers from within. I take a deep breath and slowly open the door. My legs are heavy as they make their way out of the car and toward my own personal hell.

FIVE

Lilah

We walk silently inside. He glares at the elevator doors as if condemning them to eternal damnation. His spine straight, jaw clenched, he looks ready to obliterate anyone standing in his way. We make it to my floor in no time.

As I'm fidgeting with my keys, trying to open the door, he stands behind me, his breath hot and heavy on my neck. I close my eyes and open the door. He pushes me in with his chest and locks up. Needing to keep my distance, I make my way to the bedroom without looking back, my entire body trembling. I know something bad is about to happen.

He quietly follows me inside and shuts the door. "Strip."

Stunned, I turn around wide-eyed. "What?"

He stomps forward, feet heavy, and lifts my chin with his thumb in one hard thrust. My eyes meet his, searching for something, anything that tells me what his intentions are.

His eyes bore soullessly into mine. "You heard me, I said strip." His voice is cold and even. "Don't make me ask you again."

"You're acting crazy. I'm tired. I'm going to bed." I slowly make my way past him to go to the bathroom in the hallway. A sharp sting of pain registers in my scalp before I even realize he has my hair clutched tightly in his fist. My heart pounds in my chest, and I try to jerk away but I can't. He's too strong. Cold dread enters the pit of my stomach.

He throws me on the bed and presses his knee hard into my belly. The pain is unbearable. I whimper in protest, an ache rising in my throat and a sob escapes.

"I didn't realize I was dating such a slut." He digs his knee in deeper. I cry out in pain. "First, you flirt with your neighbor and then you flirt with our waiter, *and* right in front of me!" My breathing is labored, as fear from the toxin in his voice seeps through my flesh.

"I think you enjoy getting a rise out of me. Is that it, baby? Answer me!" His palm lands hard on my cheek. My face is on fire while sharp knives slice through my gut. The tears spill openly now. I can't control the sobbing if I tried.

"You're hurting me," I cry out, but he ignores it. Had I been flirting with the waiter? No. No, this isn't my fault. Maybe I smiled too long? Did I make too much eye contact? *Shit*! I know how he gets. I should've been more careful. I'm such an idiot. When will I learn? It's hard to gauge how far he'll go when he's this angry. Sometimes, he stops before it gets out of hand, but other times, there are bruises. Lots of them.

I shake my head in protest. "I'm sorry baby, you're right. I didn't realize how stupid I was for smiling at him. I'm *so* sorry that I hurt you. Can you please forgive me, Ash?" I plead, hoping he'll at least take his knee off my stomach or maybe ease the pressure he's exuding a bit, but he only pushes it deeper.

"How many times have I told you not to flirt with other men?" he spits out, pulling my hair harshly. Everything hurts. *Someone make it stop. Please.*

He leans in closer until we're centimeters away, until I feel his breath on my face. "Do you like making them hard with those innocent fuck-me eyes? Do you picture them stroking themselves thinking of you?"

"Of course not! You're the only one I want, baby. Please, believe me!" The tears fall freely from the corners of my eyes, but he laughs, mocking me.

"See, the problem is I *don't* believe you." Letting go of my head, he makes lazy circles right between my breasts, and then he flattens his hand against my chest. It slowly begins to crawl up a little more each time and within seconds, he has my throat under his unrelenting grasp. He squeezes. Tightly.

My hands flail uncontrollably, the shock of being unable to breathe sends hot lava right into the middle of my chest. *Is this how it ends?* Maybe it's for the best, maybe it's the only way to escape him.

"Next time you decide to be a little whore, remember how easily I can kill you." That tone is frightening as he finally lets go of my neck and stands up. His laughter fills the room while my chest fills back with oxygen. I place my palms over my chest, feeling every heartbeat. I was wrong. I don't want to die.

"The look on your face! Do you not like being choked? I thought sluts like it kinky. I think we should try that next time we fuck. What do you think?" He backs up against the door and his gaze narrows. He slowly removes his belt and unzips his black slacks. My body goes rigid. *No!* He pulls down his pants and boxers, revealing that he's semi-hard. My skin crawls. I close my eyes, wishing this night to end.

"Take off your dress. Now. Then get on your knees. You can keep your panties on. I just need your mouth."

Nausea fills my stomach and I quell it. All I have to do is get this over with and he'll leave. *Please, leave,* I silently beg. He never sleeps over. He hates my small apartment.

I sit and begin taking off my shoes. "No, keep those on."

Wrapping my arms around my trembling body, I make my way to him. I give him my back while quickly peeling off my dress. I kneel in front of him as my body breaks into a tremor. He grips my hair painfully in his palm and pulls my head back, so he can see my face.

I wonder if he sees the shattered shell of the woman I once was. The one he met so long ago. *What happened?* I miss her, the girl I used to be, but I know I can't go back in time. This is who I am now.

He wasn't always like this. He was kind. He loved me. I felt it. It wasn't just in my head. He'd make me breakfast in bed at his place, and at night we'd cuddle and talk. He'd stare deeply into my eyes and devour every word I said, like I truly mattered.

He slowly turned into a monster. It started innocently, with sarcastic remarks whenever I talked to or so much as looked at other men. It then progressed to grabbing my wrists a little too hard or gripping my hair a little too rough. The violence escalated quickly after that.

Leaving isn't an option. He has something on me that could destroy my entire life, and I can't let that happen. I just can't. I face a dead end regardless of which road I choose, so I stay in this version of hell.

"Open your mouth." I do what he wants. I always do. He grips the back of my head and pushes himself hard into me. My throat's on fire all over again, reminding me he had just choked me. My eyes are heavy as more tears quietly cascade down my face.

Tightening his grasp on my hair, he pulls just enough to hurt me. "Nice and slow and use your tongue, or I'll do that again." *Please don't.* I can feel when he's almost done. I try to pull him out, but he keeps a firm grip on my head. My eyes close as his semen shoots into my throat.

"Mmm, that was good," he murmurs, sounding completely blissed out. Meanwhile, I try not to throw up. He pulls out, but I stay on my knees. Frozen. My eyes are glued to the floor while my heartbeat roars from within.

"Go clean yourself up. You look like shit." He finishes pulling his pants up. "I have to get home. I'll call you tomorrow, baby. Sorry if I was a bit rough on you. You know I only do it for your own good. If you flirt with the wrong man, he could do far worse. I love you." I feel a light kiss on the top of my head. Then he's gone.

Damian

SIX

I can't get the image of Lilah looking afraid out of my head. I wanted to dismember him, limb by bloody limb. He doesn't love her; it was obvious from the way he spoke to her. If I find out he hurt her in any way, he's dead.

I grab a full bag of trash and carry it out into the hallway to throw it out, but I abruptly stop and drop it beside my door. There's a faint wailing sound coming from across the hall. *What the fuck?* My heart races and I pace back and forth undecidedly for a few moments, torn between whether to check on her or to wait. Deciding I can't listen to those cries another second, I make my way toward her door. I knock a few times, but she doesn't answer. Her cries turn silent as my knocks grow more urgent.

"Hey it's me, Damian. Are you okay? Open up." Still no answer. *Shit.* A sense of dread rolls through me. "Fine, ignore me. But I'll be standing in front of your door until you answer. Once I see you're all right I'll go, if that's what you want."

A couple of minutes later, I hear the click of the lock. My gut tells me something isn't right. My spine stiffens and I'm on high alert. I take some deep, steady breaths before gently turning the knob and opening the door. My training kicks in as I take in the room. There's a small entrance table to my left with a sparkling, crystal vase still intact. The pink and yellow tulips taunt me with their beauty. Nothing looks out of place.

The living room is straight ahead, right past the entryway. I spot her sitting on a burgundy couch, the top of her head my only view. He isn't here. He would've made himself known by now. I'm sure of it.

"Lilah, what's wrong?" She doesn't make a sound. *She's not my mother*, I keep reminding myself. Just because I don't like her boyfriend doesn't mean he's anything like my father. But my gut's telling me something isn't right here and I always trust my gut.

I take tentative steps forward, hearing nothing but the tapping of my own shoes against the entryway tile. A few more steps and I'm right behind her. I stop, needing time to compose myself because I know I won't like what I find.

I round the corner and... *Fuck*. Her bloodshot eyes are expressionless, but brimmed with tears as she stares into nothing. The left side of her cheek is slightly red. But her neck? It's angry and bruised. The image of my mother stabbed in the same spot plagues my mind so violently it's as though I'm seeing her instead. *This isn't happening again.*

I'm back to that little boy who watched his mother suffer for years before he found her bloody and dead. But I'm not a little boy anymore. My body is that of a man, and I refuse to let another woman lose her life because of a spineless prick.

I move in closer, just a step, and she flinches. "Lilah…" She looks down at her hands, fidgeting with her thumbs. "This isn't your fault. I need you to know that." I don't want to scare her even more, but she has to know that the fault lies squarely with that motherfucker.

I recall all the times my mom blamed herself, as if the scars were her own doing. Fuck that. I won't let Lilah feel that way. Not if I have anything to do about it. I wish he was here right now. I'd take his fucking head off.

She brings her robe up trying to cover the bruises that I've already seen. "May I sit? I won't touch you. Not unless you tell me it's okay." The desire to comfort her is overwhelming.

She nods without lifting her head. I sit on the other end of the sofa and wait for her to say something, anything. The silence is deafening. My fists clench against my thighs and it's hard to breathe. I can't seem to calm down.

"I'm here. I'm not going anywhere." She continues to stare straight ahead. "I can be here all night if you want. I can stay on the sofa or the floor. We don't have to talk if you don't want to." She still hasn't looked at me, but I catch the fresh tears rolling down her cheeks. My heart shatters right there on her floor. Her eyes close as she cradles her arms around her body. I want to be the one to hold her.

"How about I make you some coffee?" I get up before she answers. I have to do something so I can stave off this unyielding need to break every one of his bones. But she's what matters right now. I'll worry about him later.

Lilah looks up at me, eyes glossy. Her head shakes side to side. "My throat hurts. I can't drink anything." Hearing her voice so hoarse turns my blood black, fueling my body until anger is the only thing I feel.

"I don't want to push you to do anything right now, but you can't let him get away with this." I know I told her we didn't have to discuss it but damn this is killing me.

She remains silent, staring off into nothing again. "Okay, we won't talk about this right now. How about we find something funny to watch." She bites her lip and nods. I lock her door, shutting off the lights, and then grab the remote off the coffee table, turning on the TV.

She stares at the screen, while I stare at her neck. It's not my mother's bloody body I see this time, it's Lilah's. Her lifeless eyes stare at me as she bleeds on the floor. My throat constricts, making it difficult to inhale. I can't let that become her future. I won't.

She brings the heel of her palms to her eyes and silently shatters, her body vibrating with tears. I want to move in closer, to wrap my body around hers like a shield, but I can't.

"It's okay, let it all out. Cry, scream, hell I'll even let you punch me. Anything you need, and I do mean anything." I try to keep my voice steady, but I'm irreversibly gutted. I can't see a woman hurt without being affected, especially her. She affects me on a deep subconscious level, filling me with this sense of possessiveness I've never felt for another woman.

She sniffles then turns to me. I reach my hand out for her, wanting to take all that hurt away, even for a little bit. She looks at it, as if unsure whether it will snap her in half or give her comfort. Then she places her soft hand on top of mine and her tight grip lets me know she's still in there somewhere.

We watch TV holding hands for a while, until she begins to move in a bit closer. She looks at me, brows pulled together in question. I gaze deep into those broken eyes and whisper, "Come here."

She lets go of my hand and moves in close, until her body is pressed up against the warmth of mine. I encircle my arms around her and hold her tight, while her body sags against me, like it knows she's safe. She digs her face into my shoulder and cries. Every sob is another twist to my gut. "I'm here. I'll keep you safe. You don't need to worry anymore." I hold her tighter, never wanting to let go, needing to protect her like I couldn't protect my mother.

She looks up at me then, tears sliding down her cheeks, "You can't help me," she trembles. "No one can."

Lilah

He makes me feel so safe. It's as if he has the power to take me away from my torturous life. I trust him instinctively. I simply don't understand why, but I do. I don't recall the last time I felt truly cared for.

I'm always walking on eggshells around Ash. Watching everything I do and everything I say. Any time he touches me, I flinch because even an innocent touch can turn violent in the blink of an eye.

Sometimes we refuse to see people for who they truly are, only seeing them for who we wish they were. That was my problem when he first began hurting me. Now, my eyes are wide open. But his grip is like cement. He won't let me go until I lose a piece of myself in the process.

The night I met Damian at the bar, Ash had lost his temper because I'd forgotten to add beef to my baked ziti. He'd grabbed me around the back of my neck and shoved my face into the hot tray of food, until I felt the steam burning my face. He'd held me there while he'd hurled insults. *You're a brain-dead bitch. You ruined my fucking dinner.* Once his rage was spent, he pushed me down onto the floor, spat at me, and walked out. The emotional abuse hurts the most. Those scars never heal.

As soon as he left, I grabbed my keys and called Lexi to meet me at the bar we go to after work sometimes. She's a paralegal in my office and we were hired at the same time. I'm so grateful we hit it off from the start because she has turned out to be my only friend.

Lexi knows about the verbal abuse but not the other stuff. She has urged me to leave numerous times, but she doesn't know why I stay. Maybe if she did, she'd understand why I let him chip away at my soul until he leaves nothing behind but a shadow.

I sink into Damian's neck and let the tears fall. He kisses the top of my head; his arms envelop me in a barrier of strength. The affection he gives splits me in half and has me crying even more. *Why couldn't I meet you first?*

His hand glides up and down my back. The touch is so comforting. I want to bottle it up so I can use it when I need it most. My eyes start to feel heavy, not only from the crying but from the need to sleep. "Stay." I whisper across his neck. "I can't sleep here alone."

"Let me carry you to bed. I'll sleep on the couch."

My breath dies in my throat as I untangle myself and fix my gaze upon him. "No! I can't sleep in there alone. Can you—sleep in the bed with me?" My chest feels like it's on fire. He can't leave me alone in that room tonight. I won't survive it. I know I'm making a strange request from someone I barely know but I'm comfortable around him and I need that right now.

"Whatever you want. I told you, I wasn't going anywhere. But if it's easier, you can sleep at my place."

"Yeah, that'd be great. Thanks." It's like he knows what I need without me having to say it. "Look in the peephole please. Make sure he's not out there."

He looks at me as he captures my cheek in his palm, the same one Ash hurt, and there I see my pain reflected in his eyes. "You don't need to be scared anymore. I'm here now. He won't be able to lay one finger on you, not without going through me first."

He lets me go and does what I asked anyway. As he gets up, I brush the tips of my fingers against my cheek, committing his touch to memory.

Once he returns, he reaches out his hand for mine just as I grab my cell phone. "Let's go, baby girl." His words drape me with warmth, while his hand provides me with a lifeline. I cling onto both with no intention of letting them go.

SEVEN

I take out one of my white T-shirts and place it on the bed. "This is for you, just in case you need it. I didn't think you wanted to go back to your apartment to grab something to sleep in." Her eyes are the windows to my own personal hell. They should never look so wrecked.

Her lower lip trembles. "Thank you. For everything."

Unable to resist, I walk up and glide the back of my hand against the curve of her chin and gently tilt her face up to me. "No need to thank me." My thumb reaches for her lower lip, but I pull back. *What the hell is wrong with me?* That's not what she needs right now. My undeniable desire for her can take a back seat. She needs a friend.

"You'll have the entire bed to yourself. I'll stay on the couch." She wraps her arms around herself and nods. "Let me go get you a bottle of water in case you wake up thirsty, the cool liquid might help ease your throat too." I exit the room to give her some time to herself.

As I enter the kitchen, my mind becomes afflicted with images of her being choked, fighting him off to get free. My jaw clenches until my teeth ache.

He's fucking dead. I'm going to enjoy torturing him. See, one thing I learned from the Army, is how to make even the toughest piece of shit piss his pants. I'd love to watch that self-righteous asshole cry out in agony as I tie up his neck and bash his face into a wall over and over until he begs for mercy. But would I stop? Hell no. I bet he didn't stop when she begged him. We'll see how he likes it.

The moment I saw her bruised and battered, she became important to me. I have to help her get out of this relationship before it's too late. If she's anything like my mother, she won't want the police involved. But if she does nothing, he's going to keep hurting her. That's a fact. I intend to talk to her about it tomorrow, because the next time she may not come out of this breathing.

I make my way back to the bedroom and knock gently. "May I come in? I got your ahh—water." As she opens the door, the sight of her in my shirt brings me to my knees. That gentleman I thought I was five minutes ago has turned into a starving beast. I hunch over a little, hiding what I know is a growing erection.

The shirt is so massive, it swallows her, stopping by her mid-thigh. It's the sexiest thing I've ever seen. I look up, trying desperately to avoid looking at her smooth legs or the apex of her thighs.

My eyes hold hers hostage. She's so beautiful, even with her makeup smeared all over. I take a deep breath, trying to get some control back. "Umm, do you need pajama pants or anything? You know, in case you're cold?"

She smooths my shirt down, avoiding my gaze. "I have shorts on under here. I'll be okay."

"Alright then, I'll just grab some clothes and then I'll be out of your hair." I move toward the dresser and take out a T-shirt and sweatpants. "If you need anything at all, just wake me up, all right?" Yeah, I definitely need to get out of here before I get a case of blue balls.

She looks up at me then, tears in her eyes. *Ah, damn it.* I can't watch this woman cry, not without being ripped apart. I move in close, erasing the space between us.

"Hey, hey, what are those for, huh?" I catch every tear that manages to escape and wrap her in my arms.

"You're just so nice to me," she grips my shirt, her forehead against my chest, "and I gave you the finger. Twice."

I chuckle, needing to make her smile. "Don't worry, I know that's your way of telling me you like me." She stills, then pulls back just enough to look at me. She weaves our hands together while her eyes trace every inch of my face. My smile melts away under the intensity.

"You've been so kind to me when you don't even know me. I'm grateful." She looks down at our hands, biting her lip. "And yes, maybe if I was someone else, someone not tethered to this life, I'd let myself fall for you, freely and completely. But I'm not. I can't fall for you." She closes her eyes, pain carved on her face. "You're a good person. You'll make someone really happy someday."

My muscles go tight, her words slamming hard into my chest. If she only knew how unlikely that is. But I don't say a word, she has plenty on her plate without needing to hear my life story.

Her tiny hands drift away until I'm empty. The sensation of her touch is still there, torturing me. My body wants her back. Well too bad, because she isn't mine.

"I'll let you get some rest. I've bothered you enough for one day," she says.

"You're not a bother. Plus, I knocked on *your* door, remember?" Smiling, I try to lighten the mood. She tucks her hair behind her ear and shrugs. "Get some rest. I'll be right out there." I point to the living room. She nods and I close the door behind me.

I change my clothes, then grab a pillow and an extra comforter from the hallway closet and make myself comfortable on the couch. But I spend all that time wishing I was in bed with her. It's like my mind's playing a game of hot or cold. One second I want her, and the other second, I'm terrified. Terrified that if I have her, I'll hurt her like that asshole has.

I've never allowed myself to get close to a woman before. I didn't want to find out if being an abusive asshole is genetic, so I always played it safe. But she makes me want to question everything. What if I'm different? I feel this need to protect her, even though I don't even know her. That must count for something. But is it worth the risk?

I toss and turn for an hour, not used to sleeping out here. Getting up, I grab something to drink. When I near the bedroom door, her muffled cries bring a fresh slice of agony to my chest. They're like a spear poking at my heart. I gently knock on the door. "Hey, I just—I'm sorry I should leave you alone."

"Don't go," she sniffles, sitting up just as I open the door. "I'm scared to sleep alone. Every time I try, my mind races with horrible thoughts." Her tears grow heavier, like a monsoon in the jungle. "Ahh, why can't I stop crying?!" She grabs the hem of my T-shirt and balls it in her fists, exposing more of her tanned, lean legs. I grind my teeth to control my attraction to her.

I come inside and sit on the edge of the bed. "Do you want me to stay?" Blue balls can go fuck themselves.

"Yes." Her voice is so low I barely hear it.

"Then I'll stay." She moves over to make room for me and I slide onto the bed with her, the heat of her body moving closer to mine, only mere inches separate us now. Her back is to me and her heavy breaths match mine. I discreetly adjust my pants, the erection straining to get out.

Before I know what I'm doing, my fingertips trace her arm. Her soft skin is so intoxicating. How could anyone want to destroy all this? Her sigh just encourages me more.

Moving my hand up into her hair, I work her scalp. She lets out a little moan and I clear my throat. I should stop but I don't want to. I'd do anything to make her feel better, even when it causes me misery.

She scoots closer. Unease rolls through me like an intense, dark wave. "Lilah…"

A sigh escapes her. "Sorry. I'll move."

I wrap my arm tightly around her instead, not giving a shit how hard this is for me. "Come closer." My dick can fuck off right now. She needs someone and hell if I'd let that be anyone else.

She doesn't hesitate, not even for a second. I don't know how she has faith in a stranger when she was just hurt by someone who's supposed to love her. My heart swells with admiration. She's braver than I ever could be.

All I want to do is capture every ounce of her pain and burn it to the ground. She deserves so much better than this, just like my mother did. I refuse to stand by and let history repeat itself.

I flip to my back and take her with me. I'll make sure to keep my dick in check. She doesn't need to know how much I want her. She tucks herself right onto my chest, like she has always belonged. Maybe she does. No, she isn't mine, even if she feels like it.

I wish my life had started out differently. But I know that my demons are lurking under all that chivalry, just waiting for their time out in the sun. I won't let them come out to play. They need to stay buried. Forever.

Lilah

I gnaw at my lip until the sting of pain slices through. How did I get here? In the arms of a man who isn't my boyfriend, consoling me, because the man who promised to love me hurts me instead. He may claim he cares, but words only take the heart so far.

I don't know how much more of this life I can take. My only option is to move away, change my name, and start over. Even then, I think Ash's blackmail would still haunt me. He has my entire life in his clutches. And what he's threatened to reveal would shatter whatever's left of my existence.

I tuck myself closer to Damian's hard body and welcome the cocoon that he's created around mine. I look up, making sure my movements haven't roused him from his sleep. My breathing begins to slow to a normal pace. His proximity calms me. He may not be able to help me out of my shitty predicament, but him being there for me is more than I could ever repay.

The way he looks at me, it's like he wants to be the one to send all my pain to the fiery pits of Hell. I wish he could. I wish he was my savior, but I'm beyond saving.

Trying to think about something else, I survey every inch of his face wanting to recognize him. Being unable to is eating at me. Where could we have possibly met? I'll figure it out one day but right now all that matters is how good he makes me feel. I burrow myself closer, needing to make his arms my home.

He's now the only person who knows what Ash is truly capable of. The realization makes me both grateful and devastated. I'm relieved that someone finally knows what I've been going through, but I'm also embarrassed. He must think I'm pitiful for staying, for not being strong enough to slay my own dragons, not that I could blame him. I am. I take deep breaths and close my eyes, hoping my dreams are better than my reality.

Lilah

EIGHT

I snap awake to the glare of sunlight that filters through the sheer, grey curtains. The rays mock me with their cheerfulness. My eyelids feel like a ton of bricks while my throat aches. My entire body feels as though it went to war and lost.

It takes me a second to realize where I am and that Damian's no longer in bed with me. I squint around the room. "Damian, are you here?" I swing my feet out of his grey upholstered bed and am ready to rush out looking for him, when I spot a note on the nightstand.

Hey, I went to get us some breakfast and to run a quick errand. You're safe here. I programmed my number into your cell just in case you need me. See ya in a bit.

I plop back down on the bed and grab his pillow and cuddle it to my chest. It still smells like him. I shut my eyes, savoring the faint, woodsy smell of his cologne. I wish I could stay here forever, but this isn't my life.

I drag my feet out of his warm bed and stride toward the kitchen in search of a coffee machine. Once I find it, I make enough for the both of us. It's the only thing I can do to show some gratitude for all his kindness.

I edge my way toward the white swivel stool next to the marbled counter, then place my hot cup down and look through my phone. There are four missed calls from Ash and one from my mom. The voicemail icon glares at me and I know it'll be him on the other end. I wrestle with whether to listen to it or not, but in the end the masochist in me wins.

"Hey babe, I just wanted to tell you I love you. Call me back."

Fuck you, asshole.

"Baby, it's me again. Are you okay? Just call me so we can talk."

I glare at the screen for a few seconds before I press the button for the next message.

"You better call me back. Now. I'm not playing games anymore or I'll show up at your place."

The bitterness drips from every word. He thinks everything he does is justified, so it's not a surprise that he isn't the least bit apologetic. I hit next again.

"I swear to you, if you don't call me back by this afternoon, I'm going to show everyone everything that you've been so afraid of. Don't fucking play with me, Lilah. Believe me you'll lose."

I expected this, but that doesn't make the sudden jolt of fear in my chest hurt any less. It's sad to see what has become of us. I know it shouldn't, but it does. Once, there was so much love there. Was it always rotten? Always veiled? Was I just foolish? I swallow the hurt away.

I have no doubt that he'll reveal what I wish he wouldn't. He's capable of destroying me, we both know it. I reach for the phone again and send him a text.

> **Lilah:** I need time. Just give me that. A few days, that's all I ask.

> **Ash:** Nice to finally hear from you. I'll give you until Saturday, but not a day more. I have work to do anyways. I need my girl. Love you.

> **Lilah:** Fine. Love you.

My stomach heaves and I fight the urge to throw up. I hate telling him I love him, but sometimes I have to. I don't want to risk angering him further.

I notice another voicemail, but it's from my mom. I shut my eyes and hit play.

"Hey honey, it's your mother. You know the woman who gave birth to all nine pounds of you? I haven't seen you in months, sweetheart, and you barely call me these days. And no, texts don't count, young lady. Is everything okay, baby? I miss you. Call your mama."

My mother is the only family I have, and we are deeply close. But I try to limit how often I speak to her these days because I'm afraid. The fear that she'll find out what's going on eats at me every day. I can just see it, me hyperventilating on the phone, describing every detail of my life with Ash. It would destroy her. She'd demand I involve the police and wouldn't accept no for an answer. I can't let that happen. My entire world would crumble.

I pinch the bridge of my nose to stop the pool of tears from streaking down my face. I'm so sick of crying. I release a long sigh.

I need some music. I find the exact song I want on my phone and let the words carry me away.

Damian

I make my way back to the apartment carrying croissants and a variety of bagels. I wasn't sure what she liked, so I bought a little bit of everything. I worried about leaving her alone, but I needed to go to the bank to deposit a check I completely forgot about.

As I approach the door, I notice an extravagant flower delivery left next to Lilah's door. I pick it up so that I can bring it to her, and then I spot the note.

For my only girl. I love you, baby.
Ash

Fucking bastard. My breathing turns savage. So, he thinks he can beat her and then send flowers? As if that'll erase the damage. Rage fills my body and poisons me from the inside out. I gotta get a hold of myself before I see her. I thought of throwing these damn flowers away, but I can't. If she finds out I did that behind her back, she may never trust me.

Finally, a bit calmer, I realize there's music playing from inside my apartment. I reach into my pocket, finding my keys, and open the door. Her back is to me as she sways to the beat of a sad song, my shirt still on her body. Walking inside, I quietly close the door behind me and place the flowers down.

I lean against the wall watching her, captivated by the curves of her body. My tongue darts out, licking my lips. I can't look away. She bends to the beat, circling her hips to the haunting words about giving up but not wanting to.

Her hands grip the hem of the shirt, lifting it a little as she moves. The urge to replace my hands with hers is so strong. What I wouldn't give to feel her tight curves gliding against me.

The music continues to play as her body moves rhythmically, matching every beat. Her hands slowly slither from the sides of her full breasts and down to her thighs. I feel like a voyeur, but I can't stop. She's so perfect.

Throwing her head back, she whirls around. With her eyes closed and hands weaved in her hair, she's lost to the sound. Just as quickly, her eyelids flutter open and go wide, redness creeping into her cheeks. She lunges for the phone on the kitchen counter to turn off the music.

Steering toward her, I cage her with my body until we're almost touching. I want her to keep dancing. I can tell she needs it and so do I. "Turn it back on," I say, placing my hand over her trembling one. Her back is to me as I lean down and whisper in her ear, "You looked like you were having fun. Don't stop on my account. Plus, I kind of liked the view." *Why the hell did I just say that?*

She reluctantly turns around after putting on the music, her pink cheeks getting redder by the second. I smirk, unable to help myself. I don't know what it is about her that does me in.

The music keeps playing as I put out my hand to her. "Dance with me." She regards it for a moment and then takes it.

I pull her in nice and close, loving the feel of her curves flush against me. Her hands loop around my neck as we move to the music like two lovers reuniting. I slide my hands down her back, wrapping her tightly around me. I want her to know that a man's touch doesn't have to hurt. I want her to feel it. She lays her head against my chest telling me she knows.

In this very moment, it's just me and her. My fears and my past be damned. But once the music stops playing and this moment ceases to exist, I know my mind will tell me not to trust my heart.

"I don't think this is such a good idea," she murmurs, lifting her head and interrupting my thoughts.

Scanning her face, I detect no sign of regret. "What are you afraid of?"

She traces her thumb along my jaw. "You." Her bottom lip is caught between her teeth, as if she's at war with what her body wants and what her mind is telling her, just like I am.

I loosen my hold. "We aren't doing anything wrong." But that's a lie. This feels wrong, but damn if it doesn't feel all kinds of right too.

Her eyes close briefly, as if knowing the truth. "Aren't we?"

Fuck. She's right, because I can't stop thinking about her in ways I shouldn't, and they all involve her naked.

I release a strained sigh. "Damn, you're right. I'm sorry." I detangle myself from her warmth and start to leave but her tight grip around my arm stops me.

"Forget I said that. Just— just don't go." She entwines her hand with mine and comes closer. Her brows pinch together while heavy breaths escape her mouth. "We weren't done dancing."

"Are you sure? Because I could dance with you forever." The words are low as though I'm afraid to say them out loud, my arms already enclosed around her.

"I'm sure. So sure. You make me feel so many things, things I shouldn't. But you're also the only one who makes me forget. So please, help me forget. Just for today."

Gripping her chin between two fingers, I lift her face up to mine. "I'll give you anything you want." Her breath is caught in her throat as she blinks away tears. I catch a few stray ones and wipe them away. "Damian…"

"Don't say anything. Just dance with me." And we do. We dance for what feels like hours. Her body belongs in my arms. The thought of her with anyone else makes me want to punch a wall.

This is the first time I wish I was someone else. Someone without the scars of the past stopping him from giving his heart to another. Yet, even if I could overcome my fear of turning into my father, she'd have to end her relationship. I don't know if she's capable of that, but I'll do whatever I can to show her she's worth it.

Lilah

NINE

Dancing with Damian is the happiest I've been in a long time. Unlike Ash, he makes me want to live another day. And if today is the last day I get in this world, I'll welcome it with open arms because it's been a good day. I don't get many of those anymore.

As the last song on my playlist ends, we reluctantly untangle ourselves from the comfort of each other's arms. It's then that I notice the flowers on the floor by the door. Pointing to them I ask, "Where did those come from?"

"*He* sent them," he mutters.

"Oh. Well, just throw them out." I don't need to read the note to know what it says.

He grins as he walks over, picking up the huge bouquet. "Be right back." He takes it out the door and comes back empty handed a minute later. "Done."

"Good," I say, smiling back. He walks over to the couch and sits, motioning for me to do the same. I take my seat next to him and his jeans brush up against my knee, sending warmth down my body.

He takes my hand into his and looks deeply into my eyes causing my heart to pick up speed. "Look, maybe this isn't my business and I shouldn't say anything, but I care about you. So I won't just hold your hand and ignore what's happening. You can't let him do this to you, Lilah. You have to go to the police."

I remove my hand and motion for him to stop. "Don't ruin this day. Don't talk to me about things you know nothing about."

He stands up, nostrils flaring. "I know a little about this, so trust me when I say, you have to end this. He won't stop until you're dead and you know I'm right." He bends down onto the floor and takes my hands in his again, brows pinching together, concern written all over his face. "If you're afraid, I'll protect you," he vows, causing me to look away. His worry breaks my heart. "Lilah look at me. I'll keep you safe. You just have to want it. Tell me you want it and you won't have to do a single thing."

He can't save me. I wish I could just tell him the whole truth and be done with it all, but that's not an option. If he gets involved, Ash will ruin me then kill me, and he'll come after Damian too. I can't risk his life as well. He didn't ask for this. I need to push him away. It's the only thing I can think of.

I shove his hands away. "You're right, it's *not* your business! We barely know each other, and you don't know Ash!" I hate that I sound so cruel but I know I have to be. "He loves me. He just—lost his temper because I flirted with a waiter. It was my fault. So just drop it. I won't go to the police and if you do, I'll never speak to you again. Just let this go!"

He stands, grabbing his hair in frustration. "Don't you fucking blame yourself! Nothing about this is your fault! Why are you protecting him?"

I can't look at him anymore. Seeing his disappointment and anger is too much. Approaching me, he lowers himself onto the floor and gently cradles my chin within two fingers, with his thumb stroking back and forth. He tilts my face up just as I close my eyes, tears streaming down my face for the hundredth time. I wonder if it's possible for a person to run out of tears.

"No, you look at me." He wipes my eyes, and brings me closer until our noses kiss. My stomach flutters at the sensation, needing more of him. And for the hundredth time I wish he was mine. "You deserve to be loved by someone who knows how to love you. I don't know why you're with him but baby girl you're worth *so* much more."

Yep, there goes whatever's left of my heart. His words just cracked me wide open and my emotions are no longer under control. I'm a sobbing mess once again.

He moves in and envelopes me in a blanket of his serenity, rubbing my back as I continue to cry. "It's okay, just let it out. I'm right here." Wouldn't it be great if somehow that was enough? If he could just hold me and make all the bad stuff disappear?

I bury my face in his neck as his strong arms wrap tighter around me. He feels so good. His embrace is an anchor for my shattered soul. "I know you hate me and probably think I'm weak," I sniffle, "but please understand I'm doing this to save myself in the only way I can."

"I could never hate you, beautiful. Never. And you're not weak. Not even close. You're the strongest person I know."

"How strong could I really be when I won't leave?"

He lets out a heavy sigh and kisses the top of my head. "Because you're doing what you think is best, but there's always a way out.

Just talk to me," he pleads. "I don't think I can take seeing you like this again."

I lift my head from the comfort of his body and cup his cheek. "You don't know just how much I wish everything were different and how much I wish I had met you first, but this is my life and there's nothing I can do about it. There are things you don't know, things that keep me with him, and I can't tell you any of it. I'm sorry."

He shuts his eyes and lets me go. "I won't force you to tell me anything you don't want to, but there's no good reason to stay. What will you accomplish when you're dead?"

"He won't kill me. He just…"

He shoots up, eyes wide. "He just what, huh?! Beats you a little, chokes you. No big deal, right? Fuck!" He paces back and forth, chest heaving with fury. "Whatever it is you can't tell me shouldn't keep you with him. Because believe me, death is far worse than whatever it is you're afraid of. And if you think he won't kill you, then you're fooling yourself!"

I bury my face in my hands. The ache in my chest feels as though a swarm of bees are attacking my insides. I know he's right, but I can't tell him that.

"I gotta go take a walk. Stay here as long as you want," he says. "Call me if you need anything." He walks out the door without a second glance.

As soon as he's gone, I ball on the floor and cry.

After all my tears run dry, I send a text thanking him for everything and tell him I returned to my apartment. Then I erase it in case Ash looks through my phone. I wait for Damian to reply, but it never comes. I long to tell him everything, to trust that it'd somehow work out, but trust isn't something I could count on, not in my life. Maybe he'll come around and talk to me again. I really hope so because I can't imagine not being close to him anymore.

I jump in the shower instead of dwelling on the pain. It's nice to finally wash off the grime of last night. I scrub vigorously; my skin turns numb. Damian's right, I can't stay with Ash, but I don't have a way out. I'm stuck in every sense of the word.

I dry myself off and head to my bedroom. As I open the dresser drawer, I take in a sharp breath when I see the bruising on my neck in the mirror. It's worse than I could've imagined. I can make out his handprint. My lip trembles as I trace the angry, red mark.

I hate him. How could he do this to me? How! Is there a limit to my suffering before I give up and die at my own hands, or do I just let him kill me? I clench my hair in tight fists and let out a scream.

I think about killing myself a lot. It's always worse after a beating, even worse after the cruel words he flings at me, telling me how worthless I am. He says I should be thankful someone like *him* wants me, that with the amount of money he makes, I should be kissing his ass instead of being an ungrateful bitch. According to him, I'm nothing more than an idiot who couldn't even get a good job with a big firm. He constantly reminds me that no man will ever want me beyond just a quick fuck. *That's all you are Lilah, pretty face and a good piece of ass. There's nothing else they'd want from you.*

I rub my face, needing to erase those memories. I have to figure out how to disguise this mark at work. The warm weather makes it difficult to hide my bruises. He's usually more careful than this though, hitting me in places I can easily conceal. He's choked me before but never this bad. He's getting worse. I'll have to wear a turtleneck tomorrow. I'm too afraid it'll show through makeup. I think I have a short-sleeved one somewhere.

Just then, my cell phone vibrates with a text. I hurriedly pick it up, hoping it's Damian, but it's not. I glare at the phone. Angry flames spark to life within me as I see who the message is from.

Ash*:* Hey babe, did you get the flowers I sent?

Lilah: Do you think pretty flowers are going to erase what you did, you piece of shit! How could you hurt me so badly when you claim you love me?

Ash: I don't want to discuss this by text. I'll call you.

Lilah: Don't waste your time, I won't answer. Just be a man and let me go without any of your threats of blackmail.

Ash: I can't do that. I love you. You're mine and you'll stay that way. Maybe I should've reacted better, but you know I don't tolerate your flirting. You can take the week to cool off, but after that, Lilah, I don't want to hear shit about last night.

Lilah: You mean reacted better than choking me half to death?! Yeah, might've been a wise decision. I wasn't flirting with anyone. You're the one with the problem.

Ash: Bye Lilah. See you Saturday. Love you.

I grab a pillow from the bed and scream.

Monday rolls around and I still haven't heard from Damian. I don't think he came home last night. How's it possible to miss someone you never really had? But my heart seems to beat to lyrics only he knows. I know because not seeing him or hearing his voice has caused it to shrivel up and die.

I don't feel just mere attraction for him, it's something much deeper. It's as though I've known him all my life. Whenever he touches or holds me, his arms don't feel like that of a stranger. Maybe some people are just meant to find each other. Their souls just reach out for one another and grab on, refusing to let go.

I arrive to work ten minutes early wishing I didn't have to be here today. Lexi's already here and follows me into my office, making herself comfortable on my desk while I sit down. "Hey, Lex."

She squints. "Okay, what's wrong? You look terrible. And I mean that in the most loving of ways."

I don't know how much to tell her. I hate involving people in my drama. "I kind of haven't told you but remember the guy who sent the drinks?"

"Yeah…" She nods slowly.

"He's my new neighbor…right across the hall."

She jumps off the desk. "What? How's that even possible? Oh my God! How have you been keeping this from me?"

"He only moved in this past Saturday."

"And?" She eyes me suspiciously.

I look away and take out some files from the drawer. "And

nothing. He's nice."

"Nice how? Just spill. I've known you long enough to know you're keeping something from me." She folds her arms, head tilting to the side.

I look down, absently flipping through the files. "Ugh, Ash and I got into a bad argument Saturday night and Damian was there for me after he left. He took care of me."

"Another fight? Fuck that guy, Lilah. You got to break up with him. This isn't normal. He's always yelling and insulting you. None of that is okay."

I play with the hem of my black pencil skirt, picking off lint that isn't there. "Not you too. Damian already gave me an earful."

"Good! Maybe you'll listen to him more than you listen to me." She squeezes my hand. "I love you. But you need to let him go." She smiles sadly as she releases my hand and returns to her office.

I sit there staring at the papers I must go through. Meanwhile, my mind races with thoughts on how to leave a man who'd destroy me before he'd ever save me.

Damian

TEN

I don't remember the last time I was this hungover. The morning sun enters Gabe's living room like an uninvited guest, and I have the urge to go back to bed. My head's spinning like crazy and my thighs ache from my workout.

After Lilah told me she wouldn't break things off, I went a little crazy. I hated knowing she'd put herself at risk like that. Yet, if I was being completely honest, I was also pissed because I wanted her. Leaving her behind went against everything I was trained to do, but it was the right thing to do. I needed to get out of there before I said something I couldn't take back.

I wrack my brain trying to figure out what would cause her to stay when she clearly doesn't want to. What could possibly be worse than what he's already doing? I replay her words in my head, something about her staying to save herself. He must be holding something over her, threatening her in some way. It's the only scenario that makes sense.

After working out at home and spending two hours at the gym, I mindlessly drove around, then got drunk by myself at some pub. Yep, pathetic I know, and pretty unlike me. I called Gabe to pick me up because I was in bad shape and couldn't even use the Uber app. He didn't ask any questions. He just looked at me, sensing something was wrong, knowing I never take things that far.

Unfortunately for me, I have to head into the office today so I gotta get the alcohol out of my system. I need to finalize assignments for the week and arrange some flights, then meet with the team to give them all the details. We have a big client traveling to Washington D.C. out of New York City this weekend, so four of my people are accompanying him and his wife on a private flight.

I take some Tylenol and jump in the shower. The cold water slices through the drunken fog. Once I'm clean, I drink two cups of coffee then look in Gabe's closet for some clothes. It helps that we're the same size. After getting dressed, I feel much more human. The hum of alcohol has finally left my system.

My mind keeps traveling back to last night. Is she safe? I need to call her to make sure he hasn't returned. I haven't even looked at my phone to see if she reached out. Damn it, I'm a selfish asshole. I should've stayed with her. I should've been there. Of all people, I should know better than to expect her to simply walk away, especially if he has ammunition against her.

Once at work, I mutter hello to Judith, my secretary. "Oh, good morning, Mr. Prescott." She tilts her head to the side, studying me with narrowed focus.

Yeah, I know I look like shit. Thanks for making it obvious.

"Mr. Westbrook's in your office waiting for you. And I left some messages on your desk," she calls out behind me.

Great. "Thank you," I mutter, heading into my office without another word.

Gabe's sitting on the black leather sofa drinking coffee. "We need to talk about last night," he says as soon as I sit at my desk.

I can't do this right now. "Look man, I had a very shitty day yesterday and drank too much, that's all."

He stands and shakes his head. "Don't bullshit me. What's going on? I've never seen you drink like that."

Fuck, I don't know whether I should tell him or not, but I know I can trust him. Also, someone else knowing may be good. He may have some ideas on how to help. I run my hand through my hair as I let out a deep sigh. "Lilah's boyfriend is beating her."

"Shit." He sits down and adjusts his tie. We stay silent for a moment, until he gets up to use my phone.

"What are you doing?"

"Paging Jax. He should know too."

"Fine, you're right." We're like a pack, we usually figure things out together. He picks up the phone and dials his extension.

"Jax get in here." Gabe's voice is all business.

"Why are you in Damian's office? Are we having a playdate?"

"Just get in here, will ya?"

"Sounds serious. Coming Dad." When he walks into my office, he notices our solemn faces and folds his arms. "Whoa, this *does* look serious. What happened?"

Once they're both seated, I tell them every detail. Jax's jaw flexes so hard I think he may lose some teeth. Gabe just stares daggers into a wall, the anger is there in his grey eyes waiting to unleash.

"So, what are we going to do about this?" Jax asks.

"We?"

He punches his palm a few times. "Hell yeah, we! No woman's getting hurt while I sit around. Fuck that! You want to beat the shit out of him? Let's go. We've got some time to kill before our meeting!"

I rub my neck until it hurts. "Believe me, I thought of that. I wanted to pay him a visit, but she would've hated me or what if he hurt her again because of me? So, I got lost in a bottle of Jack Daniels instead." I can't take another second of her being with him. I just can't.

Gabe stands, pacing around the office. "If she won't press charges, she has very little chance of being safe. Hurting him won't do much except anger him, and I agree he may use that against her. We can, however, pay him a visit anyway, but we won't hurt him. We can just—put the fear of God in him a bit."

Gabe seems like the most level headed one of us, but he's also calculating and lethal. That's what made him so dangerous in the military. He can kill with his bare hands and not even flinch, but he can also show impeccable restraint when necessary.

"What do you have in mind?" I ask.

"Right now, he thinks he has the upper hand. He believes no one knows what he's doing. And he's clearly holding some sort of leverage over her, so he feels big and in control. Let's make him feel *really* small." His lips turn up into a vicious smile.

"Hell yeah, that's what I'm talking about!" Jax says.

"Neither of you have to get involved but thank you."

Jax rolls his eyes. "Oh, shut up jackass. As if we'd let you handle this alone."

"Believe me, I'm going to have fun toying with that motherfucker," Gabe says, without a trace of humor in his voice.

My muscles are tense like they're itching to get close to that piece of garbage. *Soon.* "We go tonight. Jax, get his name from Lexi. Just make some shit up and I'll find his address in our system."

I have to get my nerves under control before I come face to face with that cocksucker. I can easily kill him right now. But Gabe is right, that won't solve anything. We need to convince him it's in his best interest to leave her alone.

After a few minutes we have his name and address. Lexi gave it up without a second thought. *Ash Davis, you just fucked with the wrong woman.*

After work, we drive to his colonial home, located on the corner of a quiet block. The overcast skies are dreary and dark as we head up the steps of his home. I feel a kinship to them.

We knew he wasn't home yet because we did a bit of research. When I say a bit, I mean a shit load. We found out he had been arrested two years ago for assaulting some guy at a bar who ended up in the hospital. But he wasn't sentenced, just fined. It was his first offense and his parents got him a good lawyer. Oh, and they're loaded, and we know money talks. But, if he gets arrested for what he did to her, it may cost him.

I'm ready to get this over with. I want to hurt him in any way I can. Every time I see her soft skin marred so viciously, it haunts me, and the need to inflict pain, to avenge her, grows until it's all I feel.

We're wearing leather gloves for the occasion so as to not leave any fingerprints. Jax does the honors and quickly picks the lock to avoid drawing an audience. Setting foot inside, we look in every room for possible weapons. Finding none, we wait in his living room, which is immediately to the left of the foyer.

A partial wall separates the two areas. The rest of the room is an open floor plan. There's a black fireplace with a large TV hung on the wall above it, and a brown leather sectional on the opposite side of the room. We stand, not wanting to sit, in case that leaves behind evidence.

Twenty minutes later, the sound of a screeching car moves closer. That must be him. The engine's turned off and heavy footsteps echo on the ground outside. *Show time*. We move to hide behind the wall and remain still. Not a sound is heard but for his keys jangling as they enter the door, and then he opens it.

Peering around, I see him before he sees me. He locks up and starts walking to the kitchen, straight ahead, while looking at his phone. Only then do we make ourselves known and let the fun begin.

"I hear you like to beat women." Ash swings his head toward the sound of Gabe's voice and drops his phone, sending it skidding against the wood floor. His eyes dart frantically to the living room where a large shadow looms.

I stay hidden behind the corner, offering me a good view. Jax turns on the light and walks over next to Gabe. I love seeing Ash so visibly pale as he takes in both guys with their arms crossed against their chest. Both are tall and massive, while Ash looks like a child in comparison. He backs up against the wall like the weak, pathetic piece of shit that he is.

"Who the fuck are you?" His voice trembles with fear. I'm enjoying the sound.

They both storm forward, not giving him a chance to escape. Once he's surrounded, Jax draws near until their faces are almost touching. "It doesn't matter who we are. We're here to talk about you, friend." Every word is said with vitriolic passion, and I bet Ash feels every one of them.

Gabe bumps Jax out of the way. "Hey, my turn."

Jax draws his clenched fist and presses it against Ash's jaw as he stares him down. "Don't worry man, there's plenty to go around."

Once I know that the guys have him within their grasp, I come out of hiding. Ash's eyes connect with mine and a nervous smile appears on his face. "Well, if it isn't the neighbor. Trying to get rid of the competition so you can have her all to yourself?"

Ignoring him, I creep up close as the guys move over, giving me the one on one I've been waiting for. Balling his shirt in my fist, I lift him off the floor and slam him against the wall until his head rattles. "I'm going to say this only once so listen up motherfucker because I won't repeat myself. You're done hitting her. Stay away from her. If she so much as has a scratch on her finger, you're going to pay for it. Only a pathetic, little shit beats on a woman."

I press my forearm against his neck, constricting his airways. "Do you like that? Because she didn't." His eyes go wide and he tries to pry my arm away. *Nice try asshole.*

"The best thing you can do for yourself is to tell her that you want to end it. I can find out anything about you and use it to destroy your life. Like that arrest. Does she know about it?" I see the terror in his eyes before I toss him on the floor like the garbage he is.

He breaks into a mirthless laugh. "You think this will keep me away from her? She's mine asshole, not yours! She knows what's good for her. I never hit her. My girl likes it rough. You should feel how wet her pussy gets when I choke her while we fuck."

Rage beats in my ears like a second heartbeat and I strike. The firm punch rattles his jaw and blood spills from his busted lip. Before I get a chance to kill him, the guys pull me off. Teeth bared, nostrils flaring, I'm sure I look every inch the feral beast ready to tear him apart. I try to fight my way toward him, but their combined grips won't let me.

"Just because we stopped him this time doesn't mean we won't come after you again. Stay away from her. You've been warned," Gabe says, his voice even.

"Next time, we won't stop him, and his fists won't be the only ones in your face. Don't make us come back," Jax adds with a menacing smile. They don't wait for a response as they drag me out. I can only hope this doesn't backfire.

Damian

ELEVEN

Once I cool off at Gabe's for a bit, I go home. While laying in bed, all I want is her. The physical need to see her, to make sure she's all right, eats at me. She hasn't sent me anymore texts except the one about going back to her place. It's kind of late, so I decide to send her a message instead of just showing up at her door.

Damian: Hey.

Her reply comes immediately.

Lilah: Hi.

Damian: I'm sorry I didn't call yesterday. I had to do some things for work then went to get a drink.

Lilah: It's fine.

Damian: I want to see you. Can I come by?

Lilah: OK.

I throw on a white T-shirt and some flannel bottoms and am at her door in no time. She opens it before I even knock. I approach, wanting to hold her, to feel her warmth, but I don't get the chance. She reaches her arm out and places it on the doorframe.

We lock eyes and she stares intensely with pursed lips. Her gaze slides down the length of my body, landing on my waistband. My breaths intensify while I try to figure out if she's pissed or if she wants me.

She looks back at my face while my gaze drifts down to her luscious, pink lips. I'm unable to control the magnetism. The need to own that mouth is strong. Damn it, I want her, every fucking inch of her. My body's greedy for just one taste. One touch. One anything. That's all I need.

But who am I kidding? That'll never be enough. Not with her. With her I want everything. I want her body. Her mind. Her soul. I want all of it. All the time. Everyday. Until she breathes me and I live her.

My eyes lock in on her breasts bursting from her black top. I want to free them from their captivity and feel all that softness. I want to suck those hard nipples poking through her top and make them ache for more. I need to hear her beg me to fill her, beg me to give her the release I know she desperately wants.

Her legs are almost bare, nothing but a pair of tiny, light pink pajama shorts cover them. I want them wrapped around my face, tight and trembling as she comes all over my mouth. *Fuck.* I need to stop before I flip her over my shoulder and show her how a man really treats his woman.

I release a sharp exhale. "May I come in?"

She bites her lower lip and shakes her head. *Are you kidding me, woman? If you bite that lip again…*

"I know you've been avoiding me. So why should I let you in now? P.S. I don't believe you were working."

So, this is her form of torture? *Two can play that game, baby girl.* "Maybe I was avoiding you." I take a step toward her. "What are we going to do about that?" She swallows then lowers her hand off the doorframe, backing into her apartment as she bites her lip once more. If that wasn't an invitation, then I don't know what is.

I stalk forward as a sharp inhale escapes between her parted lips. And as she backs up further, her breasts rise and fall with each erratic breath. I kick the door closed, locking it from behind me just as she hits the wall behind her. I take my time reaching her, relishing in the sweet taste of desire within her gaze like a man who's about to enjoy his last meal on earth.

When she's finally within my grasp, I cage her in, planting a hand on each side of her head. "Do you forgive me now? Because I'm really, *really* sorry." She pants, heavy and loud, her eyes glossing over. She's so sexy all turned on like this.

I lower my hand, fingers tracing the skin of her arm. She drops her eyes, following the soft caress of my touch before I reach her hand and enlace it with mine. "Damian…" Her hot breath fans across my lips and I pull in a little closer, pressing my hard body into her soft one.

"Am I hurting you?" I whisper against her lips. My hunger is so strong, I completely forgot she was just hurt. In this moment, I exist solely for her. I'd do anything, even give her my bleeding heart if she asked.

She looks up at me as she squeezes my hand and shakes her head.

"You'll never hurt me." And right then all I want is a taste of her lips, to devour her until all she feels is what we could be together.

I move in closer now, deepening our connection until her erect nipples strain across my chest. I don't know how much more I can take. I didn't even come here for this, but this is what she does to me.

She makes me irrational, filling me with passion I've never known. She's an ember flame just waiting to engulf me. I don't know when it happened or how, but the inferno is nearing, closing in around me until I beg to burn.

But no matter how much I need her or how badly I want to overcome my past, she's still with that piece of shit. The thought consumes me.

"Lilah...I'm so close to ripping those goddamn little shorts off and fucking you right up against this wall. But I can't. You're not mine. You're still his."

She draws in a stuttered gasp and bites that lip again. I trace it with my thumb, unable to resist, before I tug it free, nearing my breaking point.

"Go sit on the couch. We need to talk." I leave the heat of her body and she scurries toward the sofa. Rubbing my face in frustration, I follow her and sit on the opposite side. I can't be near her right now, not if I intend for us to talk. But she doesn't seem to care about how much her proximity unhinges me because she moves in closer, until our legs are almost touching.

"You're wrong you know." My brows arch in question.

"You may not be mine, but I'm yours. I have been from the moment you held me close and danced with me." She intertwines our fingers, weaving them together and it's as though our hearts are intertwined the same.

"And maybe it doesn't make any sense because we just met,

but it feels as though I've known you my entire life. If things were different, I'd choose you. I'm not his. Not in the way it matters." I cup her face, needing to touch her everywhere. Her lips continue to move and I cling to every word like a dying man needs air.

"I need you to know you're the one I think about. You're the one I dream about. You're the one, Damian. You're the one."

I can't speak, feeling the power of her words resound deep within the chambers of my heart. I clamp my fist to suppress the need to show her how much I belong to her too. But maybe it's time she knew just how much I really need her. Maybe it's what she needs to know she's not alone.

I release my fist, grab her by the waist, and crush her body on top of mine. I grind my length in between her thighs. "Do you feel that?"

"Yes," she cries out. "You feel so good." Her moan has me thrusting harder. She whimpers, louder this time and I don't want to stop.

I'm barely capable of holding on, but I need her to feel what I feel. "It only ever gets this hard for you."

"Damian…" My name's just another moan, torturing me.

"I'm not done, baby." I take her soft hand in mine and place it over my chest. "And my heart? It hasn't been alive for anyone until I saw you for the first time." My gaze pierces through the mist forming in her eyes.

"I feel like I know you too, yet I feel like I don't know enough, and I want to know everything. So please don't tell me you can't leave him because it'll kill me." I grab the back of her head, my fingers digging into her scalp as she looks at me, a chaotic maelstrom of desire and anguish swirling in the depth of her gaze. "I'd walk away if he treated you like you should be, but he treats you like trash. Don't stay with someone who hurts you."

I bring her closer, until her hot breath feathers across my lips. "I want to help you. I want to protect you. All you have to do—is let me." I slam her mouth into mine and make love to her lips with ferocious brutality. She's a drug I didn't know I needed, and now that I've had a taste, there's no way I could give her up.

Her hips rock back and forth against my cock as her hands slide into my hair. I nip at her lower lip and thrust harder and faster. I can't stop. I don't ever want to.

She opens her sensuous mouth, allowing my tongue to penetrate her with deep, punishing strokes. Sucking on her tongue, I fuse my fingers in her long, luscious hair, bringing her closer. Biting and kissing, my lips devour the skin along her jaw.

My mouth slides down the curve of her neck, tasting every inch of skin. I crave to consume her; the need is stealing every breath within me. So, this is how it feels to truly want a woman. There's no way I can live without her now.

Her hips press harder into my cock and I'm so close to giving us both what we want. "Damian—I need you. Fuck me."

Oh damn, I can't do this. I grab her hips and ease her off me. It'd be so easy to pretend this is okay but none of it is.

I take deep, calming breaths, and turn to face her. "The only way I'll ever fuck you is when you're all mine. I won't share you. Ever." She drops her head into her hands. "This thing between us is real. You're the first woman I've ever cared for or ever wanted this badly."

She glances over with a shocked expression on her face. "Cared for? You've never been in a relationship?"

"No, never. My past has been... That's a conversation for another time." Once my erection is no longer pulsating angrily, I reach out and hold her hand. "I can protect you Lilah. Please baby, let me." She closes her eyes, her brows furrowing while I continue. "Gabe,

Jax, and I are all ex-military, Delta Force to be specific. And now, the guys and I own a private security company and we don't lack in connections or resources. I can help with whatever he has on you."

She sighs, shaking her head. "I told you Damian, you can't help me. I have to stay with him," she whispers. "It's for the best."

It'd be less painful if she punched me in the dick.

"I know you don't understand, but I don't love him. I just can't leave. Please don't get involved," she begs.

Too late.

The blood rushes through my head and the growing need to pummel something becomes strong. If he hurts her again, I won't forgive myself, but how do I get her to finally see she has someone who can help? Cradling her face with both hands, I bring her closer until our lips are half a breath apart, and then I lean in and kiss her forehead. Before I change my mind, I let her go.

"Let me know when you decide to trust me. Until then, I can't be around like this anymore. I feel too much for you. But I'll always be here to help. You're not alone, no matter what you believe." And with that, I walk out the door.

Lilah

I'm caught between a man I desperately want and a man I can't escape. I haven't seen Damian since that day, four days ago. I've cried so much; my eyes feel strange without any tears pouring out of them. I went to work and tried to pretend I was all right, but Lexi wasn't fooled. She kept asking what had caused such a drastic mood shift, but I couldn't tell her.

He hasn't been in his apartment; I know because I would've heard him. He decided he had enough, and I don't blame him. I hate myself just as much as he does.

But if I tell him the truth, he'll want to kill Ash. I know it. I don't want to risk him getting hurt or going to prison. I have to figure out a plan on my own. I can't keep stalling whenever Ash brings up the future. He won't accept no as an answer for too long and then who knows what he'll do to me.

I lay in bed, unable to stop thinking about Damian. The last few days have given me a glimpse of what my life would be like without him and it's devastating. Somehow, he came into my world when I needed him most and I can no longer picture it without him.

He's right though, this isn't fair to him. It doesn't matter that I sleep with Ash because I have no choice. He deserves to have me all to himself, but that'll never happen.

I keep thinking back to that night when we almost slept together. I just don't know what got into me. Missing him so much made me crazy, crazier than I've ever been for any man. But I was also kind of angry he left and never texted me, even though I understood why. Once I saw him, all my feelings kind of jumbled together.

The way he pinned me up against the wall… that intoxicating kiss. *Oh God.* He stole the breath right out of my lungs. It's so hard to feel what I feel for him, knowing he wants me too, yet knowing we can't be together. I want to stop being afraid, but I can't.

My body aches, needing him under me again. It felt like we belonged, like it was always just us. I never knew it could be like that with a man. Sex between Ash and I only has one goal: the climax. There's never much frenzy or heat, not even in the beginning. But with Damian… He just makes me feel so good. I could only imagine what sex with him would be like. I don't think I'll ever recover.

Heat creeps up my body whenever I recall his hard shaft pressing in between my thighs or those strong hips thrusting into me with such depravity, I almost came.

I slide a hand down the length of my body until I feel the arousal coating my fingertips. I brush them over my clit imagining it's his long tongue caressing me, making me arch up for more.

Plunging two fingers inside of me with one hand, I grab my breast with the other. Twisting my nipple between my fingers, I picture his teeth biting my pebbled flesh.

I thrust my fingers harder, faster until my orgasm hits like lighting and my toes curl. Every nerve ending is on fire. I close my eyes, hips arching up from the burst of pleasure. It takes a few minutes to come down from the high.

Not nearly satiated, I toss and turn until I get somewhat comfortable. I'll never get the real Damian so I'll take him in any capacity I can get.

Damian

TWELVE

T he last few days have been hell. Staying away from her has been almost impossible. I've been leaving my place early and coming home late just to avoid her. I've picked up the phone numerous times, typing out texts that were never sent. It's hard to keep my distance when she's all I think about.

The black punching bag whips around violently as I throw jab after jab. Heavy sweat drips down my body as my breaths come out labored. I've been at it for hours and I can't seem to stop.

How the hell do I miss her so much when I've only known her for a few days? For her, I want to let go of the past and learn to trust myself. It figures when I finally meet a woman I want to slay my demons, she ends up belonging to a villain.

Bouncing on my feet, the bag flies back and forth from the force of my punches. My clenched fists ache underneath my gloved hands, but imagining that asshole's face as I beat the bag to a pulp makes the pain worth it.

"Yo D, you planning on murdering that thing or what?" Jax asks from behind.

Gabe had some work to do so he couldn't join us. Ignoring him, I keep slamming it until my muscles feel as battered as my heart.

She could die. *Punch.*

She doesn't want me more than she wants to keep her fucking secrets. *Punch.*

He gets to be inside her when he doesn't deserve it. *Punch. Punch. Punch.*

"Ahhhh," I roar. I'm not in the right headspace to be around anyone right now.

"C'mon D, I think you've had enough. We're leaving." He throws a white towel at me and waits.

My heart pounds inside my chest, my lungs on fire while I take deep breaths to slow down my strained breathing. I wipe my face then place the towel over my shoulder.

Maybe I should call her and try to get through to her one more time. Damn it, here I go again. She made her decision. I can't force her to do anything she doesn't want to do. And I sure as hell can't be around her without wanting her.

To keep her safe, I assigned Logan to watch over her. He's one of our leading bodyguards. Just because I can't be there doesn't mean I won't take care of her somehow. But I worry he won't be able to do shit if he can't hear or see a struggle. All he could do is follow her or park next door to one of Ash's neighbors whenever she's there. He's told me she hasn't seen the prick but that won't last long.

After the gym I head home. I can't keep hanging out at Gabe or Jax's like I've been doing after work. I know I'll eventually have to face her.

I walk out of the elevator and head toward my place just as she's closing her door. I freeze as our eyes meet, and my heart makes itself known, beating for the only woman it's ever wanted.

My entire body comes to life as though it's been starved for just one look. My eyes shamelessly travel down the full length of her body, admiring how her tight, white denim jeans emphasize her full hips and the way the hot pink crop top rides up, exposing a bit of her toned stomach. My cock swells at the thought of pinning her against the door and touching that body everywhere her clothes cover.

"Hey, how are you?" I ask, swallowing away the heaviness in my throat, wondering if she can hear my raging pulse. She looks down at my pants and tries to pull her shirt down. Well, guess there's no hiding that bad boy. I steal a glance at her neck, not seeing any remnants of a bruise. *Thank fuck.*

"Hey—umm I'm fine. I hope you've been well too?"

"No, I'm not well at all, but thanks for asking." I won't pretend just to make this easy on her. I need her to know I'm miserable and want her in every way. She's the cure to my darkness, the one I never thought I'd find, so I'm not about to let her go, not without a fight.

She closes her eyes, summoning a deep breath; and as she lets it out, she peers at me, her eyes full of broken and lonely pieces, crushing me all over again. "You were right, Damian. This wasn't fair to you. I let my feelings run away with me last time and it won't happen again. But I want us to be friends. Somehow."

Tightening the hold on her beige purse, she fidgets on her feet while I stare silently into those blue eyes I love. I don't move an inch, I just listen. I missed her voice. I missed everything.

"I know you've been avoiding me, and I understand why," she continues, fingering the soft tendrils of her hair, reminding me how it felt to have all that luscious hair within my palm. "I guess what I'm trying to say is that—I've missed having you around."

I start to creep closer. She backs herself up against the door and opens her mouth just slightly, her breasts rising and falling rapidly with each breath. I'm aware of the power I hold over her body and that just makes me want her even more.

I stop myself when we're a few feet apart, knowing if I get any closer, I'm in danger. I won't be able to keep my hands off her body or my mouth off of her lips. She consumes me just by existing.

"I can't be just friends with you, Lilah."

She studies me with piercing scrutiny as her brows furrow. "Why not?" I look at her and see it. I see the beauty inside her. I see her strength and her pain, and I want it all. I want everything she is and everything she will be.

My gaze cruises down her curves for the second time. "Because friends don't imagine fucking each other and I imagine fucking you all the time. I'm actually doing it right now." She gasps and I feel it in my dick, it grows and flinches in my pants.

Swallowing, she looks at my lips. "Oh…" Her chin dips low and a flush appears across her cheeks. I bet if I reached my hand down under her panties she'd be soaking.

"You're off to see him, aren't you?" I grit my teeth. *Why the hell did I ask? Of course she is.*

"We have a date." It feels as though I've been dumped into a pit of hot coals. Nah, that'd probably feel way better than this.

"He can't even pick you up!?" Every nerve ending in my body is screaming in outrage. *Leave him. He'll kill you. Be with me instead.*

"He's coming from work so it's easier if I just meet him for lunch. It's no big deal."

"You know what? Forget it. It's none of my business. Be careful. Call me if you need me." I walk inside my apartment and slam the door shut, rattling it a little.

I pace around the room, my pulse thrumming wildly. Suddenly,

I'm tormented with images of her naked body under him. They play on repeat over and over until I'm ready to bash my head into the door. Then things turn violent and now she's naked with a pool of blood around her body, turning the white sheets a bright red.

I can't stay here. I need to go back to the gym, so I have something to punch. I'm going to lose my damn mind. I find my cell and send the guys a group text.

Damian: Where are we going tonight?

Gabe: Are you saying you're coming out with us?

Jax: Our baby's all grown up.

Damian: Shut up man. I'm in no mood. Give me the location.

Gabe: The Blacksmith at 9.

I change into a pair of grey sweats and a black tank and head to the gym again. I need to release this tension before it eats me alive.

I work out for a couple of hours before my body can't take the punishment any longer. Once I'm home, I figure I'll just stay in. That is until I picture him with his hands all over her again. Clearly this won't stop. Maybe drowning in a bottle of something strong will fix it. Yeah, probably won't but I get ready to go out anyway.

I arrive at a small, dark dance club with loud music booming from all around. *What did I get myself into?* I hate this shit.

They told me they're by the bar, so I make my way there, squeezing in between people who smell like alcohol drowned in too much fragrance.

I see them with drinks in hand and they lift their chin up to me in greeting. "You guys couldn't pick something a little more low key?" I holler over the music, finally reaching them.

"We did tell you the name. Google's your friend my man," Jax shouts. "Suck it up buttercup. You need a change of pace anyway," he continues, ordering me a shot of something. "Here. Drink. You've been a miserable shit for days." I close my eyes and down the shot, the vodka burning inside and I crave more, anything to drown out the pain she's left me with.

Where is she right now? Is he hurting her? Are they fucking? I clench and unclench my fists and order another shot. It slides down my throat, coating me with liquid fire. After the fourth one, I definitely feel the alcohol, the buzz setting in.

"Have you spoken to her at all since what happened with you two?" Gabe asks. They both know how close I came to burying myself inside her.

Nostrils flared, I crack my knuckles and take shaky breaths. "I saw her today. She was going to meet him earlier, and is probably still with that motherfucker." Neither of them says a word, probably seeing the anger on my face.

I order another shot with plans to go home after because I have no desire for a repeat of drunken Damian. As I wait for my order, a small hand wraps around my abs. I look down to find long, red fingernails digging into my stomach as she rubs me from side to side. I turn to the right, throwing the guys a questioning look. Jax's mouth edges up into a half-smile while Gabe just shrugs. My pulse quickens. *Is it her*? I don't remember if her nails were red today.

I slowly rotate to find a stranger. My heart descends back to the despair I was in a minute ago.

She slides her hand up to my neck and brings my face close until her lips press against my ear. "Hey there, handsome. I'm Brittany. I've been watching you for a bit and was hoping you'd want to dance," her voice drips with desire. "Pretty please?"

I pull back and finally get a good look at her. She has long, jet black hair, and light blue eyes. She doesn't look like Lilah but in my mind, she's a close second. I want Lilah so badly I'd probably conjure her up from mid-air.

My first instinct is to tell this girl, no, to say I have a girlfriend. But I don't. The woman I want is with a scumbag. *Screw this*. I grab her hand and pull her slender body flush against me. "Let's go." Her eyes go wide before a small grin appears across her red lips.

I take her to the dance floor and she drapes her arms around my neck. Her hips gyrate seductively to some song about a man who wants a woman belonging to someone else. *How fucking fitting*. The words add to my rage until I'm drowning in it.

Pretending it's Lilah's body I'm holding, I tighten my grip around her lower back, pressing her to me. Even the alcohol can't keep my thoughts off Lilah. How could she do this to herself? To us? Doesn't she realize what I'd do for her?

Needing an escape, I flip Brittany around, so her ass is thrust up against my thighs. My fingers dip into her hips and hers dig into my hands, while she slides her body up and down against me, suggestively.

After the song ends, she turns my way. Licking her lips, pink tongue darting out, I know she wants me, and I need to forget Lilah. Maybe this girl could help me forget.

I lean into her ear, "Come home with me." She covers my mouth with hers giving me all the answer I need. I don't even wave goodbye to the guys before we go, but I see their wide-eyed expressions as we leave.

Damian

THIRTEEN

Brittany and I wait for the elevator on the way up to my place. She reclines her head against my shoulder as the doors open, unconcerned with the other two people already there. Ash wears a mocking smile, arms wrapped around Lilah from behind as she silently gasps. I notice tears brimming in her eyes, but she tries to blink them away. I wish I could kiss away her suffering. *I'm hurting too, baby.*

We came so close to falling, I could just taste our love. She took root inside me, made it her home, her safe haven, but then she tore herself away, and now I'm here. Empty.

"Hey, neighbor," Ash mocks, but I refuse to answer, letting my hate-filled eyes do the talking.

We walk in and I steal a glimpse at Lilah, but she looks right past me, as if I'm no longer there. Her trembling jaw is the only visible evidence of pain.

Brittany and I stand at the back of the elevator. She doesn't ask any questions, oblivious to our exchange.

We travel the rest of the way in stark silence. He grasps her hand and they walk out first. Anger surges through me at seeing his vile hand on her, so I wrap an arm around Brittany, following them.

Lilah hands Ash the keys and while he opens the door, she casts a quick look my way. Her face is fraught with anger and pain. The agony in it claws at my insides and crawls up my veins entwining with my own brokenness.

I want to take her away, to forget where we are and who we're with, but I can't. I turn away and open my door as she enters hers.

Brittany loops her arms around me, "Take me to bed," she says, her voice thick with lust. I look at the direction of Lilah's apartment and the guilt eats at me, but I have nothing to be ashamed about. She's in there with him.

I lead Brittany to my bedroom and push her down onto the bed. She caresses my comforter against her palms. "Mmm, this is a nice, large bed you have here." I lean over, pressing my body on top of hers, needing her to shut up. I don't want to be reminded of whom I'm with.

I kiss the column of her neck while she unbuttons my jeans. Closing my eyes, I imagine it's Lilah's breasts I kneed in my hands, her nipples I twist, her moans I hear, and her hand stroking my cock.

But once I lift my head away from Brittany's body and look in her eyes, my heart shrivels up taking my dick with it. Every piece of me belongs to another whether she wants it or not.

Brittany glances up. Her brows dip into a confused frown. "What's wrong?"

Pressing my fingers into my eyes, I stand. "Look, I'm sorry but I can't do this. Let me call you a car."

She jumps off the bed, grabbing her shirt and bra. "Are you fucking kidding me? You asshole! I don't need your fucking car. I can get my own!" She swiftly gets dressed and huffs out of my bedroom. The entry door slams shut as she leaves. I fall back on the bed, hoping sleep can swallow me into oblivion.

Lilah

I need to get myself together before Ash realizes I'm upset. Heartbroken is more like it. I scrub at my face in the bathroom mirror, wiping away tears, as if that'll erase the horror I saw in the elevator.

I can't believe Damian moved on already. Who the hell is she? I want to know every detail and at the same time I don't want to hear a word. My heart is raw, its protective layer ripped apart as it bleeds for what could've been.

I know we were never a couple, but it still hurts so much. Seeing him with another, picturing them together feels as though I'm suffocating on the rancid taste of something spoiled. My stomach contracts violently but I force the bile down.

Taking a few deep breaths, I twist the brass knob and open the door. Ash stands against the wall, arms crossed over his chest, the anger radiating from his skin.

"Took you long enough," he spits out, stalking toward me, his face cold and rigid. I recoil inward, wishing I was invisible. But I can't just disappear. There's nowhere I could go where he won't find me. I back away. He moves forward, grabbing my chin, his fingers like sharp blades digging into my flesh.

He eyes me, his nostrils twitching angrily. "So, tell me, have you been speaking to your neighbor about us?"

"What?" My pulse beats wildly. "Which neighbor?"

His free palm lands hard across my face. The sharp pain explodes up my cheek. Hot tears rise up and I want to swallow them back, not show my weakness, but it's too late. They drizzle down, leaving a cold path in their wake.

"I hate when you act stupid. Are you stupid, Lilah? Of course you are, why do I even bother asking." The cruel words chip away at my dignity, or whatever's left of it, leaving me naked. "You know which one. Stop playing games with me." He pinches my chin tighter until it burns.

"You mean, Damian?" My voice crumbles and I don't recognize it.

"See, you knew who I was talking about. If you stopped pretending to be an idiot we could've avoided all this."

"I'm sorry. Please, you're hurting me."

"I don't give a fuck, you stupid bitch. If I find out you've been telling anyone about us, let's just say it won't be good for you. Do you understand me?"

I nod. "I haven't said anything to anyone. I promise." My skin prickles with fear. *I can't go through this again.*

He caresses my chin, and then let's go. "Good girl. Come on, let's go to bed."

Nausea rips at the pit of my stomach but I follow him anyway and remove my clothes while he sits on the bed, watching me strip. I know what he wants, best to avoid any more fighting.

His hooded gaze drips down my naked body. He reaches for my hip and pulls me close, fingering my slit. Once he's satisfied, he throws me on the bed, looming over me.

"Take off my clothes," he demands. And I do. I'm too afraid to do anything else.

Once he's naked, he spreads my thighs and enters me and all I feel is the white, hot pain shooting through my core. I clench my teeth, stifling the pain, while he grunts in my ear like an animal.

Once upon a time when I mattered, he used to care whether I enjoyed our love making, but now I'm just a hole he uses to get off.

Closing my eyes, I imagine it's Damian inside of me. His devotion shining through every touch, every kiss, every thrust we share. That's the only way I can survive this.

I feel when he's on the brink, his orgasm nearing. "Fuuuuck." *Finally.* He's done.

He gets off me then gets dressed, while I just lay there, eyes shut, wishing for him to hurry and leave.

"Remember what I said, Lilah. Not a word to anyone." I nod my head furiously.

"No, I wanna hear you say it so there's no confusion."

"I won't say anything. You don't have to worry."

"Good. I'll see you soon." I breathe out a sigh of relief but it's only temporary, I know that.

As soon as he's gone, I grab a towel from the closet and head for the bathroom, needing to wash the filth of him away. Turning on the hot water, I watch the steam dance around before slipping off the red towel.

Boom. Boom. Boom. Heavy pounding batters at my door. My eyes go wide and I freeze in place as my pulse picks up speed.

The pounding continues. I should just open it. He won't leave until I do. I grab the towel, wrapping it around me, and drift toward the sound. My hand freezes on the gold lock, turning it slowly. Fear skitters up my fingers as it unlocks. Holding my breath, I grip the copper knob and twist.

Lilah

FOURTEEN

I find Damian standing there, but he doesn't notice the relief that washes over me at finding him at my door; instead, he's focused on his own turbulent mood. His breaths are ragged, his jaw tightening like he's mad at the world. My relief quickly morphs into anger when I remember the woman who was draped all over him. "What the hell are you doing here? Shouldn't you be with *her*?" The word tastes awful in my mouth.

Drumming his fingers against the doorframe, he studies me with a darkened expression, all the while looking me up and down, leaving a pathway of heat in his wake. He blows out a frustrated breath before stalking forward. I back away, clutching my towel as he walks inside and locks the door as though he owns the place. "Have you washed the smell of him off of you yet?" he asks, looking back and forth between my lips and my thighs.

"Have you washed the taste of her from your mouth?!"

He cocks his head to the side, the curve of his lips deepen into a smirk. "Are you jealous? Because if not, I can tell you how hard her tits bounced as she rode my cock. Or, maybe you'd like to know what her pussy tasted like when she came all over my mouth. Oh, I know, maybe you want to know how—"

"Fuck you! I get it. You hate me and want to punish me. Done. Now get the hell out!" My heart pounds with need, anger, and sadness. I'm a mess of turbulent thoughts but one thing is clear, the need wins.

"I'm not going anywhere." Eyes narrowing, he begins to take small steps forward while I take small steps back. Our own twisted version of catch me if you can, except I want to be caught very, very badly.

Step. "How could you do that, huh?" I practically shout, every breath heavy and painful. "How do you sleep with someone else so soon after what happened between us?"

Step. "The same way you manage to fuck him when I bet you can't stand it." The truth of it slams right into my chest, pushing me back further.

Step. "Do you pretend it's my cock inside you?" *Every time.*

Step. "Does he even make you come?" *Never.*

Another step, our bodies almost touching. "Does he fuck you with his tongue before he fucks you with his body?" *No, he doesn't, but you should. Right now, would be good.*

His last step pushes me against the couch. My heart beats wildly inside and my desire for him pools in between my thighs.

His fingers scrape along my bare thigh, sending goosebumps skittering throughout my body. My head's spinning and my knees are about to give out.

How dare he touch me this way after just being with someone

else? But I don't want him to stop. I'd be lying to myself if I said I did. So, when images of him with her invade my mind and when the tears threaten to break free, I push them away and focus on us. Because it's my fault he was with her. I don't blame him.

His breath whispers across my neck as he releases a painful sigh. "I'm sorry. God, you're so beautiful." He cups my face and looks into the deepest part of my soul. "I lied. I couldn't fuck her, baby. She wasn't you." Choking on a sob, I pull back, needing to see the truth and all I see is brutal honesty.

"I couldn't stop thinking about how much I wanted you. Only you. Every single time. So, I told her to go home. Because you own me, every single part. Everything I am is yours. And I want it all—with you, just you, because no one even comes close and no one ever will."

There are words that can break you and there are words that can put you back together, but then there are words that can do both at the same time. These are those words and I'm broken, piecing myself back, trying to recall where each fragment fits.

How do I save us? How do I walk away from him when it would cost me everything good?

He leans over and kisses my forehead. I want to savor the feel of his warm lips for as long as I can.

"I'm sorry..." I don't know what else to say or where to start. I cover my trembling mouth; my heart is an achy mess of twisted emotions. Tears rain down my face and I don't care. I want him to know how much I hurt.

He deserves better than what I've put him through. I could be selfless, tell him I'll never be his, to find someone else instead of staying shackled to me when I can't give him a future. But I won't do that, because if seeing him with a random girl hurt this much, I won't survive if he falls in love with anyone but me.

"Don't say anything else. I know, baby, I know." He leans his forehead against mine and we stay like that for long moments until our breaths turn rapidly unsteady.

He rubs his nose against my temple then lower until his tongue licks the curve of my earlobe. He wraps his warm mouth around it, flicking it with his tongue.

"You make me feel so good, Damian."

"All I want to do is make you feel good." He continues to torment me with his mouth, and I moan loudly enough for the neighbors to hear, but I don't care, not even a little.

"I always thought I'd be single forever." His strong, masculine hand snakes up my back and weaves into my hair. "But then you came out of nowhere and ruined all my plans. What am I supposed to do now?"

I groan. The feel of his hands on my body and the rasp in his voice sends warmth surging between my thighs.

He flips me around and bends me over the couch. The cool air hits my ass and goosebumps line the skin of my bare legs, yet I still feel hot all over. I don't know what's happening right now, but I need more.

He tugs my hair with just enough force to make me like it, while his other hand travels slowly up my thigh and stops. His fingers take over and dip into my needy flesh making my core clench impatiently. Lifting the towel over me, his hand skims each one of my ass cheeks, brushing his fingers up and down, leaving a tingle of anticipation behind. He grabs a handful, kneading it, wringing every ounce of pleasure from my flesh until all I know is him.

Damian

I curl over her, driving her further into the couch. "I could fuck you so easily right now," I growl into her ear. She shudders against me and it feels so fucking good knowing what I can make her do.

"Then what are you waiting for?" she prods, pushing herself into me.

I slide my fingers down the curve of her ass, lower and lower, until I trace her wet slit with one finger. My cock flinches, hard and desperate to be inside her. I want to take her like this, right now, hard and fast. She needs it and so do I, so why not just end this misery for the both of us?

My hand lands hard against her heart-shaped ass, the contact echoing through the room. Then I do it again, harder this time, her skin turning a nice shade of pink.

"Ahh, yes!" she cries out, fingers clenching against the couch.

"Fuck, now look what you made me do." Leaning over, I press my cock against her, wanting her to feel what she does to me.

"I've wanted this ass ever since I saw you the first time." She draws in a weak breath.

"You were so pissed, yet so sexy." Brushing her hair away, I allow my mouth free rein over the delicate skin of her neck. She whimpers something incomprehensible as I take small bites, nibbling along the column of her neck. "Do you know what I wanted to do to you after you gave me the finger?" A groan is her only answer. I plant my hands on each side of her wanting to make her even more desperate.

"I wanted to take you into the bathroom, wrap that ponytail

around my wrist, and fuck that attitude right out of you, until you screamed my name."

"Please, Damian. Do it." She reaches for my hand and leads it to her breast. *Fuck.* I squeeze, unable to resist, and as I find her pebbled nipple through the towel, I pinch it hard between two fingers. She curses, pushing herself further into my touch.

My dick pulsates savagely, and I don't know how much more of this I could take. But I need to control myself because the first time we're together will be when she's all mine and I'm all hers. Nothing less will do.

She tries to squeeze her legs together, but I put my thigh in between. I want her to feel every second of tension until she's completely drunk on the high that's only us.

"Damian, what are you doing to me?"

I flip her back up and we face one another, raw hunger escapes from our breaths, melding into one. I brush a thumb against her cheek and as we lock eyes, I see our future, our love story, the one that hasn't happened yet but the one that will.

My gaze rakes her body while she holds the towel in place. "You're so damn perfect. You're made for me."

"You're all I want," she says. "I just wish—" I lean in, and we're forehead to forehead again.

"I wish it too, baby." She sighs and I consume every breath. We're just two fucked up hearts who desperately want salvation. I'm not sure if I'm the one to give it to her, but I'd gladly go to hell to save her.

My fingers rest over her hand, the one barely holding that towel in place, and I begin to pry each one of her fingers apart until there's just one left. I lift the last one off the towel and send it drifting to the ground.

"Goddamn." I can't look away. Those sensuous curves captivate me. Her nipples grow hard while I take in all of her. She bites her lip, squeezing her inner thighs together while my eyes swear to memorize every inch and every contour.

The things I would do to that tight, little body if I could. My hands beg to touch her just for a moment, so I do.

I palm both breasts and squeeze them together. My thumbs rub her nipples and she flips her head back. "Ahhh...yes." Her voice is nothing more than a raspy moan.

Just one little taste and I'll stop. I dive in and take one of her breasts into my mouth, licking her nipple slowly before grabbing it hard between my teeth. She lets out a loud gasp. I hear her frenzied heartbeats like they're my own.

Maybe one more taste. I can't neglect her other nipple. What kind of man would I be? I bring it close to my mouth, my hot breath skims across it before I suck hard, pulling it into my mouth while flicking relentlessly. She struggles to stand, her legs become unsteady, so she grabs my shoulders to stable herself, the sharp points of her nails digging into me.

Enclosing my arms around her, I lean in, her hot breaths grazing against my lips. I run my fingers along her jaw. "Did he kiss you tonight?"

"No," she whispers, "He didn't kiss me anywhere." *Thank fuck.*

There's no prelude, not a second wasted as I dive in and take her mouth. Our hunger and desperation lives in our kiss. We kiss hard. We kiss fast. We kiss like it's our last.

Her fingers scrape along my back, while mine grind into her scalp. I pull away just enough to see her mouth struggling to breathe. I need more, a piece of her that's only mine.

"I want to watch you come."

"What?" She swallows but doesn't take her eyes off of me.

"I want to see you come apart just for me."

"I've—I've never done that before." She bites her lip.

I groan at the thought of being the only person she's ever touched herself for.

Grabbing her hand, I lead her into the bedroom. Once we're inside, I press a firm kiss to her knuckles and let go. "Get on the bed and spread your thighs. Show me how wet you are for me."

She slides onto the bed nervously and opens her legs. I can't turn away. *Oh damn.* Why did I ever think this was a good idea? My muscles grow tight while my cock aches, desperate to be in between those thighs. "Fuck, baby. You're so wet. Is that really all for me?" I squeeze a hand over the front of my sweats, and she cups her tits.

"Every last drop."

I growl, sounding more animal than man. Her hand lowers down to her pussy and she swirls her clit with her fingers. Her hips buck wildly, flying off the bed.

"Put your fingers inside of you. Fuck that wet, little pussy for me." She thrusts them in fully and plunges in and out slowly. Man, I'm in so much trouble with this woman.

"Fuck yourself hard for me." And she does, sliding in and out with furious determination. I press a hand over my cock, squeezing the head, wanting to fill her with every inch.

"Take off your pants. I want to see it," she demands, a sultry fire burning in her gaze, no shyness there. She's so close. I can see it.

"See what, baby? I need to hear you say it."

"Your cock. Show me what I'm missing." *Oh fuck, now why did she have to say that?*

I pull down the sweats and my dick springs forward. She can't take her eyes off it, parting her mouth then licking her bottom lip. I squeeze the base between my thumb and finger. "Damian…"

I sit on the corner of the bed, stroking myself nice and fast as I watch her touch herself. I've never wanted to fuck a woman this badly before. "Do you feel me thrusting inside of you, fucking you, hard and deep?"

Her cries grow urgent. She thrashes around unrestrained, while her fingers dive in and out, the other hand flicking her clit. "Yes... yes I want you," she moans, her voice tense as she watches me touch myself.

"Do you know how badly I want to fuck you? God baby, the things I'd do." My strokes grow ruthless, my cock throbbing, needing to come.

And then her hips arch up, toes curling as she comes violently. "Yessss, Damian..."

My cock tightens, my balls catch on fire and I come fiercely for her, the only woman who's ever made me want more of everything.

"You've broken me for all men," she says, trying to catch her breath, while I catch mine.

"You've broken me, period. I've never came so hard in my life, and I haven't even fucked you," I growl, my eyes raking the length of her body with equal parts frustration and desire.

"Stop looking at me like that," she mutters, grinning through heated eyes.

"Like what?" I smirk, doing it again.

"Like you want to devour me."

"That's because I do." I stand, walking over to her while I take off my dirty shirt and tuck myself back in. "I want your skin on my lips, your taste on my tongue, and that beautiful pussy wrapped around me." My hand skims up her chest, leaving goosebumps along her skin, until I reach her lips.

I part her mouth and dip my finger inside. She sucks it deep, swirling her hot tongue around it, our gazes locked, burning with desire not yet quenched.

"I need you like I need to breathe, Lilah. But I know once we're together, there's no way I'll allow anyone else to have you." I remove my finger from her mouth and kiss her cheek. She looks at me the same way I just looked at her and my stomach contracts sending blood rushing back to my cock.

"Stop looking at me like that," I say, the corners of my lips curving into a smile.

She grabs a pillow and screams into it in frustration, then tosses it, shooting me a playful, yet agitated look. Moving closer, I sit beside her, reaching for a strand of loose hair, and tuck it behind her ear. Her eyes narrow and lips part, releasing a raggedy breath. Our hunger for each other can't be tamed. It longs to live, to breathe, lighting up every molecule within our soul.

I stand, reluctantly preparing to leave but before I go, I capture her eyes. "I've been fooling myself into believing I could stay away from you. I'm no longer going to try."

FIFTEEN

I jolt awake to the sound of my ringing phone but make no attempts to see who's calling. My body still feels like jello from the night before. He makes me feel that good.

I'm stuck at a crossroads. My heart wants Damian but my head's clouded with fear. In my dreams, I reach out to touch him, even though the warning bells scream at me to stay away, but when he's finally near, it's Ash I see. Angry. Menacing. Threatening.

Go ahead. Ruin me. That's what I wish I could say, but never do.

My cell phone rings again, the annoying sound has me wanting to shut it off. I pick it up anyway and my gut sinks when I see who it is.

"Hey."

"Morning babe." Ash's voice drifts across the line. "I was thinking we might grab some lunch today. I want to talk to you about some things."

Oh no. If he brings up moving in or worse, marriage, I don't know how I'll be able to avoid his temper when I turn him down. He won't stay patient much longer. He'll expect me to do what he wants eventually. I can't live in this cage anymore. I have to find a way out.

"Oh. What about?"

"Let's save that for later. I can pick you up at one. Make sure you wear your hair up; I like it that way. And no heels."

"Fine." I hang up before he replies. I squeeze the phone so hard the blood drains from my palm. *I hate him!* It's not enough he belittles and hurts me, but he expects to dictate what I look like too, like I'm a doll to be dressed for his pleasure. I drop the phone on the bed and tug at my hair, staring at the ceiling. When will I be free?

The one consistent thing about Ash is he's always on time, except when he's early. Today is one of those days. He arrives twenty minutes before I expected him, leaving me scrambling to finish. He hates when I make him wait so I don't need reasons to anger him.

My hair is up like he ordered, and I'm wearing dark denim jeans with a white tank, and red flats. I add another coat of mascara and rush out of my apartment. I pause briefly, looking over at Damian's place, yearning to be with him instead.

I hurry for the elevator, which arrives quickly. Making my way to his car, I notice him typing on his phone, but as soon as I open the door, he puts it away. His bright smile doesn't say much about his intentions. He can switch his mood like a chameleon, a master of disguise. I can name countless times where I foolishly thought I was safe from his rage-filled outbursts, then suddenly I'd be trapped under him with his hands wrapped around my throat or his fist punching my stomach.

Every time he's around, I wonder what I ever saw in him. I long to go back in time and tell my stupidly infatuated self to run the hell away.

As I sit, he takes my hand in his and kisses the top of it, making my insides curdle like spoiled milk.

"You look absolutely stunning."

Unease crawls through me and I shift uncomfortably in the seat. "Thanks."

Is this some lame attempt at getting me to hate him less? Because nothing he does will ever change the past. He's broken me, shattered my soul into so many tiny pieces, they're lost to the wind. He'll never find them.

"Where are we going?"

"Some buddies from work mentioned this southern type restaurant with good food. Figured we could try it."

"Ok." He takes my hand in his and places it on his thigh. I don't dare move it, keeping it firmly in place as he drives us away.

After twenty long minutes, we arrive at a small, charming place in south Brooklyn. The rustic feel of the decor, from its wooden chairs to its tables adorned with light pink and ivory roses tied with a burlap string, makes it perfect for a casual date. We sit across from each other and a young, attractive man hands us our menus. *Note to self: Don't speak to any male waiters.*

"So, I brought you here to discuss the way our relationship has been going." My mouth starts to fly open, but I close it quickly.

"I realize my temper has gotten out of control and I'm not the kind of boyfriend you deserve. I want to change, baby, I really do. I decided to see a therapist starting tomorrow."

I jerk my head back, a dazed look upon my face, unable to hide my emotions. "I already made an appointment. The doctor's name is Robert Figueroa on West Twenty-Third." This sounds nothing like him. *What's his angle?* He has never taken responsibility for his actions. Never.

"I love you and I want a future for us, baby. It's always been you for me," he continues, as he takes a sip of his iced tea. That must be it, he's afraid I won't marry him. It makes perfect sense.

Our future flashes before me, a life worse than purgatory. I already see the bruises, the deep scars, my swollen belly holding in our child as he beats me, ignoring my desperate pleas to stop for the sake of our baby. No, I won't bring a child into this. I would rather die first.

I must be strong, standing up for myself is all I have left. Being ruled by fear can't be my default. Not anymore. I must stop letting him suffocate me. I have to fight.

"I'm glad you want to get help, I do, but that doesn't erase anything you've done to me." His jaw tightens as he scratches the back of his neck. "If you want to show me you're trying to change then let me go. Without your threats." My hands fidget under the table, while my stomach twists into tight knots of fear.

"Is that what you want? You want to leave me?" His brows squeeze together as if the questions pain him. Is he that delusional? This isn't the first time I've told him I wanted to leave. I've done it twice before, even though I was terrified, but each time he threatened to out my secrets. Does he think I actually love him after everything he's put me through? The love we once shared flew away with my soul. It'll never come back.

Chin high, I fix him with a stare full of confidence and give him my truth. "Yes. I'm done, Ash. I've been done for a while."

He pinches the bridge of his nose. "I can't just let you go as though all these years meant nothing, Lilah. I want you to become my wife. I'm trying to change so I can be a good husband. Give me a chance. Please." I knew he'd never set me free. This is a ruse, a way to seduce me into believing a fairy tale, which will never exist.

"Can you at least give me a month?" he pleads.

"And then you'll let me go without a fight?"

He squeezes his eyes shut for a second. "Yes. I swear. But you'll see I'll be a better man."

"Okay. I can give you a month. But if you hurt me in anyway, I'm done. Tell everyone you want. I no longer care." Giving him this time is probably stupid, but if there's even a small chance he can be helped, then it's worth it. Not for him, but for any woman he may encounter after me. No one deserves to go through what I've been through.

If he decides to go public with the blackmail, I'll manage the consequences. I'm strong, I convince myself, but knowing Damian will be by my side makes me braver.

"Thanks for hearing me out, babe." He places his hand on the table, palm side up, asking for mine. "I promise I'll be a new man. You matter so much to me." I remain silent but give him my hand. Those same fingers that have hurt me countless times before, gently caress my skin. I derive no pleasure from the contact; his touch makes my skin crawl with thousands of tiny spiders.

The car ride back to my place is luckily quick. Just as I'm about to exit, he grabs my arm. His fingers dig into my skin, sending a chill deep into my bones. "I love you so much, baby."

"Let go, Ash," I spit out. And he does. "Hope therapy goes well tomorrow." I get out and slam the door shut. I don't know who this new girl is, but I love her.

SIXTEEN

I'm thoughtlessly flipping through the channels, trying to find something to distract me from needing to see her. I don't want to text her just in case she's with him. The thought of them together slams me with such hatred; it's hard to focus on anything else. My phone vibrates with a message, so I pick it up hoping it's her. It's not.

Jax: Who is up for a good time tonight? There's a new lounge I want to check out.

Damian: I'm good.

Jax: I bet you are. That girl was hot, D. Want a repeat tonight or are you married already?

Damian: Nothing happened.

Gabe: What? Why?

Damian: I wasn't feelin' it.

Jax: Coulda fooled me, brother. You two were all over each other. It's her isn't it? Lilah's got her hands wrapped around your dick? Did she break up with the asshole yet? If not, then you gotta get over her.

Gabe: As much as it pains me to agree with him, he's right. There's only so much you can do, D. Clearly, threatening him didn't work.

Damian: Yeah, get over it. I'll get right on that. Whenever you find a woman you give a shit about, Jax, we'll see how quickly you'll get over it when you can't have her.

Jax: Just looking out, man. I know I joke and shit, but I don't like seeing you looking like a mess.

Damian: Thanks. But I got this.

Gabe: OK, D. Let us know if you change your mind about tonight.

Damian: I will.

I know they mean well, but they don't know what I feel for her. She has such a hold on me. It's as though she's always been there, in every part of my life. I can't even remember my life without her.

Jax doesn't get it. He's never been in a serious relationship. But Gabe should understand what I'm going through. He was once in love and it looked good on him. That is until his ex-girlfriend broke the fuck out of his heart. The poor bastard never moved on. But if there's hope for me, there's hope for him too.

The soft knocking on my door jolts me out of my thoughts. Hoping that it's who I think it is, I fly for the door and open it.

She's standing there looking hot as hell with her hair up in a ponytail like the first night we met. I note her wide-eyed expression as she taps her thumbs together, nervously. I reach for her hand, bringing her inside.

"What's wrong? Did he hurt you?" I look her up and down not seeing any signs that she's hurt. She lets go of me and paces back and forth. "I finally did it."

"Did what, baby girl?" My voice does nothing to calm her, she continues to pace while I continue to worry. "Lilah, come here." Moving to the couch, I sit in hopes she joins me.

"Ugh, what did you say?" She stops to look at me but it's as though she doesn't see me at all. Her eyes are clouded, covered by a fog.

"Sit with me baby, tell me what happened."

She's deep in thought as she grabs her ponytail, twisting the ends, just like she did the first time I saw her at the bar, the night she was upset over that bastard. "Okay. Sorry. I'm just—"

"Don't apologize," I pat the seat next to me, "just come here."

She finally sits and tells me everything that happened. Her voice carries so much fear and worry, it kills me to hear it.

But I'm glad she doesn't believe he's getting help. I'll bet anything he's lying. Even if he wasn't, so what? Therapy rarely ever works for abusers. It's something I researched. More than once.

I wish she'd just get out now, forget this one-month bullshit, but

I refuse to pressure her anymore. I want this to be her decision no matter how sick it makes me.

I circle an arm around her, protectively. "I'm proud of you, babe."

She leans her head against my shoulder and releases a heavy breath. Her voice trembles and I feel the tremor as I hold her, making all the muscles within me go rigid. "I'm scared, Damian. I know him better than anyone," she confesses. "He won't just let me go."

I taste her fear like it's my own. It rips me apart, utterly and completely. But my need to protect her also makes me stronger, a soldier who'd kill anyone who tries to hurt her.

Most of my life, I've worried about taking the leap and falling for a woman. I've always kept my distance, to protect them from me, finding it difficult to see myself as anything but my father's son. But lately, I've come to realize there's no way we're alike. How can we be if I never saw him worry or care for my mother? The only priority he ever had was finding new ways to beat her down. She was his toy, nothing more.

I can't see myself ever treating Lilah that way. I'd cut off my arms before I lay a finger on her. Whenever I see her in pain, it makes me vengeful. The need within me to slice, to burn, to obliterate anyone who causes her suffering becomes undeniable whenever she hurts.

We may share some of the same DNA, my father and I, but we're two different people. We have to be. I have to believe that.

I grab her hand and bring it to my lips, pressing a soft kiss to her palm. Finally relaxed, she lifts her head, a pained smile on her beautiful face.

I bring her hand up to my chest so she can feel my heart beating for her. "I'll keep you safe. Do you hear me? You're not alone anymore. I'll be here for your worst days and your best days. I'm not going anywhere. Ever. You have me."

Her fingers reach out and glide against the outer edges of my lips. Closing my eyes, I revel in her touch, craving more. Her fingers are suddenly replaced by the warmth of her lips as she kisses me slow, as if learning my mouth for the first time. I let her take control, let her take whatever she wants because all I am is hers.

As we separate, our eyes connect and it's as though they're speaking a language of their own, lost in each other's pain and need. "I never believed in fate but then came you," she says, caressing my face. "You've been sent to me and I never want to give you back. You overshadow all the awfulness that has been my life for too long." Her words are like fuel for my damaged heart. "You're everything I need, Damian, and soon it'll be just us."

I never imagined I'd feel the raw power of those words being uttered to me by a woman, especially one I want this much. Maybe being with her would be easier if it wasn't filled with all these complications, but nothing worth a damn is ever easy. And she's worth all this shit. So even knowing everything I know now, I still want her because this woman, she's everything.

I grab her waist and flip her on top of me, needing her close. My eyes roam her face, tracing every line, inscribing her beauty into my subconscious. "You're everything I wished for but never thought I'd have. You've turned my world upside down without even knowing."

Her breaths turn shallow as she leans forward connecting our bodies until our lips connect the same. This time it isn't slow. We kiss hard and deep, our tongues colliding, creating a life of their own. Our fingers claw at our skin, wanting our bodies to be just as close.

She brings out the needy bastard in me. My hunger for her is carnal, the fire burns so strong nothing could ever destroy its power.

Her hips rock back and forth as she straddles my legs tightly within hers. Her tongue scans across mine and I thrust my erection against her, swallowing a whimper. Clutching the back of her head,

I pull her closer, deepening our kiss, never wanting it to stop. Her hands grip my T-shirt as she moans my name, and that sound is better than anything in this damn world.

"You own me, you know that?" I whisper across her lips.

She pulls away just a little and gazes into my eyes. "I better." Her mouth lifts into a sexy smirk matching mine.

I clutch the back of her head. "You better, huh?"

She pants, the smile now gone. "That's right," she mutters.

I bring her closer. "Don't worry, baby. You'll own me until the day that I die." Her mouth lands hard on mine and our kiss turns savage once again. She fists my shirt with both hands while her hips grind against my hard-on.

Her long nails dig into my skin as she says, "I need you, Damian." I need her too. So badly. I want to watch that face twist in pleasure the first time I thrust inside her. "Oh God— this is...this is better than my fantasies," she whispers.

Wait? What was that? I pull back a little to peer at her. "You've touched yourself thinking of me?" I growl.

Eyes hooded, her tongue darts out licking her lips. "I've fingered myself to you so many times I've lost count."

Oh damn. That's all it takes to send me over the edge.

I stand, lifting her with me. Her hands clench my hair as her raspy voice asks, "Where are we going?"

"My bed, baby girl." She leans into me and kisses my chest, while I indulge in the feel of her in my arms.

Once we reach my bedroom, I turn on the light and toss her gently on top of my bed. Lowering down, I settle my weight over her body, loving the feel of her fingers sinking into the flesh of my back.

Her hands land on my biceps as she strokes them. Grazing her cheek with the back of my hand, I peer down at her, tasting her hunger as it echoes mine. "I want you, baby, so much." Her pulse rages against my lips as I kiss up her neck. "But I'll take anything I can get. And right now," my thumb brushes against her bottom lip, "that's you coming all over my mouth." She gasps and I don't give her a second to do anything else as my mouth swallows her groans. *Yeah baby, this is happening.*

I grind my dick in between her thighs as she wraps her legs around my hips, pushing us closer together. "I'm trying so hard not to fuck you," my lips graze against hers, "but damn it you make it difficult. If you only knew all the ways I wanna make you come." She curses, biting her lip, making my dick flinch in response.

I keep my eyes on hers as I slowly kiss my way down the center of her body until I reach her jeans. She cups her breasts as she watches me pop open the button and lower down her zipper. Squirming underneath me, almost breathless, she arches into my touch. "Eager, aren't we?" I give her my cockiest smile before going down and licking the skin right above her sheer, white, lace panties.

She grabs my head, nails digging into my scalp, her voice unrecognizable. "You're torturing me." *Hell yeah, I am.*

I climb back up her body, lowering myself on top of her. "And I'm loving every second." I stroke her cheek with my thumb, edging closer until I kiss the lips that make me hard as a rock every time she bites them. Her tongue fights mine, punishing me for not finishing what I've started. Our hungry moans and tangled limbs feed our kiss as it grows more demanding.

I release her mouth just as her hips thrust hard into my erection. "You're killing me, beautiful." I tug her ear with my lips, my self-control on the verge of collapsing. "I'm two seconds away from tearing off your clothes with my teeth and filling you with my cock. I want to watch that pretty mouth say my name as you come."

Her nails scrape against my back, "Yessss, please." *Soon baby, but not tonight.*

Her heart pounds under my lips as I trail kisses down her neck to the valley between her breasts.

I pull her tank top down, exposing a white lacy bra. "I like this." My mouth lands on her breasts, kissing them over the thin material.

"Just take it off, Damian, please."

Lifting my eyes up, I shake my head, "Not yet, baby." I don't know what our future holds so today I go slow, needing to stretch out every moment.

She groans as my thumbs brush over her nipples. I cup the undersides of her breasts, taking a hard tip into my mouth, biting just enough to make her feel it, just enough to make her cry out in pleasure. Needing more, I unclip the front of the bra and let her breasts spring free.

"I'll never get enough of you." I take a pebbled nipple into my mouth, clasping it between my teeth before moving on to the other. She writhes underneath me as I suck each one, rubbing my tongue against them. She grips the back of my head as I lower down her body, my hot breath telegraphing my every move, until I reach her hips.

"Lift up." And she does. I pull down her jeans and panties, tossing them somewhere on the floor. Gripping her knees, I spread her apart and she opens up willingly. She's dripping and it's about to be all mine. "Tell me what you want, baby. Give me the words."

She rolls her hips as I kiss up the inside of her thigh. "I want to come...all over your mouth." *Fuck.* I hook my arms under her thighs and brush my lips across her pussy. I want to take it slow, want to make her wait for the pleasure I'm about to give, but as she cries out for my mouth again, I give my woman what she needs.

I fuck her with my tongue over and over as my thumb brushes her clit. She grips the bedspread, screaming out for more. So, I do it again, and again, until her cries get closer together. Her fingers interlace with her hair just as her eyes flutter shut.

"Look at me. I want your eyes." She opens up for me, and the hungry haze within them tangles with my own dark need. Not breaking the connection, I continue to torture her, devouring the taste of her while she twists in agony trying hard not to look away.

I want her so damn much, but I know fucking her now isn't a good idea. Once I'm inside her, things will never be the same. She'll feel more mine than she does already, and I'd tie her to my bed before I'd let him touch her again.

"You taste so fucking good, baby. I need to savor every little drop, so I'm not ready to let you come, not yet." I swirl my tongue around her clit and she swears under her breath. "I'm way too busy enjoying myself."

I pin her wrists to the bed and thrust my tongue inside her again, plunging in and out hard and fast, until she's close, then I slow it down. I keep her on the brink until she's dripping down her ass.

"Damian, yes, yes...don't stop!" She clenches her hands, her feet digging into my back as I swipe my tongue up her engorged clit. And as she's about to come, I let go of her hands and fuck her with my fingers, hitting her G-spot just right.

"Oh my God, yessss!" Her pussy quakes around me, and her hips thrust up like she's possessed. Once the tremors stop, I remove my fingers and suck them dry. She watches me, her breasts rising and falling, tongue licking her lips.

"You want to see how good you taste?" She nods. I lick my way up her body. And when I reach her lips, I kiss slow, making love to her mouth as my desire for her fuses with the taste of her own. Our lips finally untangle, and I lay next to her still painfully hard but utterly fulfilled.

"Damian...wha...um...what about you?" Then she sighs like speaking is just too difficult. That sound is worth all the blue balls.

I should be used to it by now though because this woman gives me plenty of them.

"I love the sound of you speechless." I kiss her temple. "Don't worry about me. That was all about you, baby." If she puts that mouth anywhere near my cock. It's game over. She's getting fucked.

"Mmm, okay," she says, a satisfied smile on her face, her eyes fluttering from exhaustion.

"Go to sleep, beautiful. I'll be right here." She cuddles against my side, her head on my heart and my arm around her. Right now, all I want to do is hold her like there's nowhere else she belongs but right here.

Lilah

SEVENTEEN

I'm getting ready to go on a date with the man I can't stand while thinking about the one I actually want. The two weeks following the passionate night Damian and I shared have flown by.

Ash claims he's still in therapy, but whenever I ask to go with him, he says the therapist prefers he comes to his sessions alone so he can share his feelings openly. I doubt my going one time would impede his recovery. Not that I want to go but I'd like to know whether he's being honest about attending. There's still a tiny spark of hope in me that wants to believe him, but it's hard to.

As soon as I had the doctor's name, I looked him up. Last week, I considered sitting at a coffee shop across the street from the office just to see if he'd show up for his appointment, but then at the last minute I chickened out. I was too worried of the repercussions of getting caught. He'd never tolerate my checking up on him. He'd hurt me…or worse.

Ash and I have seen each other a few times since he began his quest for change. My body recoils every time he touches me but it's so much worse when he's inside me. I feel like I'm cheating—on Damian —and my gut heaves each time.

I want this month to be over so badly. How do I survive another second of this charade? I'm teetering on such a thin line and I just want to fall. Fall into the unknown where he doesn't exist because I know Damian will be there to catch me. He's always there.

I'm falling in love with him. Head over heels. The whole shebang. Every cliché I've ever read about, I feel it. He's the music that keeps me dancing. Every part of me is his for the taking. But I can't tell him. Not yet. When I'm free from Ash, I'll show him how much he means to me, both with words and with my body. Right now, I have to play the devil's game.

Damian and I've been spending almost every day together. Any free hours we have after work or on the weekend we spend with each other. We talk about mundane things like our favorite colors or things we love to do. Pretty much all the basics we can think of. It's like we're in our own little bubble of bliss.

Sometimes, I have weak moments where I doubt myself, afraid of trusting my instincts about men, considering how wrong I was about Ash, but I stifle those dangerous thoughts. Not all men hurt women. Most importantly, Damian wouldn't hurt me. He just wouldn't. I refuse to live in a world where that would ever be true. He's the one who's turned on the light in the dark cave I've been living in for years. Now, I refuse to return to the darkness. I crave to be in his light. I've been without it too long.

We've been trying to tame our passion for one another. We both know how close we are to sleeping together. But it hasn't been easy, especially for me. That man has way better self-control than I do.

I wish I didn't have to go tonight. I wish I didn't have to see the man who stole years from my life, and my chance at real happiness, but I have to. I'm proud that I stood up to him that day. I went from being a scared little girl to a woman who no longer gives a shit, one who's sick of being afraid. When I saw what he did to my neck that night, something fractured within me and it's been chiseling off bit by bit, leaving me with an open wound.

I put on a black, sleeveless, sheath dress with a silver belt and black stilettos. He told me he has something special planned, so this seemed appropriate. I'm surprised he didn't pick my outfit for me. I mean I would've just worn yoga pants and sneakers but that would've caused a major fight. I'm not *that* brave.

I'm supposed to meet him at his place first. He apparently has some sort of surprise for me. Can't say I'm not majorly apprehensive about what that may be.

I grab my cell to check the time and notice I've missed a few texts from Damian.

> **Damian:** I miss you.
>
> **Damian:** I hate that you're going to see him.
>
> **Damian:** Please be careful, baby girl.

My heart squeezes inside me at his words and my chest aches, knowing how much pain I'm causing him.

> **Lilah:** I'm sorry, Damian. For everything. I can't wait for all this to end. I'm counting down the minutes until we can be together. I've been running for years, always looking over my

shoulder. I can't wait to stop running. I can't wait to be yours.

Damian: I feel the same, baby. You've come into my life at the most unexpected time. I need you. There's so much I want to tell you, but I want to do it in person. Come over later tonight. I'll stay up.

How could a man be so masculine, yet be so forthcoming with his feelings? He's all sorts of perfect and I get to keep him all for myself.

Lilah: I want to tell you more too. I'll see you tonight. I'll be thinking about you the entire time.

Damian: I know.

I put myself in his place, imagining him being inside another woman, even one he doesn't want, and it kills me, my heart would explode. I don't know how he's surviving this. Two more weeks. That's all. Then I can finally be done with this game and find happiness with the only man who can mend my broken spirit.

I look in the full-length mirror one last time, smoothing out my dress, and head out. The drive's short, so I arrive in front of Ash's door ten minutes later. I get ready to knock but pull back. Unease creeps up my body. *I can do this. I can do this. Everything will be all right.* Closing my eyes, I take a deep breath, then hold it and release. I quickly knock before I change my mind. The door swings open within seconds and he's there, all smiles and pleasantries.

He devours my body with a heated gaze. "Damn, I'm one lucky son of a bitch."

132

I plaster a fake smile on my face. "Thank you." I've been faking it for so long it comes naturally when I want it to. As I walk inside, the fragrant smell of garlic mingled with the sweet smell of tomatoes attack my nose. There's noise coming from the kitchen. It sounds like someone is mixing something in a bowl. That's strange. Who'd be here cooking? I didn't see any other car in the driveway. "It smells nice. Is someone here?"

The corner of his mouth curls upward into a deep smile. "That's actually part of your surprise. Close your eyes." I look at him speculatively, unsure of what to expect. I do as he asked, and sense him moving to my left, looping his arm around mine as he guides me forward, toward the kitchen. Once we stop, he says, "You can open your eyes now."

I pry them open to find a short, grey haired man dressed in a chef's uniform preparing something on the stove. The man stops what he's doing, wipes his hands on his apron, and walks over to us. He extends his hand to me in greeting and I shake it. A natural, inviting smile brightens his face making his olive-colored eyes gleam.

"Hello, I'm Chef Roberto. I've heard a lot about you. All good things, of course." I smile back as he continues. "I've prepared a wonderful three-course meal for you two, as well as a chocolate lava cake for dessert. I hope you're hungry."

"I'm definitely famished, thank you. I'm sure everything is delicious," I remark, looking around at his preparations. He nods his head and walks toward what looks like a large bowl of pesto. "You two may have a seat. I will be serving your first course shortly."

"Thank you, chef. We're looking forward to it," Ash says, as he curls his arm around my waist, pulling me close. We make our way to the dining room. The table's adorned with a red tablecloth, gold flatware, and crystal wine glasses. The center is scattered with white rose petals and the large votive candles provide a very romantic ambiance.

I'm not sure what any of this means. He's never gone out of his way to be romantic in the last few years, not since the abuse became more aggressive. I hope I'm wrong and this is sincere. Maybe he truly doesn't like being so angry all the time, maybe all this is a positive sign for the both of us, for our own separate futures.

He pulls a brown leather chair for me and takes his seat directly across. "Would you like some wine?" he asks, pointing to the two bottles already on the table.

I try not to drink too much when I'm with him, afraid of losing my inhibitions, but a few sips won't hurt. "Sure, that'd be great."

"Red or white, babe?"

"Red. And thanks for planning all of this." I don't want to appear rude or ungrateful. I want this night to go as smoothly as possible.

He stands, deftly opens the wine bottle, then picks up my wine glass, pouring some into it, and does the same to his. He grins as he sits back down. "Only the best for my girl. Instead of going out, I brought the restaurant to us. He's supposed to be one of the best."

"Well, I'm definitely surprised. Thank you. I'm sure the food will be amazing. Do you know what he's making?" As long as it's made quickly, allowing me to leave sooner, I really don't care.

He picks up his glass and takes a few sips. "I told him to surprise us, so your guess is as good as mine." He extends his hand toward the middle of the table, asking for mine. I give it to him, even though everything inside me screams no.

He moves to the edge of his seat, straightening his spine, and stares at me with piercing focus. "I love you, Lilah. I only want the best for you, and for us. You're it for me babe and I'm so sorry for everything I've done to you. Therapy has really shown me how to manage my temper in more productive ways."

I go still as my stomach rolls and my heart picks up speed. He wants the best for *us? There's no us!* What can I say without leading him on? My knee bounces under the table while I formulate a response.

"I'm glad therapy is helping. I want the best for you too." I remove my hand from his and reach for my glass. *Where is the damn food?* I take a big gulp of wine while Ash glares, unflinchingly. His expression is completely devoid of elation as he lets out a harsh breath and looks past me straight toward the kitchen. *Oh no. Did he pick up on my words? Oh my God, he did.*

Just as I'm about to wonder how long it will take for the food to arrive, Roberto approaches, carrying two white plates, setting them before us. "Your first course is a pesto and garlic shrimp bruschetta with feta cheese and a balsamic glaze. Enjoy."

Then he retreats to the kitchen, letting us savor our meal alone. We remain quiet through our appetizer, which tastes delicious, but I'm barely enjoying it, too worried about what Ash is thinking.

The next course is a scallop and carrot salad with some sort of grapefruit dressing. I wish I was enjoying the food because this man can really cook, but I can't seem to settle my nerves. "How are you liking the food?" Ash asks, finally breaking our silence.

"It's delicious." I smile. "Thanks again." He cracks a grin and returns to his food. Phew, maybe this night won't be as bad as I thought.

Finally, for our main entree, we're served filet mignon with crushed tomato and garlic sauce with a side of sweet potato fries. I quickly move to finish it, praying I can get out of here after dessert. My desire for this night to end is much stronger than my love of food, and I *really* love food.

Roberto comes back to collect our plates and brings us our dessert. "It was a pleasure cooking for you this evening. Enjoy the rest of your night." Ash hands him an envelope with what I assume is cash inside, then our chef is gone, leaving us in weighty silence.

I take one small bite of the cake, so not to insult Ash, and push away my plate. I'm so stuffed anyway; I don't think I could eat anymore even if I wanted to.

He clears his throat, watching me. "You're not going to have the rest of your cake?"

"It looks good, but I'm still so full from all that tasty food."

"Why don't you try to have a few more bites," he begs. "The middle is the best." He cuts into his slice showing me the gooey chocolate filling in the center and puts a piece into his mouth.

Damn it. That does look good. I guess I can make some room for *that*. As I begin cutting into my cake, he gets up to get some more napkins. I keep digging around but don't find any chocolate filling in the center. I want some melty chocolate goodness too. Breaking it up some more, I find nothing but more cake. I turn around intending to tell Ash my cake is broken, except I don't find him in the kitchen, instead I find him on the floor behind me.

EIGHTEEN

I gasp, clutching my chest with both hands. *No, no this can't be happening*! He said I'd have one month to decide if I wanted to stay with him. So why's he down on one knee with hope burning brightly in his eyes. "Ash?"

He motions toward my plate. "Look in the cake, baby." A beaming smile is pasted on his face. I look back at the cake. Picking up my fork, I dig through it with such ferocity I'm afraid I'll chip the plate. But then I finally see it. The ring.

Fishing it out, I wipe the crumbs off it with my fingertips. A large, solitaire, princess cut stares at me, the tiny diamonds cascade down the band, sparkling in the light. I turn to him and he's still on the floor, smiling like all the pieces of his life are about to fall into place.

"Ash, what is this?"

"Lilah, you and I have been through a lot together. Being without you even a day is too much for me. I want you in my life, not just as my girlfriend but my wife. I love you so much. Will you marry me?"

No. No. No. The nausea creeps up my throat. I'm definitely going to be sick. My hands are clammy and my throat goes dry. What do I say without angering him? "I appreciate everything you've done tonight," I voice softly, running a hand nervously through my hair, "and for your willingness to see a therapist, but you told me I'd have a month to decide whether I wanted to be with you. That month isn't up yet, so I—I don't understand what's happening."

He's still on the floor on bended knee but his smile is now gone. "I know it hasn't been a month, but I thought you might be open to the possibility of starting your life with me *now*, seeing as how I changed. The last two weeks have been so good, haven't they?"

I clutch the ring tightly in my fist, its sharp edges cutting into my hand. "Ash, a person can't change overnight." I try to smile but my lips tremble. "You have to give it time. There's no rush, babe. It takes months, probably years, for a person to ahh—overcome these problems."

He lowers his other knee and looks blankly at me. "Are you saying you won't marry me?"

I gulp down the fear scratching its way up my throat. "All I'm saying is that it isn't fair to push this on me when you've promised to give me more time to decide."

He stands, inching closer. Dread pushes itself inside me while my hands shake. I clasp them together in hopes they stop, but it's useless. He lowers his mouth to my ear. "You have to be *pushed* into marrying me?" His voice is a sting across my flesh, like sharpened knives carving into me slowly.

I clear my throat as it tightens. "That's, umm, not what I meant." A cluster of goosebumps coat every inch of my skin, and as I try to breathe, no air enters my lungs. I try harder until I feel my chest rising with hollow breaths. I sink deeper into the chair wishing I could somehow melt into it and disappear.

"Nothing is ever fucking good enough for you is it, you cunt?" He screams the words loudly, his spit lashing me across the face. My watery eyes enlarge as my body breaks out into a cold sweat.

What have I done?

He backs away just a little. I shrink inward, staring at his black loafers not daring to look at his face, too afraid of what I'll find.

"Ash, I'm not saying no." I attempt to clear my parched throat again, trying to get the words out before he loses the tenuous hold on his temper. "I love you. You know I do. I'm just— I'm just saying not right now. That's all, I promise." *Do I sound believable? Does it even matter at this point?*

He untucks his shirt and my pulse quickens. He moves to the back of my chair and I fear I may pass out. I need to figure a way out of this. But before I have a chance to consider my options, he drags the chair forcefully across the floor with me still in it.

"Stop! What are you doing?!" I scream, while holding on, afraid of falling. My heart pounds like a fist inside my chest, the thumping so loud I can hear it like a warning in my ears.

He drops the chair in the middle of the dining room and walks around, encircling me, while I cower in pure terror. "You know, I thought convincing you I began going to therapy would make you more willing to start a life with me, but I now see nothing will. You just don't want me." He stands behind me again, smelling the back of my head, inhaling deeply. He wraps a lock of hair around his finger momentarily, before setting it free.

"Yeah, that's right, you dumb bitch. I never went to therapy." A cold chill skirts up my spine and I close my eyes as tears fall down my cheeks. *I knew it.*

"Did you think I'd lower myself to do something like that? As if I'm some loser with issues? I don't have problems." His hand touches my neck and I flinch as he slides his fingers up and down the side, probably enjoying the way my pulse thrums frantically.

"*You're* the reason I'm like this. You've been a horrible girlfriend for years, always talking to other men, fucking that asshole behind my back! I *know* you are. You're gonna pay for all of it."

I want to run, to scream, but I can't do anything. The sharp bite of his voice seals off any viable exit. I'm frozen in place, no longer human.

I need you, Damian. I shut my eyes hoping this is just a nightmare. I don't want to die. Not like this. I want my chance at happiness. I want to live.

Damian. I call to him again, the sound echoing in my brain, summoning him. I see his face, that handsome face smiling at me and it inflicts more tears. They fall silently, each one representing the days I may never get with him.

Still standing behind me, Ash's hand creeps up the back of my neck until he reaches my hair and he viciously yanks my head back. I stare into his eyes filled with hateful disdain, his pupils dilating like sharp daggers from the anger flowing throughout his body. It's as though every part of him is a weapon meant to destroy me.

"I know you're fucking that asshole. Just admit it!" He roars into my face and I try to shake my head, but his grip is tight making my scalp throb. I sob, every word he utters breaking me down a little at a time.

"Did he tell you him and his buddies paid me a visit and threatened me to stay away from you? I know you told him. You're out to destroy my life, pretending you're some victim! But. You're. Not. He'd beat the shit out of you too if he knew what a whore you are."

I taste every one of his words, feeling their jagged edges cutting into me. "I never slept with him," I croak out, my neck hurting from being bent in such an awkward position, making it difficult to speak. "I don't know— why he'd do that. Maybe he saw my throat in passing. I'm—I'm sorry."

"You think I'm stupid?" he laughs diabolically, "I can't believe I ever loved you. You disgust me." Insults fly from his mouth like rocks from an angry horde of people seeking retribution.

"What did you think? You were going to leave me for him? Guess what? You're not getting a fucking happily ever after." My eyes widen. W*hat does that mean? What's he going to do?* He lets go of my hair and I hear what I think is him ripping off his shirt behind me.

The next thing I know is the taste of his cologne mixed with my salty tears as he ties his button down around my mouth. I scream and scream while trying to suppress a wave of nausea that hits me.

"Shut up. No one can hear you," he says calmly as he comes around. But I scream anyway. I scream until I can't scream anymore, until all that escapes is silence.

Once he's convinced I'm tightly bound, he grabs a chunk of my hair and without warning, snatches me off the chair. My body hits the floor hard as he drags me across it while I scream again, but all that comes out is a muffled cry. No one'll hear me as I die.

I'm sorry Mama.

He drops me on the floor like a sack of unwanted junk. My cheek hits the ground as he climbs on top of my back. Fear and panic mingle inside every inch of my body.

He pulls my hair once again, pulling until the back of my head touches his chest. "Does that hurt?" The air stalls in my lungs and I try to nod, but I can't move my head. I hope it ends quickly, but I know he'll kill me slow, enjoying every tear of skin and every drop of blood.

"How about this?" I don't even have a second to register what he just said before he slams my face onto the cold, hard floor. An explosion of pain shoots from my nose and I taste what I think is blood dripping down my throat.

I can't breathe! I can't breathe!

My chest is ablaze. I'm going to drown in my own blood. My nose hurts. I think he broke it. Pushing my face up just an inch brings some air back into my lungs. That's when I notice the pool of blood on the ground where my nose had been. There's so much of it but it doesn't stop, I keep losing more.

His hands grab at my thighs as he lifts my dress and shoves my panties down and off my legs. I know what he's about to take from me but I'm too worried about dying to care. Grabbing my hair, his voice slithers against my neck. "If you fight me, if you so much as do anything I don't like, I'm going to make this hurt. So be a good little slut and spread your legs."

He drops my head, slamming my face back on the floor against the blood produced from my suffering. A sickness rises in my throat, its power so strong I choke on my own vomit.

Just keep breathing. It'll be over soon.

I close my eyes needing to shut off my brain for what's about to happen. He pulls down his zipper, the rasp so loud it resounds in my head. "On your knees," he demands. I try to move as fast as I can but the agonizing pain in my face slows me down. My body shatters with maddening cries.

"I said on your fucking knees." Losing patience, he grips my hips and lifts them up as his fingers dig into my flesh. Once he has me positioned the way he likes, he slams his full penis into me. My fingers clench and I scream, gagging on the shirt, but no one can hear me. I hurt everywhere but I focus on the large drops of blood pouring out of my face instead.

Drip.

Drip.

Drip.

I count each one. How much blood can a person lose before it gets to be too much?

Drip.

Drip.

Drip.

Will he leave me here after he kills me? Or will he find somewhere to hide my body? I hope my loved ones aren't the ones to find me. I don't want that for them.

"Fuuuck." He finally finishes as I reach sixty-eight. That number will be carved into my consciousness for as long as I live.

Before I even have a chance to recover from what he just did, he flips me over. Looking straight into my eyes, I see no regret, just remnants of a wild storm that's not fully satiated.

He lifts his arm and more pain rips through my face as he slams his fist into my cheek. "You couldn't even pretend to enjoy it? I bet you would've if his dick was fucking you, you dirty whore!" His words rip at my insides while his hands destroy whatever's left of my outside. The burning pain across my face is unlike anything I've ever felt before. It's as though he's hammered my face into the ground.

The blood leaks into my throat and I begin to gag. *Just keep breathing. You're still alive.* But my chest is too heavy.

He stands up and my eyes follow him as he walks to the kitchen, opening the refrigerator door, his back to me. This is my chance. I can make a run for it. All I have to do is crawl a short distance toward the door, then run like hell. The need to live gives me adrenaline I didn't have minutes before.

I remove the blood-soaked shirt from my mouth and slink slowly across the floor as quietly as a child afraid that her mother will catch her doing something bad.

Almost there.

Just another inch.

Once I reach the door, I climb up, but my legs are so wobbly I almost fall. I steady myself holding on to the knob and I twist the lock open, when suddenly a loud smash, like that of glass breaking, causes me to spin back around.

I pound on the door and scream for help just as he picks up a piece of a broken plate and runs at me. "You bitch!" I'm panting, trying the knob but it won't budge. *Open, damn it!* I manage to bang on the door a few more times before he jerks me away and throws me up against the wall. He presses the sharp edge into my neck, and I feel a slight pinch, knowing he cut me.

"Go ahead you son of a bitch, do it!" I yell, finding strength I didn't know I had. "You can't kill someone who's already dead!"

He drops the weapon and clutches my neck in his fist. "You don't know what death is, but you will." He bashes the back of my head into the wall and my vision goes blurry as he drops me onto the floor.

Someone pounds at the door and then a man says my name, but it's a distant sound, like a dream. I flicker in and out of consciousness as the same voice says my name again, closer now, but I don't recognize it. Gentle hands pick up my head, and I hear more words being spoken but I can't make them out. *It's too late,* I want to tell him. But instead, I close my eyes surrendering to the darkness.

Damian

NINETEEN

How long is this damn date? It's almost ten and I haven't heard from her yet. Maybe he forced her to sleep over. She's probably scared. I pace back and forth, unable to calm my nerves. She's fine, I keep telling myself, she has to be. Even knowing Logan is watching her doesn't relax me. I should've had him plant a camera inside the bastard's home. I told Logan to break down the door if he hears any suspicious noise coming from inside. No news must mean good news, at least I fucking hope so.

I'm so close to losing my mind, I've even considered going by the house myself. But if Ash sees me, it'll put her in jeopardy, and I won't risk her life. I already took a gamble by threatening him and I refuse to do it again.

If something happens to her, I won't survive it. She's got my heart in her soft, little hands and if she dies, it dies with her. *Fuck*.

She's not gonna die. I have to stop thinking that way.

I decide to take a shower in hopes it helps me pass the time. I need to see her, to feel her heartbeat, to know she's okay.

I enter the bathroom, turning the dial, releasing the hot water as the steam fights its way out, wafting everywhere. Stepping out of my black sweats and white T-shirt, I open the glass door and welcome the slicing of heat against my back.

As I close my eyes, I'm bombarded with images of her. The water does nothing to calm me. It's the opposite. All I see is her, hurt and alone. It's as though someone is snapping polaroids and gluing them inside my head. I fist my hands across the brown, ceramic tile as my mind is torn apart. I bang my forehead against the wall to clear my mind, but I keep drowning in morbid thoughts.

I pour the shampoo into my palm and scrub my scalp until it's sore. *Where are you, baby?* I have to tell her how I feel, tell her I'm falling in love with her. That feeling, it's been there for a few days now, but I've wanted to wait to tell her, wait until we're together. But now with everything going on, I can't wait anymore.

I finish scrubbing my body and turn off the water. Towel wrapped around my hips, I walk back to my bedroom to get some clothes. The small, white bedside lamp provides the only light as I get dressed. I look around for my cell before remembering I left it in the kitchen. Hoping not to miss her call, I rush to retrieve it.

I enter the passcode into the keypad and the phone finally unlocks. I blink hard at the three missed calls and numerous texts from Logan and the guys. The room spins as I read the first message.

Logan: She's hurt. It's bad, Damian, really bad. I'm sorry, man, so damn sorry. I got to her too late. I'm with her in the ambulance and we're going to Montclair Hospital. I called Gabe and Jax when you didn't answer and told them

> what happened. They're on their way to pick you up. The bastard ran off as soon as he had the chance, but I didn't want to leave her and go after him. She needed medical attention ASAP. The police are looking for him. I'll be out searching too as soon as you get here.

My heart pounds heavily, like it's being detonated from within. I grip the counter, forcing air into my lungs but they won't work. My chest is heavy with suffocation, as though a weight is pressing into my throat. I need to go to her, but I can't seem to move, reading his words over and over until my eyes bleed, wishing this was just a nightmare.

It's my fault! "Fuck!" My clenched fist rams into the counter as my knuckles bleed. There's a distant pain in my hand but I ignore it. I grab my phone and keys, rushing out of my apartment not bothering with waiting for the elevator, taking the four flights down the stairs like a mad man. Once I'm out, I sprint for my car.

"Damian! Get in!" Jax yells while honking. I hadn't even noticed him because my block is so congested with vehicles. I race for his car, finding Gabe in the passenger seat, and climb in the back.

He guns the engine and we speed off. The ride is quiet except for my own thoughts screaming at me. I've failed another woman in my life. Another one will die because I was too useless to do anything. I should've done more, should've protected her instead of letting her do things her way. Why the fuck did I let her go alone tonight? Pain settles behind my eyes and I squeeze them shut, while the night wind whips across my face like angry lashes punishing me. I deserve worse. So much worse.

I can't lose her; can't bury another woman I love. I won't survive it. *I'm sorry, baby. So sorry I wasn't there to save you.* I bury my face in my hands, feeling my eyes burn like acid, unsure if they're from unshed tears or the images of him punching her that assail my mind.

After a few more minutes, the car makes a sharp right as the tires screech in protest. I see the hospital up ahead, the large beige building getting ever closer. Jax stomps on the brake pedal once we're in front of the Emergency Room and the car careens to a stop.

I jump out, racing toward answers, hoping it's not as bad as I think it is. Once inside, I jog straight ahead to the front desk. I approach an older woman, who looks up at me through red-rimmed glasses.

"Lilah McDaniels was brought in earlier." I grip the cold counter, taking slow, shallow breaths, the heaviness back in my chest. "Tell me where she is. I need to see her."

She continues to stare, her brown eyes filling with compassion. "Are you a friend or family member?"

"I'm her—boyfriend." It feels wrong to say we're friends. I fucking love her. I won't lie anymore.

"Okay. One moment. Let me check."

I tap my fingers impatiently while she types on her keyboard, every stroke driving me further into insanity. *Hurry up.* My Lilah is here somewhere. Is she conscious? She must be so scared.

I take out the phone from my pocket and send a text to Logan.

> **Damian:** We're here. Where are you? Is she OK? Meet us at the front waiting room.

The reply comes immediately.

> **Logan:** She's in surgery. I've been sitting in the waiting area inside, but they haven't told me shit. I'm coming now.

Surgery? *Fuck*! My stomach tightens while madness rolls through me like violent waves in a tsunami. I need to find him and cut off every limb until he's nothing but a head. He won't get away with this.

Just then footsteps approach. I turn around and the guys are there with Lexi. Jax holds her as she cries, her hand gripping his T-shirt. "I got you, babe," he says, looking down at her, while she wipes at her face. And for the first time since I've known him, I see something that I've never seen before. He cares for her. I'm too worried about Lilah to think about what this means.

I turn back around and stare to the right at the double doors that lead further into the hospital. I should make a run for it. Maybe security won't get to me before I find her. Suddenly, the doors open, and Logan comes out. His hands and the knees of his jeans are covered in blood.

Her blood.

His black T-shirt is probably stained too but it's impossible to see. I can't keep my eyes off of his hands as he stands next to me. *What did he do to you, baby*? An ache lodges in my throat but I quash it down.

"I'm sorry, Damian. I should've done more." I can hear the guilt in his voice, but this isn't his fault, it's mine. I did this.

"There's nothing you could've done, you got her out of there," I say, flatly. He lets out a deep sigh and places his bloody hands in his pockets.

"I'm sorry, sir," the receptionist says getting our attention, "but all I can tell you is she went into surgery a little while ago. The doctor will be out to speak with you all as soon as she can."

I grind my teeth, breathing heavily. We already knew that shit. The receptionist continues to stare, like she's unsure if I'll need a doctor of my own. "How long will the surgery be?" I ask, my chest expanding and deflating like a ton of bricks.

"I don't know but I will notify the doctor's team to send someone out to update you all ASAP, okay? I wish I could help more but I don't have the authority or the information."

I mutter a thanks and park my ass on one of the green chairs, my weight heavy against it. Everyone else follows suit, Lexi sitting next to me, while Gabe and Jax make their way across from us. There are about ten other people in the waiting room, some together some alone, scattered into their own circle of doom.

"I had no idea he was hitting her," Lexi says, her voice cracking. "How could I not know, Damian? I'm supposed to be her best friend. I only knew about the verbal abuse and begged her to leave. I should've done more, but I—I just didn't know what." Her body breaks into a tremble and she buries her face into my shoulder and sobs.

I drape an arm around her, not having anything else to give in return. No tears of my own, no words of comfort, no empathy. I'm barely holding on, just a bomb ready to detonate, taking out everyone in its path. I need this doctor to come out and tell me what the hell is going on before I go and find out on my own.

Lexi lifts her face up, sniffling while wiping her eyes. "I called her mom before I got here. She's on her way." She leans her head back against the wall, clearly not expecting a response.

The double doors open again but this time a tall, slender woman walks out, probably in her fifties and wearing navy scrubs.

"I'm looking for family of Lilah McDaniels." *Finally.*

Lexi jumps up getting her attention. "Right here!" The doctor walks over, glancing at each one of us, her face stern but sympathetic, as she delivers what I suspect to be bad news.

Damian

TWENTY

"**H**ello, I'm Dr. Martinez. I'm sorry we kept you waiting." She looks at each of us, her brows wrinkling, the lines between them standing out prominently. "I know how stressed you must be but this is where we are right now. Ms. McDaniels suffered a traumatic injury to her nose, which caused it to break requiring immediate surgery. The surgery will take about three hours." Lexi draws in a sharp breath while I try to squash the rage seeping into my veins. He hurt my baby, and he hurt her badly. He'd better hope they find him before I do because I'll kill him, I'll drain the life out of him slowly, until he begs to die.

"I know this is upsetting but we will do everything we can for her." She jams her hands into the pockets of her scrubs as she continues. "There was also a hematoma in her nose that required drainage, but there were no complications." She could've died on her own blood. *Oh fuck.* I push my fingers into my eyes, the anger within my body growing.

The doctor stares at me for a second as she clears her throat. "Her left cheek suffered trauma as well, but nothing is fractured, which is good news. She does have a bone bruise there, however, but that will heal on its own. There is also a small nick on her neck, which has been cleaned up and bandaged. I want you all to be aware that she has extensive damage to her face. One of her eyes is partially swollen shut and there are black and blues around both eyes, not just from the incident, but from the surgery as well."

"Oh Lilah," Lexi cries.

"Shit." I think that was Jax behind me, but everything sounds muted as my heart pounds noisily within my ears. *How could I let this happen?*

"I'm sorry for upsetting you all but I don't want anyone to react with shock in front of her."

"We understand, Doctor," Lexi whimpers.

"My other concern is a possible concussion. She has swelling on the back of her head so I will be keeping a close eye on that. If she does have a concussion, I suspect it's mild. However, we will monitor it just to be sure. The CT scan thankfully revealed no brain bleed." I cup my mouth, the muscles inside me spasm, ricocheting throughout my body until it feels as though my bones will snap.

"Once she's released, she will need someone to stay with her for a few days. Does she have anyone who would be willing to jump in and help?"

"She has me. I'll stay with her," I say. I don't know where her mother lives, but with that piece of shit on the loose I'm not letting her out of my sight.

"Okay. Very good. I will be back with another update after the surgery is complete." She walks back inside, and I pray like hell she can help Lilah. She doesn't deserve any of this. She deserves to smile, to be taken care of, and to be loved.

I ball my hands into tight fists, turning to the guys needing them to mobilize and start a hunting party. His parents have plenty of resources to help him get out of the country and it'll be a cold day in hell before I let that happen. "I appreciate you guys being here but—"

"You don't have to say it man," Gabe says, cutting me off, "we're off to find him. I texted Samantha and a few others earlier to help with the search. She texted us the addresses of all the homes his family owns, and a few members of the team have already began looking."

He crosses his arms over his chest. "She also contacted the private plane company they use, so if any member of the family decides to take a sudden vacation, we'll know about it." He clasps my shoulder as I release a deep breath, feeling a little bit of relief. I have no doubt our team will locate him.

If someone is out there, Samantha will find them. She's our killer hacker and bomb expert, who joined the company when it first began. Ash is fucking screwed. I wish I could see his face when he's captured.

"We'll find him brother," Jax adds. "I promise you that." His eyes swear an oath, one I know he'll carry through or die trying. "You just stay here and take care of your girl. We'll keep you posted."

"I need to know as soon as you find him."

"Don't worry, we'll send you a picture." An evil smirk breaks across his lips. "And I'll make him nice and pretty for you." I hope Ash feels every bit of pain she felt when he beat her without mercy. His time is coming.

Sitting next to Lexi, I peer at my cell noticing it's already almost two. It's been over three hours; she should've been out of surgery by now. *Did something go wrong?* I hope not. She's suffered enough.

Closing my eyes, I see him laughing in my face, the image so clear from the day we broke into his place. I picture myself alone with him, just us, no one to stop me this time. I crouch down smelling his fear as he cowers away. Gripping his shirt, I lift him up, slamming him against the wall. I tighten my other hand into a fist and pound it against his jaw, smashing his teeth in. But in my vision, I don't stop. My fists crack his nose as he bleeds. And as he laughs, coughing up blood, I throw him on the ground then press my shoe into his nose, hearing it crack some more under the pressure.

My barbaric pulse beats at the vivid imagery. That's what I should've done. I should've gone back and beat him, squashed him like a bug before he ever had the chance to hurt her again. Instead, she's here suffering because I couldn't defend another woman who depended on me to keep her safe.

I pinch the bridge of my nose, attempting to ease the pressure building in my head. *What the hell is taking so long?* I'm about to curse out loud but stop myself at the sight of a child sitting across from me, just staring. He looks to be no more than six, and when he catches me looking back, he grins, lifting his hand to show me a yellow hot wheel. I remember loving them as a kid. Man, I had so many I lost count.

I force a smile as he races the car in the air. One of the women next to him must be his mother. I assume it's the younger one since the other woman looks to be his grandmother's age. The two of them cry as they console each other, but the boy is in his own world. *Enjoy it kid. It doesn't last long.*

"Lexi! How is she?" My thoughts are interrupted by a slim woman who I assume is Lilah's mom. They look so much alike except she has dark brown eyes and her brown hair is filled with streaks of blonde highlights.

She sits next to Lexi who updates her on everything, but as she hears all the graphic details, she completely shatters. Placing her head into her hands, she sobs. I walk over to the fountain grabbing a cup of water, and make my way over to her.

"Hi, I'm Damian, Lilah's neighbor. I live across the hall from her." I don't know what she knows but I don't think telling her I'm in love with her daughter is appropriate right now. She glances up, wiping her face.

"This is for you." I hand her the cup and she takes it.

"Thank you. I'm sorry, I didn't realize you were here for Lilah. She's never mentioned you, but then again it seems like she hasn't told me a lot." She blots at her eyes with the soaked tissue in her hands.

"That's okay. We just met recently." I pause, needing to find the right words. "I found out about what he's been doing and tried to get him to leave her alone." I rub at the stabbing pricks within my chest and look straight into her tear-filled eyes. "I'm sorry I didn't try harder."

Pulling her brows together, she shakes her head. "Oh no, don't do that. Don't blame yourself." She reaches for my hand, grasping it in her cold one. "If anything, this is my fault. I'm her mother and—" her voice cracks. "I had no idea she was with someone who was capable of doing something so vicious."

I glance at Lexi attempting to covertly wipe away her own tears.

"You can't blame yourself either ma'am. You had no way of knowing," here she is dealing with her own suffering but instead she's comforting me.

She reminds me a little of my mother who constantly looked out for others no matter what she was going through. She loved to volunteer, always taking me with her. One of my favorite things to do with my mom was to go to the local animal shelter every week. She'd show me how to bottle-feed the kittens while they eagerly sucked out every ounce. I'll never forget sitting down, letting them climb up my shirt. Their tiny paws reaching up my neck as their tongues licked me all over. My mother always smiled, watching my laughter fill the room. Those were some of my happiest memories of her, the ones not filled with bruises or screams. If I'm ever lucky enough to have children of my own, I hope to make them as happy as I was on those days.

Lilah's mother sighs, letting go of my hand. Walking back, I sit and rub at my heavy-lidded eyes.

"Do you think everything is okay?" Lexi asks quietly. "It's taking a long time." I can see the worry on her face. It's obvious she truly cares about Lilah.

"I don't know but they better tell us soon or I'm going to find out myself." Just as I'm about to stand up to get an update, Dr. Martinez comes out. Her tight smile doesn't tell me shit. Approaching us, she sits next to Lilah's mother.

"How's my baby, Doctor?"

"Your daughter did great. We fixed her nose without any complications. Like I told them earlier," she looks to me and Lexi, "I just want to monitor for a possible concussion and do further testing. If everything goes well, she can go home with you, Mr.—"

"Prescott." Lilah's mom turns to me with a widened expression. She probably thinks it's strange for a neighbor her daughter barely knows to stay and take care of her. I guess she'll learn about my feelings for Lilah sooner rather than later because my woman isn't leaving my side.

Rising to her feet, the doctor rubs her hands against her scrubs. "Once the anesthesia wears off and she's moved up to the recovery room, you all will be able to see her."

After she leaves, I walk over to Lilah's mother and sit beside her. "I'm sorry if I overstepped by suggesting I stay with her, but I figured it's easier if she was close to her things and —"

"No, no, it's fine. I'm glad my daughter has someone who clearly cares for her. She needs that." She releases a sigh. "I'm going to stay a couple of days though. I can't leave her right now."

"You don't need my permission ma'am. I just want to make sure she's safe. I promise to give you as much alone time with her as you need. But I can't promise I won't check in on her, a lot." The corner of my mouth curls into a smile. "So, you'll have to do your best to tolerate me."

She chuckles through her tear-filled eyes. "Oh no, you can stay. But if you expect me to tolerate you then you better never call me ma'am again," the sides of her eyes crinkle. "Please call me Karen."

"I can do that."

"Good. Now tell me, how long have you been in love with my daughter?"

Damn.

Lilah

TWENTY-ONE

Beep. Beep. Beep. *What is that noise? Where am I?* I try to open my eyes, but they're heavy. A bright, yellow light seeps through, though the effort to keep my eyes open is too great, so I shut them again.

There's a dull pain across my entire face, then I remember why. *Where is he? How am I alive?*

My stomach tumbles around like a dryer and I suppress the need to vomit. I reach for my belly but a sharp prickling in the crook of my elbow stops me.

"Ms. McDaniels, welcome back. I'm Katie your nurse." Her voice is low, like she's afraid anything louder would scare me.

Did she say nurse? I got away? Did the man bring me here? The last memory I have is of his voice. He must've rescued me.

"Let me dim the overhead lights for you." The light thumping of her shoes moves further away, then the room gets darker. "Okay, that should be better. How are you feeling? Any pain?" I bat my eyes but only one flutters open. A short, red headed woman stands at the right side of my bed.

"Medicine," I mutter, my voice sounding hoarse like I've caught a bout of the flu. Another wave of nausea hits me and my stomach rolls. "Nauseated."

"Okay, let me page your doctor because I can't give you anything without her permission. I'll be right back." I close my eyes, hoping it calms my stomach, but it doesn't. As I take a deep breath, my nostrils flare at the strong stench of antiseptic and Pine-Sol, which doesn't help the nausea at all.

I try to distract myself by focusing on the intercom calling out codes I don't understand, and the clacking of a keyboard somewhere outside of my room.

There's a squeaking of shoes growing closer and closer. Turning my head toward the door, I open my eyes and find the nurse with a tall woman in a white coat holding a bright green folder. She pulls her brows together in concentration, her lips forming a sympathetic smile.

"Hi there, I'm Dr. Martinez, I heard you're not feeling so well." I nod.

"That's to be expected. We'll give you a little Zofran in your IV now, and you can rest some more."

"Wait," I beg. My brain is cloudy, yet I have so many questions, but only one really matters to me right now.

"How bad?"

She clears her throat. "I don't want to overwhelm you with details now, but I want you to know you're okay. Your nose was fractured but we fixed it, and your left eye is swollen. But right now, all I need you to worry about is resting and healing. We'll talk more when you feel a little better, and I promise I will answer any questions you have, okay?"

I squeeze my hands into tight fists as my chin trembles, feeling my walls collapsing around me, the ones barely holding me together, the ones blocking out everything he did to me. "Say it—say it again. Please say I'm okay." Tears rise up, drifting down my cheeks leaving a chill behind.

She moves closer and clasps my hand into hers. "You're okay. You survived. You're a warrior, remember that." I push my head back against the bed and sob, breath ragged, gasping for life. She squeezes my hand, and doesn't let go, not until every tear is dry, not even as I fall asleep.

I wake up to the steady beeping reminding me I'm still in the hospital. They must all know by now, probably here worried sick. I wish they didn't have to see me this way, it's probably a scary sight.

I feel around for the nurse call system and press my thumb against the button. A moment later, Katie arrives. "Hey, how are you feeling now?"

"I feel much better. May I have some water? My throat feels dry."

"Of course. I'll go get you some and page the doctor, letting her know you're awake."

I glance at the clock on the wall straight ahead. *Six in the morning? How long have I been here?* Katie returns with a cup in hand and walks over to me. "I'm going to put your bed in a sitting position first."

"Okay." The bed buzzes as my head moves up. When she's satisfied, she hands me the cup, and after I drink the entire thing in a matter of seconds, she gets me another one.

Just as I finish, the doctor walks in. "I'm so glad you're feeling better."

I nod. "Is my mom here?"

"Yes, she's right outside with a few others. They've been here the whole time. You have an army of support waiting for you when you're ready."

I take a deep breath. "My mom must be so angry with me. She didn't know. She didn't know what he was doing to me." My lip trembles imagining how she felt when she first found out what happened.

Dr. Martinez approaches the bed and sits on the chair beside me. "From where I was sitting, I only saw love, no anger, none at all."

I flex my fingers, feeling nervous but knowing I need them. "Thank you, Doctor. I'd like to see them now."

She stares, eyes filled with kindness. "Of course, but before you do, I want to discuss a few things. Some police officers are here, and they want your statement."

"Oh." Am I ready to relive everything? But what choice do I have if I no longer want to be weak, if I no longer want him to take everything else from me? Those bruises on my soul may hurt now, but with time they'll heal, I know they will, until they're nothing but a reminder that I went to war and won.

"I can tell them you're not ready yet."

"No. I want to. I won't let him control me anymore. But before I speak to them, I want to speak to my loved ones." I owe them the entire truth. It's time they knew everything. No more secrets.

After she fills me in on the more pertinent details about my injuries, she goes to get my family. That's what they all are to me, family. I never had anyone but my mother. It's always been just us two, but not anymore.

"Hey Mom." She comes in alone, her hand trembling over her lips. Seeing her so pained rips at my heart.

"Oh baby." She rushes forward and gently envelopes me in her love. I lean my cheek against her chest and warmth fills me. I'm back to that little girl whose mother's hugs could solve all of life's problems.

"I'm so sorry, Mom." I let out a sob, my body shattering.

"Shh, don't you dare apologize for anything. You hear me?" She caresses my hair while I nod. "We're going to get him for this, baby. Don't worry about anything." I lift my head away from her warmth, and wince as my face throbs.

She pulls up the yellow chair beside my bed and sits. "Are the pain meds helping? If not, I'll go and make them give you more. I don't want you hurting."

"No, I'm okay. I promise. Is Lexi and Damian here too?"

"Yes, honey." She squeezes my hand. "Do you want me to get them?"

"Yes, I want to talk to all of you." It's time to lay all my cards out on the table and tell everyone the truth even though I may not want to. Guess it's a good thing I can't see as well. Glass half full kind of moment.

She kisses my hand then shifts the chair, its legs scraping against the floor. "Of course, sweetheart. I'll be right back." A sudden chill runs up my arms, sending goosebumps in its wake. *I can do this.*

The light thud of multiple footsteps gets closer and closer as my stomach twists into knots.

I take a deep breath and exhale slowly as they all walk in. Lexi approaches, while Damian stops dead in his tracks huffing in and out. My eyes begin to water at seeing him so upset, but I will them away, wanting to appear stronger.

"I'm so glad you're okay," Lexi cries, placing her cheek against my shoulder. "I'll let you two have a moment," she whispers against my ear.

"Thanks Lex." She joins my mother on the other side of the room, to give us some privacy I'm sure.

Still finding him frozen by the doorway I call to him, needing to feel him close. "Come here." Hand gripping the back of his head, he approaches while attempting to smile, but unlike me he's terrible at faking it.

Once he's near, he leans down and kisses my forehead. "So, on a scale of one to you'd fuck me right now, how good do I look?" I whisper, smiling through the pain. Would he even want me if I'm ugly? Ash always told me that the only thing I ever had going for me were my looks. Without them, he'd say, no man would ever want me. Maybe he wasn't wrong.

"Baby. Fuck. I'm gonna kill him." His voice is low, but I hear the anguish as if it was clearly written across every word.

He leans down, close to my ear, his hot breath against my skin. "But if you think you'd ever turn me off, you must not know how I feel about you. I want to kiss you so badly, it hurts." I try not to cry but his words hit me hard. I never felt this wanted before. I never felt like I was enough. I finally do.

"What's stopping you?" I ask.

"I don't want to hurt you."

"You won't. That's the one place I'm not broken."

He doesn't hesitate, his breath skates across my cheek and reaches my parted mouth, just as his hand lands softly across my neck. Full lips wrap around mine, moving slow, measured but in perfect sync together. The world melts away with each breath we exchange, and in this moment my mind only knows him. He breathes life into me once more, like the day he heard me cry and stilled the ever-growing storm. The quickening of his breath matches mine as we kiss deeply, not wanting it to end.

"Get a room, you two…Oh wait." Lexi laughs.

We part quickly, but not before he gives me another kiss. "I missed you so much, baby." Lexi and my mom let out a collective aww. Yep, he's all mine. Even on my dark days, he finds a way to make me smile.

"Well, it's my turn. I'm sure I could do better than that though," Lexi says as I choke out a laugh, covering my mouth. I adore her. She's the kind of friend every girl needs. Damian raises his hands in defeat, a small smile on his face as he sits on the sofa, and my mom joins him.

"Lex, thank you for being here." She sits on the bed beside me. "It means so much to me."

"Shut up. You're going to make me cry." She wipes some stray tears away. "I'll always be here for you." She lays her head against my chest and wraps an arm around me.

"I should've told you everything, but I was scared."

She kisses my shoulder. "You don't owe me an explanation. But I'm here now."

Having them around fills me with so much courage to seek justice. I want him punished for everything he did. For ravaging my body, destroying my worth, gutting my self-esteem, and consuming my soul. I felt powerless, like a butterfly with a broken wing, but with these people by my side, I'm stronger. But more than anything, I just want peace. I just want to be free.

Lexi lets me go and sits next to Damian and my mom. I release a deep, weighted sigh. "I have so much to say. It's hard."

"Take your time, honey," Mom says.

"I want you guys to know I'm not stupid. I didn't stay with him because I thought he could change or because I loved him. I've despised him for years. I stayed because I didn't see a way out." I swallow the painful lump in my throat, needing to compose myself before revealing what I've been afraid of for so many years.

"I've tried to break things off numerous times, but he threatened me, so I chose to suffer thinking it's better than the alternative."

Damian angles his body forward, head propped on his clenched fists. "Threatened you how, baby?"

I cling to the hope that they won't see me any different, that they won't blame me. "He has pictures and videos of me...he promised to make them public if I left."

TWENTY-TWO

"**W**hat sort of pictures, sweetheart?" Mom asks gently.

Just say it. Get it over with.

"Throughout the beginning of our relationship he kept a hidden camera in his bedroom and recorded us... having sex."

"Motherfucker," Damian spits out.

Lexi's mouth twists in disgust. "What a sick bastard!"

My mom just looks at me, covering her mouth.

I swallow a quick breath. "That's not all. There's also another video from a college party he recorded where some people were doing drugs. I didn't participate at all, but I'm sitting among them." I chew on my lip, finding it difficult to continue. "He—he said if he releases it no one would believe I didn't use, and I'd never work in the legal field again. I couldn't allow the videos to get out. I just couldn't."

"Oh God," Mom cries, probably so ashamed of me. But she would've found out in court anyway, I'm sure. Better she knows now.

"I'm sorry, Mom," my voice was weighted down with embarrassment.

"Oh, sweetheart no," she stands and sits beside me. "This isn't your fault. He's a sick man. I'm sorry I didn't push harder to see you. I should've known something was wrong, we always made time for each other in the past. But at the same time, I didn't want to be overbearing. I thought you had just gotten busy with work and life." She puts her face on top of my hand, her wet lashes ghosting against my skin, and then she cries, her pain ripping across the room and right into my heart.

Holding her close, I say, "It's not your fault, Mom. I wouldn't have listened to you anyway."

She lifts her head up, sniffling.

"Have you seen them?" Lexi asks.

"Yeah, I've seen all the photos and videos on his laptop, so I know he isn't lying. He also told me it would never get back to him. He has a hacker friend who would ensure of that."

Damian comes over to the other side of me. "Don't let him scare you, baby. I have hackers on my payroll, and I promise you that ours are better." He kisses the top of my hand, his lips warm against my cool skin. "We'll find and destroy the videos before he ever gets the chance. I'll break into his house if I have to and take every goddamn computer he owns."

I want to believe him, but it's not that simple. "What if it gets out before you have the chance? Once something is online it's never truly gone." Fear claws through me. "What will I do if my boss sees it before it's removed? I'll lose my job. Who'd ever hire me?"

"Then I'll take care of you."

"Be serious, Damian."

"I *am* serious. If you're worried about money you don't have to be. You got me, Lilah. I never want you to worry about that."

"That means a lot to me, but I can't let you do that. Plus, I love my job." I don't like the idea of depending on anyone for money. Not that I don't trust him, but it feels good to make my own. It feels good to use my brain for something I enjoy. I don't want Ash to take that from me too. Damian is an amazing man and I know in my heart he means what he says, but I want to stand on my own two feet.

"And if this job is stupid enough to let you go for this then you'll find something else, but until then you have me. So stop fighting it, woman."

I glance upon my mom, grinning happily even through the tears. She likes him. It's written all over her face. She never looked at Ash that way, not once. Maybe she had a feeling about him but kept it to herself. The only times she's been around him has been during major holidays. I did my best not to have them in the same room more than necessary. The last thing I needed was something to make him angry in front of Mom.

"Fine. If you want to be my sugar daddy who am I to stop you?"

"Ouch, baby, I'm not that old."

We all laugh, erasing a little bit of the sadness that bleeds through every wall in this room.

Being around Damian lifts me up from the depths of the hell I've longed to escape. Instead of the constant fear I've grown accustomed to, I'm safe and accepted for who I am. His touch brings passion not violence. And when he speaks, it's with adoration not indignation. He's the sort of man every woman deserves and for once I want to believe I'm that woman, the lucky one.

I hate to ruin this moment but there's more they must know.

"So," I swallow, "I'm going to speak to the police shortly but before I do, I need you guys to know something else." All three pairs of eyes search my face, concern growing as they listen.

"After he bashed my face against the floor, he raped me."

"Oh, baby no," Mom says. Holding my hand, she tries not to cry again but she's unable to hide her pain. My own heart slices open reliving what I thought would be the last few moments of my life.

Lexi moves in next to us, hand covering her mouth, as silent tears roll down her face like a river.

I look at Damian pacing back and forth, breathing in and out like he's breathing fire.

"I'm sorry, I wanted to tell you before you hear it in court," my voice cracks. "I'm going to tell the police everything I can remember, but none of you have to stay for that conversation." Can the police even help? He's still out there and he can find me. My stomach churns in sudden fear. Will I ever truly feel safe?

"I'm sure I speak for all of us when I say we aren't going anywhere," Lexi says, brows furrowing.

"If you want us here, we'll stay, honey."

"I do, Mom, I really do."

Once Damian is a little calmer, he comes over and kisses me. "I'd never leave your side. I'll go get them when you're ready."

"I'm ready."

Two officers walk in, the female with black hair in a tight bun opens her pad, pen poised to take notes. "Ms. McDaniels, I'm Officer Jenkins and this is Officer Reed." She points to the blond-haired man next to her.

"I know you've been through an ordeal, so thank you for speaking with us. We won't take up too much of your time." Her long lashes flutter as she looks at me, her expression soft. "We need to know everything that happened based on your recollection. Then we'll take photos of your injuries."

"Okay." I go through detail after excruciating detail of the night and everything that happened before. All the years of suffering, the bruises I know I won't be able to prove, to the videos and pictures he's threatened me with. It all comes pouring out of me, like my blood on his floor. I thought I'd cry but I don't shed a single tear. I feel free.

The camera flashes, capturing wounds I wish to forget. They take picture after picture from every angle, and then they're done.

"Thank you for all the information. We got everything we need." Her partner nods silently and they begin to walk away.

"Wait." They turn around. "I forgot to ask if you knew who found me." She flips her pad checking her notes. "A Logan Campbell. He's a bodyguard and said he was hired to protect you."

"Okay, thanks." There's only one man who would go through such lengths. As the officers leave, I look to Damian.

"I'm sorry if you're mad, baby." He comes close and sits beside me. "I just couldn't sit around and do nothing. I wanted to—"

"I'm not mad," I cut in. Lifting my hand slowly, I reach for his. He takes it, kissing each one of my fingers. "If it weren't for you and Logan, I'd probably be dead. You saved me." He interlaces our hands, holding mine tightly in his.

"Thank you. Thank you for loving my baby," Mom says, voice shaking, overwhelmed with emotion.

His eyes meet mine and I know we both feel the intensity of our love without needing to utter the words.

"How's our patient? Any pain?" my doctor asks, standing next to Katie. I hadn't even heard them come in.

"I'm okay. Probably look a lot worse than I feel. The meds are helping."

"That's great. I'm glad to hear that. I need to discuss some personal things with you. Would you like to do that in private?"

I gaze at Damian, still sitting beside me, and back at the doctor. "No, they can stay."

"Sure. I want to perform an exam to check for a concussion. After that, the rape kit will be administered. Does that sound, okay?"

A shiver runs down my body, wishing there was a way to avoid the intrusive test, but I know I have to do this. "Yes."

"All right. Let's get started." She checks my eye movement and response to light, and then she asks me a bunch of basic questions about myself. During the next phase of testing, my stomach growls. Now that I no longer feel sick, my body's crying out for some food, but I have no appetite. I just want to go home.

"I don't see any immediate evidence of a concussion. However, I will give you a list of things to look for once you're home," she then says to Damian, "If she experiences any one of them, I want you to call my office."

Brows pulling together, I glance at him, not understanding why she'd be telling him that.

"Thanks Doctor, I will. Her mom will be staying with her too, so between the both of us she'll be monitored around the clock." Mom smiles and nods in agreement. Clearly, I missed a lot.

"The more eyes the better," Dr. Martinez says. "So, we're going to ask you all to leave now for the exam. You may wait in the area right outside."

I look at their solemn faces and force what I believe is a convincing smile. "I'll be fine. I'll see you all in a little bit and then you can help me break out of this joint."

Damian flexes his jaw before coming over and kissing my forehead, his soft lips leaving a tingle before brushing over my ear. "You're so strong, baby. You amaze me." My throat clenches. *Don't cry. Don't cry.* If he only knew how badly I'm crumbling inside.

As he moves aside, my mom comes forth. "We'll be right out there if you need us. I love you." She hugs me tight, my arms enclosing around her too.

I never realized how much I needed her until now. Whenever I had a nightmare as a child, I'd run to her bed and bury myself in her chest, feeling instantly safe, like I was under her protection. It feels that way now.

She stands up, straightening her grey T-shirt and walks out with Damian. Lexi is the last one there. She doesn't say a word, but her hands over her chest tell me everything I need to know. I bite the inside of my lip to stop the tears burning within. I'm so close to breaking apart, their love and their sadness is permeating my every cell, but I need to keep it together for them.

As soon as they're all gone, that's when I collapse. My hands tingle as my chest tightens, making each breath harder to take than the one before. *Keep breathing. It's just a panic attack.* The doctor's warm touch brings me back to reality and as I look into her compassionate eyes, all the agony I was attempting to bury comes retching out. My tears are heavy yet silent, rocking my body as she holds my hand, allowing me to open my soul and feel the pain without worrying about anyone but myself.

After what feels like forever, my body finally stills. I look up at her, taking deep breaths, my heartbeat slowing to normal. "Okay, I'm ready. Do it. Do the exam."

TWENTY-THREE

I've always heard that rape victims feel as though they're being re-victimized when under one of these examinations. They're not lying. I lay there open, while my most intimate parts are poked and prodded, like I'm some sort of experiment in a lab. My body tenses and I bite my lip, trying to keep my anxiety in check, but nothing I do could ever make this bearable.

"You're doing great. This next part will feel like a pap smear, and this device right here," pointing to a large machine with a TV screen attached, "will take photos of inside to document any lesions or bruises."

"Okay." I close my eyes at the first bit of pressure, taking slow breaths in an attempt to relax, but it's impossible. My heart's pounding against my ribs, threatening to rip out of me.

"You're doing great," she says, adding more pressure, and I

wince at the burning pain. Just then flashes of that night appear before me. I feel his fist against my cheek, his groans as he invades me, it all comes crashing back. Exhaling in a short series of breaths, I try to squash the panic swelling inside me.

"Almost done." *Not soon enough.*

"Please, just hurry."

"Okay. Done." I groan as she removes the device out of me. "I'm sorry you had to go through that. I just have one more thing to do." What else could they possibly want from me?

"We need to brush your hair to collect any potential evidence he may have left." That sounds a lot better than what I had just endured.

They sit me up, undo my bun and Katie runs a comb through my hair.

"We're done." They bag and seal the comb and place it next to the bags holding other evidence.

"When may I go home?" If I spend another second in this room, I'll lose whatever's left of my sanity.

"I would really recommend you stay another night."

"I can't stay here. Please, I need to go home."

She gives me a sympathetic nod. "Okay, we can start your discharge paperwork now."

"Thank you. For everything." Her kindness and compassion have helped make this horrifying process a little easier.

"You've got nothing to thank me for." A small smile tugs at the corner of her mouth, and then she walks out.

"I'll go get you those papers," says Katie.

"Thanks. I appreciate it."

"No trouble at all. Be right back." As she leaves, my three favorite people return.

"They didn't hurt you, did they sweetheart?"

"No Mom, I'm fine. Promise."

"You should try and eat, baby," Damian says, sitting beside me.

"Guys, I'm fine. I just want to get out of here." Lexi walks up to my bed holding a white shopping bag.

"And that's why I got you these goodies!" She reaches inside and pulls out a black T-shirt and black sweatpants. "The gift shop had the nicest outfits ever. I know, I know, super sexy. No need to thank me."

"But where's your matching outfit?" I tease.

"Only you could pull this off. Oh, and look at these flip flops." She shows off a pair of plain black ones as though they're a pair of the nicest stilettos. I shake my head, laughing, just as Katie returns.

"So, I have all your paperwork right here." She hands me the clipboard and I sign everything without even bothering to read it with my one good eye. After I hand it back, she removes my IV. Flexing my arm a little, I still feel the slight burning ache where the needle used to be.

Everyone leaves again so I have some privacy as Katie helps me get dressed. My legs are a little wobbly as I stand. "Let's take a little walk around the room. Let me know if you feel dizzy at any point."

"Okay." She loops her arm around mine and we take small steps.

"Other than the pain in my face, I feel fine."

"You're due for another dose of Motrin, so once you get home make sure you take it." I nod and as she sits me back on the bed and helps me get dressed all I could feel is the fear scrabbling from inside me, knowing I'm about to leave the safety of the hospital and emerge into a world where he still lives, where he still wants to kill me, where he still might.

"You guys don't have to baby me, you know?" Mom and Damian help me to the couch, their arms around me as though I've broken my legs instead of my nose. Lexi has to work tomorrow and had gone home after I had been discharged, so she's not here to keep me entertained.

"Would you let your mama take care of you?" She rolls her eyes as if I've said the most ridiculous thing. Damian chuckles as he gently helps me sit down.

"Fine, fine, only because I almost died." Damian stills, his hands on my shoulders.

Mom gasps, tears filling her eyes. "Lilah! Stop that."

I reach for her hand. "Oh Mom, I'm sorry."

She lets out a weighty sigh. "I'm just not ready to hear that." She quickly wipes her tears away and puts on a fake smile. "Anyway, does anyone want to eat? I can make some eggs or pancakes."

"Maybe later, Mom. I don't think I can eat yet."

"Okay honey, I'll just go to the supermarket and make us some chicken Parmesan for an early lunch."

"That sounds really good Miss—I mean, Karen." She narrows her gaze, the sides of her eyes crinkling as he smirks. That must've been another thing I missed. They've clearly become friends and that makes me happy.

"That sounds good, Mom. Thank you," I smile, still feeling awful for what I said.

She blows me a kiss. "I'll see you kids in a bit." Damian stands up and locks the door behind her.

As he comes back, I notice one of his hands is injured. "What happened?" I ask, pointing to it.

He looks down, as if he forgot all about it, even though it looks like a fresh wound. "Oh that? It's nothing. Just hit my counter a little too hard."

"Let me see it." He sits beside me, placing it on my lap. I lift it up to my lips and kiss his knuckles, knowing he hurt it because of me.

"Baby, I'm fine, stop worrying about me. I should be taking care of you." He gets up walking toward the kitchen. "How about I make you a snack while we wait for your mom. You have to be starving."

"I'm okay, really. I'll just eat later." I get up, making my way to the bathroom, and as I walk inside, I see something I hadn't been ready to see. I see myself and I'm barely recognizable. My legs fold as my blood runs cold. Holding on to the doorframe, I try to remember how to breathe, but every ounce of air has been knocked out from my lungs. Clinging to the wall, I steer toward Damian. "Why didn't you tell me?" I ask, tears aching behind my eyes.

Cup in hand, he turns, the smile he was wearing now replaced by concern. "What's the matter?" He places the cup on the counter and crosses the room toward me. "Tell you what, babe?"

"Why didn't you tell me that I'm hideous?!" I reply, part crying, part screaming. "How—how could you even stand to look at me?" I turn away from him in disgust, my shoulders rising and falling with my sobs.

"Don't you do that." He turns me around and lifts my face with the back of his hand, but I can't look into his eyes. "Don't you ever call yourself hideous again. You hear me?" I pry myself away from his touch.

"No, baby. Don't hide. Not from me. If you think I want you any less because of this then I obviously haven't done a good job of showing you what you mean to me. If it wasn't for your doctor warning me not to fuck you for a week, I'd be doing just that."

His words warm my heart, and as he cups my face, my lips curve up into a small smile. But when he kisses me, that's when I feel the self-loathing melting away. If a kiss were a word his would be a pledge. One of unchanging love even in an ever-changing time.

Damian

I watch her sleeping in my arms, her slow breaths even and finally calm. Knowing she feels unwanted because of her injuries, kills me. I fucking hate it and I know who's to blame. She's so beautiful and she doesn't even know it because he never made her feel like she's everything. I know the type; I know them well. Maybe he'll end up at the same prison my father is in. They'd become fast friends.

My biggest regret in life is that I didn't kill the motherfucker when I had the chance. Maybe I was too young to help my mom, but I'm no longer a kid. I could've ended him that day and she'd be fine right now.

Every time I see her face, a dark rage wraps around my body, engulfing my sense of humanity. The swelling, the deep red and purple bruising on her face is so painful to look at. I do my best not to react around her, to let her forget the pain even for a second, but fuck it's hard. Just thinking about what she went through, what she was feeling...my need for vengeance ripples through me in violent waves. It'd be so good to hurt him, really hurt him, until all he knows is suffering.

I keep texting the guys every few hours asking for updates, but there are none yet. The bastard is still in hiding. There's a warrant out for his arrest so he can't travel, but we'll find him. I just hope it's sooner rather than later.

There's a light knock on the door. I gently pull Lilah off me and lay her down on the sofa. I head for the door and look through the peephole before opening it, part of me wishing he was the one on the other side.

"She's asleep," I whisper, taking the three white bags from Karen.

"Oh, good." She speaks low, moving into the kitchen with me. "I guess I'll wait on making lunch or maybe make it for dinner. I don't want to wake her."

I empty out the bags and quietly place everything in the refrigerator. "That sounds good. I can order takeout once she's awake."

She sits on one of the stools and sighs. "You have to promise me you'll watch over her. Please, Damian, she's all I have. I can't lose my baby. I just can't." She weeps soundlessly into her hands. I flex my jaw, wishing I could take her pain away.

Sitting next to her, I offer the only thing I can, my promise. "I'll do everything in my power to keep her safe. I swear to you. That bastard will not hurt her again. He'll have to go through me first."

I grip the back of my neck. "She means everything to me. I love her." The words come so easily; I feel them in my bones. It's still hard to believe that the boy who once thought he would never take the plunge, fell so hard.

TWENTY-FOUR

Covering a yawn, I lazily squint awake, not hearing anyone in the living room. The whole place is quiet. *Why is no one here? Where are they?* My breath catches in my throat as my body goes from sleepy to awake in seconds and every bad thought is accelerated. What if Ash broke in and killed them? *Oh my God, are they dead?* I feel the tears before I even realize I'm crying. But wouldn't I've heard the screams or the fighting?

I clutch the soft blanket around me as frazzled breaths come in gasps, feeling their warmth against my face while I hide behind the covers. Is he still here, waiting to kill me next?

I want to scream out for them, but an invisible hand clasps around my mouth. *I can't breathe. Someone help!* I take slow breaths, but they're painful, it's as though the same hand squeezes my throat preventing me from drawing air into my lungs.

"Morning, baby," someone says, but the voice is muffled from the buzzing in my ears, as loud as a swarm of wasps.

"Lilah? What's wrong?" That sounded a little like Damian, I lower the blanket, but I can't speak yet. *Say something, damn it!*

"Baby it's me. I'm right here." He lowers down to the floor beside me. "I'm sorry I left you alone." *They're okay. They're okay.* "We went to sleep once it got late. I would've brought you into the bedroom with me, but I was afraid to wake you."

"I—" I breathe in and out through my nose a few times, trying to calm my heart. "It's okay. I'm sorry. I just got—" I sit up, rubbing at my forehead, not wanting to finish that sentence.

"Don't be sorry." He sits beside me and reaches his arm out. "Come here." I lean against his strong body, feeling instantly safe.

"What time is it? How long have I been asleep?" He glides his fingers up and down my arm soothing my frazzled nerves.

"It's five in the morning."

"What?" I cock my head back. "I can't believe I slept all day and night!"

"You needed it. Are you sure you're okay? Do you want to talk about it?"

"No, not right now." I sink further into him, breathing a sigh of relief. "Just hold me."

"There's nothing I'd rather do more."

We sit together silently for a while, lost in each other. How did I ever live without him? I burrow myself into him, wishing I could climb inside and hide away.

Out of nowhere, his cell phone beeps, and he fishes it out of his pocket.

He stares at the screen, sitting straighter while his hand slides away from me, mood abruptly changed. "They got him, baby. He's being arrested right now." I'm instantly light-headed, covering a sob with my hand.

"Jax sent a photo. I can show it to you but only if it'll make you feel better." Part of me wants to look at it but another part is afraid of seeing his face again. But maybe, just maybe, this is what I need to stop the panic that's been wrapping around my psyche.

I reach out a shaky hand and curl my fingers around the phone. My pulse begins to scream so I flip it face down.

"You don't have to look at it if you don't want to, but I'm here either way."

"I want to." *You can do this*. There's no amount of time which could prepare me for this moment, so I turn the phone over.

A single flame sparks to life in my gut, building and growing like a wildfire, until it twists through the rest of my body. Everything goes red and all I feel is hatred. I can't say I've ever hated anyone in my life. Sure, I've disliked plenty, but to feel a deep-rooted animosity for another person, no I never felt that, not until now. As I look into his face, blood around his nose as Jax pulls his head back for the camera, all I want is to see him dead. I hate the woman he has turned me into. The Lilah before Ash would never wish that on anyone, but I stopped being her a long time ago.

I hate you.

I hand Damian the phone back. "Do you think he'll get bail?"

He wraps his arm around me once more. "I don't know."

"So, he has a decent chance of walking free before trial?" Fear trickles through my system, slowly overwhelming me, like it's on an intravenous drip.

"Let's hope not, but I won't leave your side either way."

"I won't have to see him before the trial, right?"

"No, baby."

I swallow the knot in my throat and try to still my nerves. "I don't think I could testify." Just thinking about walking into court and seeing him again, in person, makes me ill. "I can't face him, Damian."

"You'll never be alone. I'll be there the entire time." He takes both of my hands in his and holds them tight.

"Show him that strength he didn't think you had. Fight him with the truth and tell that whole courtroom what he did to you. Don't let that motherfucker win."

Lip trembling, I choke on painful tears. Knowing he's right doesn't make the prospect of facing Ash any easier.

I hear the guest room door open, announcing Mom's up. "Good morning. How are you feeling, darling?"

"I'm okay."

"Good, honey. I'm going to make us some pancakes. You need to eat." She heads for the kitchen.

"Mom?"

She turns back around. "Yes, sweetheart?"

I stand. "They caught him."

She draws in a sharp breath and rushes to me. "Oh, thank God!" She wraps me in a tender embrace as we both cry, our relief and anguish filtering through the room. I know she needed to hear this just as much as I did.

Damian

The next day while we're all enjoying lunch thanks to Karen, my phone vibrates against the table. Seeing an incoming call from Gabe, I quickly answer, knowing what today is.

"Hey man, what's up?"

"Hey D, we're just leaving his arraignment. The son of a bitch made bail, but the judge ordered him to wear an ankle monitor."

Fuck. They say hatred is a powerful emotion. It can blur your vision, cloud your judgment, and possess your soul until you drown in it. I can feel myself being swallowed by it more and more every day. He gets to walk free after what he did, while she gets to fear for her safety. Where the fuck is the justice in that?

"I know it's not the news we were hoping for D, but at least we'll know where he is at all times."

"Yeah." I look over at Lilah as she takes tiny bites of her food, pretending she's not paying attention to my conversation. My gut twists. I don't know how I'm going to tell her.

"There's one more thing, we installed a remote access program on his laptop during our search and Samantha found the photos and videos you mentioned. She said he also sent it to his email. It's all gone now, man. Wiped clean. There were no traces of them anywhere else."

Relief washes over me. At least I can give her some good news. "Did you see them?" The thought of someone else seeing my girl that way infuriates me.

"No. Samantha is the only one who handled it. We'd never do that."

"Tell her thank you."

"Will do. Let us know if you guys need anything."

"I will."

I hang up and place the phone back on the table. There's an undeniable tension as both women face me.

"I know that had something to do with me. What happened?"

"The judge released him, but he'll have an ankle monitor the whole time."

She freezes for a second, staring at me unblinking, before turning back to her food as if I just gave her the weather forecast.

"What kind of judge would do such a thing?!" Karen snaps. She places a hand over Lilah's. "I'm sorry, honey."

Lilah clears her throat. "It's fine, Mom. I'm not surprised. His parents must've handed the judge some cash and told him what a fine, upstanding citizen Ash is." She releases a defeated sigh before continuing. "They have connections everywhere."

I pull my chair closer, wanting to tuck her within my body, to keep her safe, even though I know nothing will make her feel that way, not until he's locked away. "I wish I could do more, baby. I hate seeing you upset. But I hope the next bit of news cheers you up." She sits up straighter. "The videos and everything else are gone. You never have to worry about it again."

She drops her fork, it clatters loudly against the plate. "Wha— how?"

"Someone on my team hacked his computer and erased all evidence of them." Her bottom lip begins to tremble, and the next thing I know she flings herself over me, wrapping her soft arms around my neck, crumbling into my shirt. She weeps loudly for what feels like forever, and for once I know they're happy tears.

Pulling back, she peers at me. "I don't know how to thank you."

I gently cup the face of the woman who I believe was put onto this earth to be mine. As I gaze into her eyes, I know this moment right here is the right moment to tell her what she makes me feel, no longer caring about finding the perfect time or the perfect place because none of that exists. We create our own perfection. And right now, the way she looks at me, the way my heart beats for her, that's perfect for me.

"There's nothing I wouldn't do for you, baby." I stroke her cheeks with my thumbs just as her mom stands to clear the plates. "You mean so much to me. Now that I know what genuine love feels like, I never want to let it go. I never want to let you go. I love you, Lilah."

"Damian…" She places her hand on top of mine, the one still on her cheek. "I love you so much." I pull my lips down and kiss her, letting my mouth tell her everything that my voice forgot. Yeah, this is perfect.

Lilah

TWENTY-FIVE

A s Mom and I sit together on the couch, the sound of a running shower echoes across the room.

"Are you sure you'll be okay?" she asks, her brows wrinkling as she sips her coffee.

"I'll be fine, don't worry. I'm going to stay with Damian in his apartment." I lean my head against her shoulder.

She takes a deep breath then kisses my hair. "If I didn't have to be back at work, I would stay much longer, but I'll come back on Sunday. It should be a slow day."

"Only if you can get away. I don't want you to lose your job." I hug her tight, not wanting to let go but knowing she needs to go back home. She's a lead hairdresser at a swanky salon in Long Island, so she can't be out of work long.

"I know, I just hate not being here. I'm glad you have Damian though. He seems like a great man." My heart swells with affection at the mention of his name, but at the same time doubt rears its ugly head.

"He is. I just—"

She cocks her head back. "What is it, honey?"

"What if I'm wrong, Mom? I was so wrong about Ash. What if I just don't know how to pick the right ones?" I hear the pitter-patter of the shower, glad that Damian is still inside because the last thing I want is for him to walk in on this conversation after he just told me he loves me.

"He's good baby, so good. I see it. Don't allow one bad man to cloud what you know in your heart."

"I love him so much, but my feelings have grown so strong so fast. I'm scared it's not normal. I worry it'll all come falling down on us."

"Love doesn't work on our timetable, sweetheart. It just happens when it happens. It's okay to be afraid but don't let fear stop you from finding the type of love that's stronger than life's many struggles, because that type of love is worth everything."

"You're right," I bite the inside of my cheek. I need her to be right. I'll never overcome the pain if he hurts me too.

"If you find someone who gives you their unyielding devotion, who makes you feel more beautiful on the inside, that's who you want by your side. And I have a feeling that's him."

Just then the door creaks open and Damian comes out dressed in a tight white T-shirt and grey sweatpants hung low on his hips. His muscles are on full display and I internally drool.

"Well kids, it's time for me to go." She rises to her feet and gives Damian a hug. She whispers something in his ear, then comes over to me and squeezes me tight. "Call me if you need anything at all. You hear me? I'll rush back."

"I will, but stop worrying."

"Yeah, yeah, wait until you're a mom. The worry never stops. But let me go before I decide I rather stay."

I kiss her cheek. "You're an amazing mom. I hope you know that." She sniffles, pulling me in for another tight hug. She deserves her own happiness and her own Damian. I wish she'd meet someone to share her life with, but she never found anyone worth her time. Mom dated one man for a few years when I was around thirteen, but that was it. Maybe it'll happen when she least expects it.

Damian's powerful arms slide around me from behind as she walks out. He brushes my hair away from my shoulder as his warm breath skims across my neck, leaving soft kisses against my skin. I lean back, enjoying the feel of his hard body against mine. Just a simple kiss, and I melt into him. That's how much he owns me.

I let out a moan, low and needy. I want to remember how good we were together before I was hurt. I want to return to those moments, I want more. We can finally have that.

He slides his hands down to my hips, digging his hands into my skin. "Fuck, baby. If you keep making those noises, I won't be able to wait an entire week to be inside you."

"Well, whose fault is that?" I grind myself against him, my pulse rising with every breath.

He groans, rather loudly. "You're evil, woman." A wave of pleasure shoots down to my core as his teeth scrape along the shell of my ear. Grabbing on to his forearms, I curl my fingers around his muscles, loving how hard and unyielding they feel in my grasp.

He spins me around. We both breathe hard as we stare at one another with longing. My tongue slides out and I lick my lips, and that's all it takes for us to crash into each other, mouth first. His hand veers into my hair, clawing at my scalp, while he kisses me hard but taking great lengths not to hurt my nose. I nip at his lips with my teeth, causing him to growl low in his throat.

He pulls us apart, our breaths raw and weak. "The things I'm gonna do to that body…" he says, looking at my mouth then at my nipples, now hard against my shirt. I squeeze my legs together, feeling his words where I need him most. He draws closer, encasing his arm around me. "I really hope you're ready, because once we start, I know we'll never want to stop. Now go pack a bag because you're coming home with me."

Mouth parted, I can't seem to move. Every inch of me is desperate for him. "Now, Lilah, before I lose all self-control and fuck you right on this damn floor." As if I couldn't be anymore turned on...

"I wish you would," I whisper, kissing his lips before heading for my bedroom.

"You're killing me, baby. Killing me," he calls out. I smile, loving the way we make each other crazy.

I stuff a large tote bag with some things I'll need for a few days so I'm not constantly going back and forth, and come back out. He takes the bag from me as we exit my apartment and into his.

"Do you mind if I take a shower?" I ask.

"Of course not, baby. I could run you a bath if you want." He drops my tote on the kitchen counter.

"Oh, that sounds so good. Maybe you could join me?" There's nothing I want more right now than his hard, naked body around mine.

He shakes his head in mock disappointment. "You're clearly trying to kill me. I mean, there's no other explanation. You know very well there's no way in hell I'd be able to resist you while you're all naked…and wet." He looks me up and down as if he's already picturing me without a shred of clothing.

I walk up to him, looping my arms around his neck. "I mean do we *have* to wait a whole week? I'm completely fine. Maybe I'll call the doctor and ask for a permission slip."

He wraps his arm around my back, holding me close. "Oh yeah? And how's that conversation going to go, hmm? Hey Doc, I really want to bang my boyfriend. He makes me so desperate for his cock. Can you make an exception? I really think it would help with my recovery."

"That's not what I'd say." I lean into his neck, my tongue drifting up to his ear. He groans and grows harder against my belly.

"What would you say?" he pants.

"I'd say, hey Doc, if you saw my boyfriend naked, you'd *completely* understand."

"Fuck, I love you." His voice desperate. "Go grab some towels in my bedroom closet. Now. Because I'm about to join you in that bath."

I press my lips to his cheek, his stubble brushing up against my mouth, the friction not helping my sexual intoxication. "I love it when I win."

"I have a feeling you'll be winning a lot in this relationship. Now move that pretty ass and get us some towels."

As I head to his bedroom, he calls out, "Oh, and Lilah?"

I stop, turning around. "Yeah?"

"Maybe you can wear one of my shirts to bed, like you did that first night."

"Trying to re-create a fantasy, are we?"

"Maybe." He feigns innocence as a cocky smile crosses his lips.

I turn back around then call out over my shoulder, "I think that could be arranged."

I walk toward the white closet door, still smiling and still turned on as hell. Could tonight be the night we're finally together? I dream up ways of making him cave in the shower. So many delicious ways...

Reaching for the silver knob, I pull open the door and find two white shelves inside. Well I'm impressed; his closet is more organized than mine. There's a row of grey towels neatly folded on the lower shelf.

As I reach for them, my eyes land on a light brown stuffed animal sitting on some sheets on the shelf above, its back to me. *Aww, is this his from when he was a child?* I melt a little. Being the nosy girl that I am, I decide to retrieve it, needing to see it for myself.

I grab it, feeling its rough fur, and turn it around and… "Oh my God." Hands jumping to my chest, I involuntarily release the teddy bear. *How is this possible?* My brain stutters, unable to connect the dots. Time feels as though it's standing still and I'm frozen within it. *How could he have it? Who gave it to him?*

"Babe, our bath is ready," he calls out from the other room. "Did you find the towels?" My words refuse to take flight, I'm stuck in the past remembering the teddy I once knew well. I hear him come inside, but I'm unable to look away from the bear.

"Lilah? Lilah what's wrong?" I turn to face him, my heartbeat racing frantically.

I try to swallow the twinge in my throat. but it won't go away. "How—how do you have this?" I ask, pointing to the teddy.

"The bear? You're upset I have a bear?"

"Who gave it to you?"

"Some kid when I was young. Why? Can you tell me what's going on? You look like you've seen a ghost."

I look at the teddy again, from the missing part of her ear to the face colored in green and pink, and then I look back at him. "That bear… It's mine."

Lilah

TWENTY-SIX

"What?" He jerks his head back, standing at the doorway. "No, that's not possible. I mean, the girl who gave it to me...her name wasn't Lilah. I don't under—"

"The girl, what was her name?" He takes tentative steps forward, scratching his forehead. It can't be. It's just not possible.

"Olivia. Her name was Olivia."

"Tears pool in my eyes. "That's—that's my middle name." I can't believe this.

"Wait. What's going on right now?" He moves to the bed and sits, running his hands through his hair. "Are you saying you're her? You're the girl from the hallway?"

"Did you live in a building on 86th St. twenty years ago," I ask, "the one with the yellow—"

"Awning," we say in unison.

"Fuck. No way." His eyes lock in on the bear then on me, mouth opening but no sound comes out.

"I never told you my first name because I hated it," I explain. "No one had it and I didn't like being different. Anytime I met anyone new, I gave them my middle name."

I never thought I'd see this bear again nor the boy I gave it to. When I was young, I'd give my stuffed animals makeovers, if you could call it that. This particular bear suffered through my first attempt at a haircut, but I accidentally cut off her ear, and colored her face with marker calling it makeup. She was my favorite. I'd recognize her anywhere.

Then I met a broken, little boy sitting in front of his door while his father hurt his mom. We only lived a few doors down so I'd hear the screaming and the crying. We all did. It was usually during dinnertime, so as my mom prepared our meal, I'd sneak out to check if he was there. Sometimes he wasn't, but when he was, I always joined him. I didn't want him to be alone.

He was so mean to me at first, always pushing me away, calling me a brat, telling me I was annoying. But I just kept on coming. I was always a stubborn child with a big heart. I'd love the hell out of anyone until they'd give in. He didn't stand a chance against me, especially when I brought snacks. But even when he gave in and stopped asking me to leave, he never opened up. He stayed silent most of the time and that was fine by me. I was happy to do most of the talking.

It's hard to believe the boy I've wondered about for so many years was standing right in front of me. He gets off the bed, walking up to me. The back of his hand grazes against the curve of my jaw. "Is this real?" he asks, his voice cracking.

I nod, brushing away the tears from my eyes. "It's real."

"Do you remember what you said to me when you gave me that bear?"

I smile, recalling my words. "Wherever you are, you'll always have a friend."

He leans his forehead against mine and closes his eyes. "How could I have forgotten those eyes? From the moment we met, I wondered where I knew them from, and the answer was in my closet the whole damn time."

"It was a long time ago." I whisper. "We changed. I couldn't figure it out either and I had a major crush on you back then."

His head jerks back. "Crush, huh?"

"Oh, yeah." I loop my fingers around the back of his neck and look into his chocolate eyes. "I was a little infatuated and I didn't even know your name because *you* wouldn't give it to me." He encloses his arms around me.

"I know. I'm sorry I was a major dick to you. It wasn't because I didn't like you or didn't want you around. I was just fucked up back then. I didn't want anyone to feel sorry for me."

My heart squeezes inside my chest for the boy who suffered so much. "Oh Damian…"

Damian

I hear her door open, small steps coming closer as I huddle next to mine, his screams getting louder. "You should go home," I say without looking up. "Isn't your mom wondering where you are?"

"I don't want to go home. When are you going to realize that maybe I want to stay."

"Don't you have anything better to do than spend your fucking time with me?"

"You really shouldn't say bad words. I'm not allowed to say that."

I look up at her. "Well don't say it then."

She rolls her eyes. "Fine."

"Fine." She's so annoying.

We stay silent for a few minutes until she asks, "Can I sit next to you?" I want to say yes, please sit with me. But I don't.

"I don't know why you'd want to." I look back down to the floor.

"Why wouldn't I want to?"

"Have you met my father? No one talks to me. Even at school they know about him and stay far away from me."

"Well lucky for you I'm not them." She plops down beside me. "Everyone needs a friend, even you, and I want to be yours." She lays her head against my shoulder and holds onto my arm, and for a second, I forget that those sounds coming from inside belong to my mom.

I can't believe I'm staring at the girl who mattered to me so much growing up. I never felt like I deserved her kindness, so I'd tell her to go, but truly all I wanted was for someone to stay. And she did, she always stayed.

My father scared me more than I like to admit. I felt safer out in that hall more than I ever did hiding in my closet, so when I could get away, I'd sneak out and just sit by the door. The guilt at abandoning my mom ate at me every time, but I still did it. Fear is a powerful emotion.

Lilah was the only bright side in my dark time, and for six months she was there, pushing through my walls, making my heart her home. I guess she never left. And when Mom died and I moved away, I left a piece of myself with her.

I let her go and pick up the bear, clutching it firmly in my hand. "You were the first girl I ever loved." She leans her head to the side, her brows gathering with emotion. "The only way a fucked-up boy could love a girl, but in my own way I loved you." I take her hand in mine, leading her to the bed as we both sit.

"Every time you sat with me, every time you talked to me, you stole a piece of my heart and made it yours. But when you gave me this bear, I lost it. No one cared about me but you. I wanted to grab you and tell you what it meant to me, but I refused to let myself appear weak."

Her fingertips stroke across my cheek. "I'm so sorry for everything you went through. I hated every second of it. I begged my parents to adopt you."

I chuckle at the thought. "Maybe I should be grateful they didn't because falling in love with you would've been a problem."

She bites her lip, tugging it between her teeth. "Probably."

"Come lay with me. I want you close." Scooting back on the bed, I give her room to join me.

"What happened to you? Where did you guys move to after?" she asks as she lies on my chest, drawing small circles with her fingertips.

"You don't know?"

She looks up. "Know what?"

"About what my father did?"

She shakes her head. "No," she says stroking my face, her delicate touch makes me want to bottle up all the ugliness I'm about to share. Will she see me differently knowing my father is not only a violent criminal, but a murderer too?

I rip the Band-Aid off and tell her everything, letting the memories sting. She sobs as she learns my mom's fate, and her tears spill for the boy who had to find her. I tell her how it changed me, how I've refused to date anyone, and how lonely I've been, but also afraid of what I could become.

"I understand if this is too much. I won't blame you if you don't want to be with me anymore." It'll kill me, but I love her enough to let go. Let go of the girl who barged into my life twenty years ago and the only woman I've ever loved.

Her knuckles slide across my cheek. Closing my eyes, I relish in the feel of her touch. "Is that what you think? That somehow any of this changed what I feel for you? Because the only thing that changed is my love for you. It's so much stronger, deeper. I want you like I've never wanted anyone in my life. You're my everything."

"Lilah—" The sincerity in her words makes it difficult for me to speak, my throat clogging with emotion.

She holds out a hand stopping me. "I understand why you've been afraid but you're nothing like him or the monster I was with. You protect, not hurt those around you, and for once, I've found the kind of love I've always dreamed about." I wrap my arm around her, needing to feel her, to know this is real.

"I don't know if soulmates exist," she continues, "but I'm thankful to whatever brought us together." Leaning down, she captures my lips, lighting me on fire, the warmth spreading throughout my body.

I roll on top of her, sinking into her curves. We start out slow, but with every breath and every moan, our desire turns primal, and we're unable to contain it. In this moment, no one could destroy us. She's the half of me I've been missing, and with her I'm finally whole.

Our kiss is deep, blazing a trail of heat throughout our bodies, our hands tugging and pulling everywhere they can touch. My fingers slide down to the contours of her hips and I pull down her black shorts, taking her panties with them. She moans out my name, biting my lip and that's all it takes to lose my self-control.

"Yessss," she screams as I plunge two fingers inside her. I go hard and fast, wringing out every ounce of pleasure she has to give. She pants against my neck, her body clamping around each of my thrusts.

"Do you want more?" I ask, sucking on the fingers that were just inside her, "because I do." I slip off her tank top, grabbing her breasts in my hands, rubbing her nipples with my thumbs. She arches into me, wrapping her legs around my hips.

"Damian...don't stop." I kiss her neck, licking my way down from between her breasts to the place she wants me most.

"You're so beautiful," I whisper against her thighs, loving their softness. Just a few more days and I get to be inside her. The doc was pretty clear about her orders, but she never mentioned this.

I plunge my fingers inside her again and she whimpers, her legs trembling under my touch. Fuck, she's so wet. "I promise to make it better, baby." I descend between her thighs, flicking her clit with my tongue. Over and over I give it to her, while she cries out, no longer holding back. I reach up and grab her breast, pinching her nipple while keeping up the pace with my other hand.

"Yes, yes, don't stop," she moans, her voice raspy and trembling as her pussy clenches around me, and that's when I know she's close.

I look up, needing to watch her come. I fuck her faster, hitting her spot just right, and then she falls apart, calling out my name like a song of worship and all I want to do is give her more.

I lick her dry and travel back up, my body coming down over hers. A smile of pure contentment is written on her face as she tries to control her breathing.

"Are you ever going to let yourself feel what you make me feel? I wanted you inside me. Why didn't you—" I kiss her, interrupting those thoughts before they get me in trouble. She kisses me back, her tongue swirling with mine making my cock flinch, probably shouting at me for being an idiot.

"I want you so badly baby, but I want to make sure you get the all clear at your next doctor's appointment." I thrust my thumb in between her lips and her tongue glides up and down against it. "Once you do, there'll be no stopping the number of times I'll make you come."

I swipe my thumb against her mouth, and she kisses it. "I have no doubt."

I flip to my back and she curls against my side, her head resting on my heart, my arm wrapped around her protectively. "I love you, Lilah, so much." I still can't get over how comfortable I am saying those words, but with her it all comes easy.

"I love you too, Damian. Always." And when she drifts off to sleep, I know that in her dreams I'm still holding her close in my arms.

Lilah

TWENTY-SEVEN

I stretch around in bed, still groggy, watching Damian remove his clothes as he gets ready for the shower. He's such a sight. I'll never get enough of all those hard muscles, straining against his thick body.

"I kinda like you eye fucking me, but if you don't stop, watch what happens," he warns playfully, his deep breaths making his ab muscles contract in the most delicious way. As he steps out of his navy boxers, I bite my lip, my body instinctively running hot and achy everywhere. He growls, low and deep. "Damn it, woman. Do you know how hard I get when you bite that lip?" I lift a brow and look at his cock. *I do now*.

"You're an evil, evil little thing, aren't you?"

"Maybe?" I love knowing how turned on he gets by me. It's a powerful feeling. And I kind of love pushing him, I want him to stop

201

being so good and give in.

"Maybe, huh?" He climbs up the bed slowly and I swallow, heat blooming in my core. He flips the covers off me, groaning at my nakedness, and pins me down hard against the mattress with his body.

"Shouldn't you be in the shower?" I ask, trying to keep my voice steady, pretending the feel of him doesn't affect me at all. The only answer he gives is the press of his stiff length between my thighs, but as he slides his hardness up and down, that's when I stop pretending.

"It can wait." He rolls his cock in deep, hard circles, and I moan loud and unashamed. He just lit the match and now my skin burns everywhere. I arch into his strokes, needing him to move just a little so I can feel him push inside me.

"See the thing is, beautiful," he whispers against my ear, teasing my entrance with his blunt tip, giving me what he knows I need, "two can play that game."

What? I don't register what he said, not until he stands up, a smug grin on his face. I lay there dazed and turned on as hell. "You better come back and finish what you started," I beg, squeezing and un-squeezing my thighs.

"Or what, baby?" He grips the head of his hard-on, making me squirm. *Damn him.*

"Or...you'll never get to fuck me." I'm only like ninety-five percent joking.

"Never?" He moves closer, smirking while I squirm like a desperate little virgin.

I squint, a tight smile on my lips. "Nope."

"Oh, can't have that." As he sits on the bed, I hope he unexpectedly changed his mind about giving us the relief we clearly both need, but instead he caresses my cheek. *Damn him.* "Don't touch yourself while I'm in the shower. Save it for when I get out and I promise

I'll have you coming hard." My core clenches in protest at having to wait.

"You're lucky I love you."

"I *am* lucky," he admits. I see devotion all over his handsome face. "See you in a bit, beautiful." He kisses my lips and starts toward the bathroom.

"Hurry the hell up, will you?" I shout after him and hear a deep chuckle.

"Yes ma'am."

I lay there for a few minutes trying to bring some control back into my lust filled body. Once I feel like I can stand without crumbling, I drag myself out of bed and head for the closet, needing my tote bag. I can't remember if I brought my body scrub and I want to use it in the shower once Damian is done. I rummage through, not finding it. *Ugh.* I must've forgotten to bring it.

I hurriedly slip into a tank and yoga shorts then grab my keys and head to my place, not bothering to tell Damian. I'll be in and out, no reason to worry him, and he *will* worry. I see it every time I wake up from a nightmare, I see it as he talks to his friends about my case, and I feel it when I'm wrapped up in his body. Once this is all behind us, we'll both breathe easier.

I silently leave his apartment and reach mine, struggling with the keys, anxious to make it back before he finishes his shower.

The door clicks open at last and I leave it ajar, keys still inside the lock, and hurry to the bathroom. Opening the cabinet, I delve inside for my scrub and as I stand up the boom of my front door closing sends me jolting backwards, heart racing uncontrollably.

Ah damn, Damian must've realized I was here. "Hey babe, I'm in the bathroom. Just forgot something here." He doesn't answer. "Damian? Are you there?" Maybe the door just shut by itself. That must be it. My stomach tumbles and twists as I walk out to investigate the noise. The living room is empty.

I near the door, opening it to peer into the hallway, when out of nowhere a hand grips me tightly around my mouth and pulls me back in. I scream and scream, but it's nothing more than a pathetic whimper. No one can hear me. I'm alone. *Damian*! My hands flail and I push him away to no avail. The stranger's too strong. His other hand wraps around my waist, holding me tight to his body.

"It's *so* good to see you again," his voice slithers across my neck licking me like a venomous snake, and any fear I had a few minutes ago is nothing compared to the sheer force of terror I feel at hearing Ash's voice. He pulls me further into the room, walking backwards until we stop in the kitchen.

"I never thought this day would come. I see the face is looking better. Too bad," he growls. "I wish I killed you. I'd never be in this mess if it weren't for you, you bitch. You think you're going to testify against me?" Something pointy and sharp presses into my belly and my whole body trembles with dread. I can't look down to see what he's doing, his grip around my mouth is too powerful.

My mind is spinning with so many thoughts at once. How is he here? Where is the ankle monitor? Is he still wearing it? Will the police come? Please let the police come. Oh my God, I don't want to die. I ball my hands into tight fists to control the shudders undulating within my body.

"I've been waiting for you all night. Broke in while you were out." His breath slashes across my neck and goosebumps spread across my arms. "Do you know how easy it is to pick a lock? No, I guess you wouldn't, but man yours was easy." He digs the weapon into me, its sharp sting causing me to wince.

"Here I was sitting for hours and hours, thinking you went out, but little did I know you've been playing house with the neighbor. I knew you were a slut, always have. You've ruined my fucking life and now I'm going to ruin yours." Am I hurt? Does it even matter if what he plans to do with me is so much worse? I knew he'd find a way to get to me. An ankle monitor doesn't stand a chance against a monster who only wants one thing: to see me dead.

"Do you know how much money my parents have already spent on lawyers because of YOU!" he shouts in my ear and my heart races, strangulating my chest. The loud pounding in my ears feels as though his fists have somehow found a way to reach inside, delivering blow after blow.

My eyes burn from the tears that have managed to slip out. I scream against his hand, wanting to bite but afraid he'll kill me if I do. "Stop fucking moving!" he hollers. But I continue to fight against him, because it's all I have left.

Then out of nowhere I hear the jangle of keys that are still on my door. "Not a sound," Ash threatens while tightening his clutch around me. The knob turns ever so slowly until the door gently opens. Damian's eyes go wide for just a split second, taking in the scene of me being held against my will by someone we equally despise. But just as instantly his demeanor changes into soldier mode. Shoulders back, head high, his stance becomes deadly as he looks at Ash.

"If it isn't the neighbor! Or should I call you the new boyfriend?" His cruel laugh causes the hairs on my arms to stand in attention. "I mean it didn't take you long enough to steal what's mine."

Damian takes small steps toward us, and I struggle to breathe. *No! He'll kill you!*

"Where the hell do you think you're going? Stay the hell back or she dies! I'll take this fucking knife and gut her right in front of you." My body drips in fear just as my throat closes, while my world turns upside down.

"Look man, she means nothing to me. Really. She's just pussy," Damian tells Ash with a lopsided grin, while slowly inching forward.

What is he doing? "I'm sure you know how it is. Your beef is with me. I fucked her behind your back, and I'd do it again. What are you gonna do about it?" My eyes go wide. *No, no don't you dare do this!* Before I know it, I'm tossed aside, crumbling to the floor.

Ash lunges for Damian, one hand gripping the knife, which I now see is the one from my kitchen. I slide across the floor, huddling against the fridge, too afraid to move. What do I do? How do I save him? I don't have my phone to call for help and there's no house phone in my apartment. I watch helplessly as Ash swings the knife around, aiming at Damian, who jumps back.

"I hope her pussy was worth dying for because I'm going to enjoy killing you," Ash spits out through gritted teeth. Damian doesn't respond, instead he jumps back, and kicks Ash in the stomach causing him to tumble to the ground, the knife slipping out and crashing to the floor.

He grunts painfully, while Damian runs over to me, kneeling. "Lilah, you gotta get out of here, now." I sob, my body shaking. "No, I'm not leaving you."

"Baby, listen to me. I'll be fine. Go get help," he demands. He gives me his hand to pull me up and as I look behind him, I scream, "Watch out!" But it's too late, Ash punches him hard on the back of the head, sending him crashing down.

He doesn't waste a second as he climbs on top of Damian. "I'll gladly go to prison for killing you both," Ash admits, punching Damian, who manages to get some in too. They continue to fight as my urgency to do something grows.

I start crawling away, intending to reach his apartment and get to a phone, but just as I make my way across the floor, I notice the knife, its blade glistening in the sunlight creeping through the kitchen window. I stretch out my hand, picking it up. The paring knife is warm as I cling to it tightly in my clammy hand. I rise, quietly dragging my feet until I'm behind the man who continues to take everything from me. I won't let him take my life. I won't let him take Damian's. He has taken enough.

I kneel and don't hesitate as I stab him right in the middle of his neck, pulling the knife out on instinct. Blood splatters from the wound, hitting me everywhere, and in that instant, I don't feel relief, the only things I feel are shock and panic. *What have I done?*

His punches begin to still, then they stop as he starts falling on top of Damian, who pushes him off to the side. He sits up, wiping the blood away from his face, not his, but Ash's. The blood doesn't stop squirting out, it's like an angry fountain, as Ash lays on the floor, not moving. Damian swiftly removes his shirt, pressing it into Ash's wound.

"Lilah look at me," he demands, voice low. I stare into the eyes that always seem to calm me, but they don't have that effect right now. "We don't have much time. You have to listen. You'll tell the police that I did this. I stabbed him while we were fighting after he attacked first. Tell them that he broke in and threatened to kill you."

I blink the fog away and shake my head, "No, I'm not doing that." I won't let him take the blame. I picked up the knife. I stabbed him.

"Goddamn it, Lilah, do what I say!" he demands. "Please baby. We don't have time to argue. Tell me you'll do it." How do I let him take the blame for me? I can't take the chance that he could end up in prison. I can't lose him.

"Lilah, Fuck. Say it! I'll be fine. I'll claim self-defense." I look back and forth between Ash and Damian. I don't know what to do.

He presses into Ash's neck with one hand and checks his pulse with the other. "He's gone."

I grip my hair and pull. "Oh my God. I killed him." I should've walked out and called the police, instead I created a mess. I did this.

Me.

Damian picks up the knife and wipes the handle vigorously with his shirt. He picks up Ash's hand and places it against the handle, then grips the knife with his own hand. "Your prints should be gone now. We have to call the police. Do what I said, baby. You're mine to protect, you hear me?"

I press my fingers into my temples, the panic screaming inside. *What have I done?* "Fine—I, okay I will," I cry, my hands shuddering with fear.

"Good baby, good. Now, go back to my apartment and call 9-1-1." And I do.

TWENTY-EIGHT

They had me checked out at the hospital before bringing me to the station. The doctor said I was fine; just some lacerations on my face and then the police took me away. All the while, I thought about Lilah and how I almost lost her. Again. That motherfucker got the upper hand once more, and if I hadn't gone to her apartment the minute I realized she was gone, or if I was in the shower a little longer, who knows if she'd be alive right now.

I had failed her enough. I'm done failing. It's time I finally protect her. Maybe not from Ash anymore, but from the police and especially this woman before me. I don't want Lilah anywhere near this situation, she's suffered enough to last a lifetime. That's why I had to tell her claiming self-defense would get me off, even though I don't think that's true, not with my combat training. They'll hold me to a higher standard, so I'm probably fucked; but I'd do it all over again.

"Did you hear what I asked you, Mr. Prescott?" I look up at her and glance to the camera in the corner of the small darkly lit room. The two-way mirror stares at me and I wonder who's behind it. Never in my life had I imagined I'd be in one of these rooms, but here I am.

"I'm sorry, would you mind repeating the question, ma'am?" I ask Mrs. Thompson, the assistant district attorney assigned to my case. My foot bounces underneath the table. Man, can they turn the air on higher in this damn room? It feels like a sauna in here.

"How did you come to be in Ms. McDaniels' apartment?"

"Lilah was at my place first. I don't know what caused her to go back to hers while I was in the shower, but once I got out and saw her phone on the nightstand but found her missing, I began to worry. I exited my apartment and when I saw the keys on her door, I went inside. That's when I saw him."

"By him, who are you referring to? You need to be specific for the video, Mr. Prescott."

"Ash Davis. He was inside Lilah's apartment, gripping her from behind, holding a knife to her stomach." She sits across from me, mouth in a tight line, eyes cold enough to melt steel. "She was already bleeding from her stomach, and with him beating her to the point of death days ago, I knew I had to intervene." She writes something in her yellow notepad and glares.

"How long have you and Ms. McDaniels been together?" There's judgment in her brown eyes and I'm afraid to answer, it may make us look like the ones who've done something wrong. But I decide to go with the truth. One lie is enough.

"We met a little over a month ago. Initially, at a pub called, Whiskey, and the next day we ran into each other as I was looking at renting an apartment across from hers."

"So, you two were in a relationship throughout the month while she was still with Mr. Davis, the deceased?"

I clear my throat. "It wasn't like that. We never…had sex. Our feelings started slow and—" I don't get to finish because she interrupts me.

"I understand your father is serving time for the murder of your mother, is that correct?"

"Yes ma'am, that's correct, but—"

"And the police were called to your home many times for domestic violence and your mother refused to press charges each time, is that also correct?" She stares solemnly.

I rub at my mouth, anger simmering beneath. What is she trying to insinuate? "Yes ma'am, that's correct but that has nothing to do with Lilah."

"Really? Because that's not how I see it. The way I see it is you killed Mr. Davis because he was very much like your father, beating on a woman, who like your mother, was scared and defenseless. A woman you had feelings for, by your own admission earlier." She puts the pen down and folds her arms across her suit clad body, looking at me as if I'm the villain, as if I'm the one who terrorized Lilah, like I'm the one who broke into her home, like the murder wasn't justified, when it was.

"And when you and Mr. Davis were fighting," she continues, "you picked up the knife he almost used on her and you killed him, instead of easily defending yourself, especially with your background with, what was it? Delta Force?" she asks, squinting her hazel eyes as if she doesn't know the answer. I had no idea where this interview was going to go, or I wouldn't have waived my right to an attorney. I figured I looked like I had nothing to hide if I did.

I pinch my brows together, the movement stinging a bit, my face still hurting from the fight, and I release a heavy sigh. "You have this all wrong, but I don't think anything I say will erase the story you have already concocted in your head. I was defending myself to the best of my ability given him punching me in the back of my head earlier, which I had already explained to you before. I think it's best I call for that attorney now."

"Yes, I think that's the smartest thing you've said today." She pushes her chair back, taking her papers with her, and exits the room.

A detective I saw in the room earlier returns. "C'mon, you're going back to the cell," he mutters, like I've ruined his entire day.

"Okay, but first, could I call my friend to tell him to call my attorney? I don't remember the attorney's number."

"Yeah, fine, let's go." He leads me to the front where two black phones hang on the wall. I dial Gabe's number and he immediately answers.

"Hey Gabe, it's me. Calling from a police station so I can't talk long. I need you to get the attorney we know and have him meet me at the Third Precinct."

"Already done. Jax and I are with Lilah. She told us everything. The attorney should be there soon."

"Thanks, man. I gotta go. Tell Lilah I love her."

"She knows brother, she knows." I hang up and hope like hell the attorney knows what the fuck he's doing.

Lilah

"I'm sorry what did you say? Can you repeat that because I definitely didn't hear you right!" I clutch my hair tightly in my hands as I glower at Mr. Fields, Damian's attorney, who's informing us about the charges. I can't believe any of this is happening. It's like an awful dream I can't wake myself up from.

After meeting with Damian, Mr. Fields called Gabe wanting us all to meet at Damian's place, who instructed we be kept in the loop. I sniffle, wiping my eyes, feeling the tears against the pads of my fingers. I can't stop worrying about Damian. I hate knowing he did this for me. He shouldn't have!

"Lilah just sit down. Let him finish," Lexi urges, but I'm unable to sit still, everything inside me is revolting, like an angry riot. I replay everything from that night like it's on a never-ending loop. The many what ifs fly around in my head. What if I had went and gotten help only to find Damian dead? What if Ash got to me before I managed to dial for the police and killed me after killing Damian? What if Damian would've killed Ash himself?

Multiple pairs of eyes stare at me, waiting for me to calm down. Well, they can keep on waiting because I won't be calm, not until he's out.

Jax stands, taking tentative steps to me like I'm a wild beast who needs to be tamed. "Lilah, babe, come on. I know you're worried. We all are. But he wouldn't want to see you this way."

I sigh, attempting once again to calm the war going on inside me. Staring into his blue eyes, I can see the concern but unlike all of them I can't just relax and assume everything may work out. It sure as hell doesn't sound that way to me.

I know Damian wouldn't want to see me upset because, well, he's Damian and all he's ever wanted to do since he met me is to protect me. But he's the one who needs protection now. I have to help him. He entered my clusterfuck of a life and it ruined his. "It's fine, I'll stand. I'm too upset to sit."

He nods once and returns to take his place next to Lexi. Gabe is the only one who seems to be as concerned as I am, but unlike me, he doesn't show it so well. The only evidence of his feelings is the clenching of his fists every time the attorney speaks.

Mr. Fields brushes a hand over his grey hair and gives me a sad smile, clearing his throat. "Look guys, this assistant district attorney is the real deal. She is tough and she wins. Like I said, she initially was going to charge him with murder two but after our meeting she bumped it down to voluntary manslaughter, which carries a minimum of five years and a max of twenty-five."

"No, no way! He's not going to prison," I yell. "He did nothing wrong!" Everything hurts, every part of me aches and I burn from the inside out, the avalanche of flames growing bigger.

"She has a case, but so do we. I don't want anyone giving up, because I'm not. We have a great argument for self-defense. We'll need you as a witness, Ms. McDaniels."

"Of course. Anything he needs. What are his chances? Please, I need to know."

"I won't lie. It can go either way and juries are very unpredictable." I run a hand over my face. "My job is to prove that the amount of force he used was equal to that used by Mr. Davis, and that he had no other choice but to act to save his life. However, we have to focus on one thing at a time. He's got arraignment tomorrow. Then comes the grand jury at some point after. You all should be prepared for the fact that he won't get bail."

That's when I sit, or more like drop down, right on the floor. No bail means he'll be stuck in jail until trial, which can take months, and for the entire duration of the case. I shake my head in disbelief and anger.

This is all too much. Why didn't I just tell the truth when I had the chance? Why had I let him rope me into this damn story? The mess we've created is far greater than the one we would be in had we simply told the truth. I know that now. If I decide to tell the truth, who's to say the prosecution would even believe me, and even if they do, we lied. There's a price to pay for that, for the both of us.

Mr. Fields stands, picking up his black messenger bag. "I'll keep you all informed of any new developments. Stay positive." I just continue to sit there, refusing to say a word.

After he's gone, Lexi sits next to me, her arms wrap around my back as she leans her head against my shoulder. "I love you." That's all she says and that's all I need. The last thing I want is for anyone to tell me everything will be okay because no one knows that. Life has no guarantees and neither do trials. Innocent people go to prison all the time.

"Mom, I don't want you to lose your job. You don't have to come. Just wait for the trial," I urge her, gripping the phone tightly against my ear while lying in Damian's bed wearing one of his shirts. The woodsy smell of his cologne only makes my heart miss him more. My throat aches and I swallow it away.

I'm still staying at his place and I plan to for as long as I can. I refuse to go back to mine even after the cleaning crew Gabe and Jax hired is done. I don't care if they will make my home look like nothing happened, I won't step foot inside. The thought of ever walking inside there again makes me ill.

"Honey, I can't just leave you by yourself. I'm coming tomorrow." Her voice is full of anguish.

"Lexi's staying with me today, so I'm not alone, and Damian's friends are always around too." Of course I want her to be here but there's nothing she can do except worry.

"Oh baby," she cries again, "I can't believe any of this. When Lexi called me I—my mind went to the worst scenario. Oh Lilah, I thought I lost you again." She blows her nose before continuing. "I feel so awful for Damian. That poor boy. I know we shouldn't speak ill of the dead but I don't care. I hate Ash's guts." *So do I.* That monster doesn't deserve anyone's sympathy. Even in death he found a way to screw me and those I love. *Rot in hell!*

My mom has no idea I'm the one who killed Ash. I decided not to tell her because it would serve no purpose other than to make her more stressed out. I'm barely tolerating my own anxiety; I can't handle anyone else's. "I know, Mom. I just hope there is a Hell and I hope he's suffering," I grind my teeth, my jaw rattling from the force. She lets out a hard sigh. "Me too baby, me too."

I look up at the ceiling and close my eyes, recalling the short while ago when we were here, happy together on his bed. What I wouldn't do to go back to that, but instead we're stuck in a grim reality where nothing seems to go right. It's as though we're cursed.

"Once my schedule clears up a little in a few days, I'm going to come down to see you, okay? You're my baby. I want to be there." A deep ache starts behind my eyes, filling them with tears just begging to get out.

She sniffles, while I clear my throat trying to push down my emotions, so she doesn't know how badly I'm truly doing. "I love you too, Mom." I feel her love without needing to hear the words, because her love is there even when it isn't spoken.

"I love you, sweetheart. You call me with any news. I don't care what time it is. You hear?"

"Of course. And if I don't you *know* Lexi will." She laughs, knowing all too well. My mom adores Lexi. Those two will sometimes chat when I'm not even home. And when Mom can't find out stuff about my life, Lexi will fill her in just enough without revealing things she knows she can't. They're both so important to me, I'm glad they love each other as much as I love them.

"Okay honey, I'll let you go get some rest. Call me tomorrow."

"I will. Goodnight, Ma."

"Goodnight." I toss and turn, unable to relax, dreading tomorrow's arraignment, but at the same time wanting to see him, even if we can't touch, even if he can't hold me, even if my heart will shatter.

Lilah

TWENTY-NINE

As I face the large, white building of the courthouse, I feel nothing but a deep wave of dread and guilt attempting to claw its way out. Today is one day closer to him going to prison, one day closer to being separated, one day closer to tomorrows that'll never be. A soft hand clasps mine suspending my bitter thoughts. I look up at Lexi as her eyes reflect the direness of the situation.

"Are you ready?" she asks.

I brush a hand against my black trousers and take a deep breath. "I'll never be ready, but let's go anyway." We make our way up, our heels clacking against the stone steps. Opening the heavy, imposing doors, we pass through security who point us to the direction of the courtroom. We enter the room, filled with row after row of brown benches and anxious looking people. Jax and Gabe spot us walking toward them as they sit in the back row, and we settle next to them.

The arraignment of other defendants has already begun. A stern middle-aged judge sets bail for a man probably no older than twenty. I look at the other four defendants sitting behind a glass cage on the right of the judge, none of whom are Damian. *Where are you?* Are they treating him okay? Is he in the cell with anyone? I fiddle with my knuckles, fingers weaving in and out in my lap, and my heart? It throbs against its own cage, pushing and demanding to be noticed.

Once the judge is done with that defendant, the court clerk calls the next case. I lean my head back against the wall and close my eyes, ignoring each case that comes after. My mind's too absorbed in ways I can help Damian. I scratch at the goosebumps on my arms, wishing I had a way of knowing what would happen if I confessed, a way to know the future.

"People versus Prescott," the clerk calls out, and my body jerks forward, eyes widening as a handcuffed Damian's dragged to the front like a criminal he isn't. His eyes roam around the room, probably looking for me. I stand for a second, just enough for him to spot me and when he does, he smiles. I try to smile back but nothing comes out.

The judge looks up, showing no emotion at all as he reads the charges. His voice is dry. He doesn't care. This is just another case to him, but to us this means everything. *He's innocent! Can't you see that?* I yell to only myself.

Legs crossed, I bounce my foot furiously. My neck aches from the tension as my body grows warm, sweat dripping down my back.

"How do you plead?" *He's innocent! I did it.*

My pulse roars as my stomach twists into knots, making it difficult to inhale. *I did it, not him.*

"Not guilty your—"

Without a second thought, I jump to my feet. "I did it your honor.

Me. I killed Ash Davis."

"Lilah, what are you doing?" Lexi whisper-shouts, but I ignore her.

I ignore everyone's looks and everyone's gasps. "Damian Prescott is innocent your honor."

The judge glares at me, his brows bunched together. "Miss, please sit down and be quiet before I have you escorted out." But I don't stop.

"Your honor, didn't you hear me? You have the wrong person. He didn't kill anyone, he's protecting *me*! I should be up there, not him!"

There are whispers all around, everyone turns to look at me, including Damian who is furious.

The judge bangs on the gavel. "Order, order. I will have order now or everyone will be held in contempt!" There's finally silence until the judge begins to speak again. "Counsel, sidebar. Now."

They walk up to the bench, giving Damian a chance to look back at me, shaking his head in disapproval. *I love you,* I whisper. He can be mad, but at least he'll be free.

I love you too, he mouths back, his eyes softening, and my heart hurts knowing I can't hear those words.

Damian turns around as the attorneys return to their tables. "The arraignment is adjourned for this afternoon until both sides can figure out what is going on here. Next case." A court officer drags Damian back to the cell as tears stroll down my face. I hope I didn't make things worse. I hope we've reached the end of this horror show.

I sit back down, my hands trembling. "Lilah, what did you do?" Lexi asks, concerned.

I take a deep breath. "Do you know how difficult it's been to keep this inside and let him take the blame? I couldn't live with it. The truth is finally out and I won't stop telling it until everyone listens and until he's out." She clasps my hand in hers and squeezes.

Gabe nods in understanding, "That was brave, really brave. But you know he was mad, right?" He cocks a brow in amusement.

"Oh, I know," I say with a tight smile, "but he'll just have to get over it."

"Oh man," Jax chuckles. "I like you."

She stares, eyes squinting while she flips her pen around in her fingers. "Let me get this straight. You and Mr. Prescott decided to make up this lie instead of just telling the truth? I mean if it happened how you claim it happened you wouldn't have even been charged. You were in your home and your ex-boyfriend broke in intending to do harm. It's that simple. But now you what? Woke up and had a moral epiphany and decided to finally reveal the truth? Is that what you want me to believe?"

"Yes, that's exactly right. I know it probably seems as though I'm making it up in order to save him, but that's *not* the case. He was the one who saved *me*." I dig my nails into my hands under the table to suppress the nervous energy humming inside me.

"After Ash beat and raped me, Damian did the only thing he could do to protect me from any more pain, he took the fall. Everything happened so fast, so I just agreed. But I can't do it anymore, because you see, I just want everyone to finally know what happened. Ash was a monster, he came to kill me and when I stabbed him, I thought he'd kill Damian. I was defending him. I'll do whatever you need to show I'm being truthful. I'll take a lie detector test, I'll—"

"I appreciate you coming forward with this Ms. McDaniels, but

I am still waiting on the forensics from that day, which will take a few days, and they *will* show the truth." She glowers, then her anger is replaced by indifference.

"Oh, and lie detectors aren't admissible in court but you're welcome to take one for the police if you wish. It will be collected as evidence by them. In the meantime, I will be re-interviewing Mr. Prescott, and I will get to the bottom of this one way or another." She stands, her chair scraping loudly against the floor. "In the meantime, I suggest you get yourself an attorney."

"I don't need one."

She clears her throat, looking at me with no emotion. "That's what Mr. Prescott said before he got one. Thanks for coming in." And that's when I realize, she won't make this easy, not at all.

Damian

Later that day, I stood before the same judge who remanded me back to the courthouse jail. No bail. Not that I expected any different, but part of me was foolishly hopeful.

I miss her so damn much, wishing I could go back and savor those few moments alone we once had.

I still can't get over what she pulled in court. What the hell was she thinking? It's my damn job to protect her, not hers to protect me. My hands tingle at the thought of spanking her tight ass for what she did. Fuck, now I'm hard. Why the hell did I think it was a good idea to picture her naked in this place. *Idiot.*

"Are you listening to me, Mr. Prescott," Mrs. Thompson asks as she sits across from me, glaring with the same contempt I felt the last time.

I look up. "Don't listen to anything she said today. I did it. Just me." A detective stands in the corner observing quietly, while the camera records.

"Stop talking," my attorney advises, but he shuts up as soon as I look at him, my eyes raging.

"See, that's *not* how this works, Mr. Prescott. I already interviewed your girlfriend and her version of events sounds plausible. She offered to take a polygraph test, by the way."

"No! You can't let her do that. They're not even reliable." *Fuck!*

"I don't work for you so you don't get to tell me what to do. And you can protest all you want, but taking the lie detector test is her decision." I tap my feet against the floor, my mouth going dry. How do I stop this?

"So, unless you have something new to tell me," she continues, "we're done here." She contemplates me with boredom then rises to her feet and walks out. The detective turns off the camera and follows her, leaving me alone with my lawyer, who looks ready to read me the riot act.

"Look Damian, I'm your attorney and I'm here to help you. If you expect me to defend you properly, you must tell me everything." I glance at the table and close my eyes. I don't know what the fuck to do. "Listen to me, if she's the one who did it, she won't go to prison."

I scowl. "I don't care. I'm not putting her through this shit. She deserves better."

"Well not everything is up to you. She has a right to tell the truth and if that truth saves you both then maybe it's worth it." Doesn't he understand how much she's suffered already? How guilty I felt seeing her in that hospital bed, broken, beaten, all the while knowing I let it happen? So I chose to save her when I failed to before. And even knowing everything I do now, I'd do it again. Every single time.

"They won't arrest her. The only thing they can get you both on is obstruction of justice. But even if the district attorney presses charges against her, there's almost no chance the grand jury would even indict, so I wouldn't let that stop you from setting the record straight."

Hell no. Almost isn't good enough. "No fucking way. I'm not taking the chance that they won't press charges against her."

"How long have you been an attorney? Come on, Damian. No grand jury would indict a victim in such a case. If they indict you and you're later found guilty, it's no more than a year in prison." I clench my fists. I can do a year.

"Do you want a life with this woman? Or do you want her to move on with someone else while you waste away for something you didn't do?"

He just poured the gasoline and lit the match. She's not moving on with *anyone*. Not a chance in hell. *Fuck!* But that's not fair is it? How could I deprive her of a life?

"You have a strong woman who clearly loves you. Listen to her." Damn it, he's right. Lilah won't let this go. I know it just as much as he does.

THIRTY

Spending my morning at the police station ready to take a lie detector test isn't exactly what I had envisioned for my Saturday, but here I am, sitting beside Lexi and my attorney, Lori Silverman. The guys found her and she's supposed to be a shark by all accounts. Sipping on her coffee, she reads through my file as we wait, her short, auburn hair framing the sharp angles of her face.

She closes the file and turns to me. "They will ask you everything we discussed last night and like I told you they may try to trip you up on purpose, so don't get nervous."

She crosses her legs while I bounce mine. "I won't. I have the truth on my side."

"Well, sometimes the truth doesn't matter." Maybe she's right, but I refuse to give up and think that way. We need a win for once.

Lexi leans against my shoulder. "You got this."

I tilt my head against hers. "Thanks." We sit that way in silence until a detective calls my name. I look back at Lexi, lifting my hand in a small, nervous wave. I follow him into an interview room, the same kind I was in yesterday when I spoke with Mrs. Thompson.

A man sits on one side of a desk, his face intense. I swallow the lump in my throat as he motions for me to sit. My eyes follow the black wires sticking out of a laptop he just finished typing on. After I take my seat, he stands, wrapping a blood pressure cuff tightly around my bicep, then some sort of strap is attached around my chest. A soft panic settles over my shoulders as small, black monitors are slipped onto two fingers. This is it. *Just tell the truth. You'll be fine.*

He starts with basic questions about me, then proceeds with questions about that day. I don't know why I'm so uneasy. I have nothing to hide. But the way he looks at the computer screen, the way the detective just stands there staring as though waiting for the test to show I'm lying, unnerves me.

"Did you kill Ash Davis?"

"I—"

"Yes or no answers only. Did you kill Ash Davis?"

"Yes." My pulse beats angrily but I fight it.

"Did Damian Prescott kill Ash Davis?"

"No." I'm more confident this time.

"Did you lie to the police when you told them Damian Prescott killed Ash Davis?"

"Yes."

"Are you lying right now?"

"No."

He presses a few keystrokes and closes the laptop. "Okay, we're done." He unhooks me from the wires.

"Thank you for coming in," the detective says, and I nod, a tight smile on my face, and walk out the door. I never want to do that again.

"Did everything go well?" Ms. Silverman asks, rising as I approach. I swallow away the nerves.

"Yes, nothing out of the ordinary. You prepared me well. Thank you."

She nods. "Good. I will be in touch once the results are given to me. Please call should you have any questions in the meantime. I'm available anytime."

"I will. Thank you." She walks out ahead of us, toward the elevators as we head for the subway. Parking here is a nightmare so we decided not to drive.

"Do you want me to come over and stay the night again?" Lexi asks as we descend the steps to the station. "We can eat ice cream right out of the tub and binge on episodes of Friends all night."

"That sounds amazing. Thanks, Lex. For everything. I'm really grateful I have you, you know that?"

"Yeah, I know. I'm pretty damn awesome." We loop our arms together, waiting for the train to arrive. I'm glad I don't have to be alone this weekend.

We're on our fourth episode of Friends, our bellies still full from devouring way too much Thai food and chocolate ice cream, laughing at the show as though we haven't already seen it twenty times before. But we're both so obsessed with it, we could see it another twenty times. "Damian is your lobster isn't he?" she asks,

227

referencing what one of the characters said about lobsters mating for life.

"Yeah, he kind of is." Except I can't be with my lobster because he's stuck in shark infested waters unable to get to me. My bottom lip quivers and I bite the inside of it to stop the sounds that attempt to escape from my mouth. My eyes gloss over and I know the tears are about to break. And when they finally burst out like a waterfall, I cover my face hoping to silence them, but they refuse to be restrained.

"Oh Lilah, I'm sorry. I was trying to be cute, but I screwed up." She hugs me as I cry. The last few days have been so mentally exhausting; they're finally catching up to me.

"It's not your fault," I sniffle, looking up at her. "I'm just overwhelmed by everything and— and I just miss him so much, Lex. I need this to be over."

"I know you do. I hate this. You've been through hell and it's all fucked up. None of this is right. I'm so sorry."

I wipe my face on his blanket wrapped around us. Just then my cell phone pings with a text and I wonder who it could be as I pick it up off the coffee table.

Jax: Hey, we just wanted to check in and make sure everything went okay today.

Lilah: Thanks guys. It went fine. They asked everything I discussed with my attorney. Thank you for hiring her for me. There was no way I could ever afford one.

Gabe: No worries at all.

Jax: What he means is Damian would've killed us from jail if we didn't. So yeah, you're welcome, babe.

I giggle.

"Who's that?" Lexi squints in question.

"Gabe and Jax, just checking in."

"Oh, Jax? Great. That's nice." She blushes a little. Whoa, wait a second, how did I miss this? My friend has a crush.

I place the phone down and cross my arms. "Why is your face bright red?"

"It's not. What are you talking about? It must be the wine. Shut up."

"Sure. If we had been drinking any." I smirk. "Are you feeling all right or has Jax gotten you a little hot and bothered?" With everything going on, I hadn't even realized she had a thing for him. I need a distraction from my own life, so I plan to have a little more fun with this.

I don't know much about Jax, but he seems like a nice enough guy. Lexi could use a good man in her life for once. She's had casual dates here or there, but nothing ever comes of it. Her heart is still badly bruised, so she tends not to give men a fair shot. I guess finding your fiancé screwing a secretary on top of his desk will do that to a girl.

I smile mischievously then go back to my phone.

She scowls. "Why do you have that look on your face?"

"Oh, no reason." I start typing on my phone.

"Lilah, what are you up to?"

"Absolutely nothing." I bite my tongue to suppress a laugh.

Lilah: Thanks either way guys. Well let me go back to Lexi. She keeps wondering who I'm speaking to.

Gabe: Okay, no problem. We'll talk to you soon.

Jax: Wait, Lexi is there? Tell her I said hi, will you?

Well, this crush is definitely not a one-way street. It'd be awesome if my friend and Damian's friend ended up together. The little teenage girl inside my head is jumping up and down at the thought. This is the first idea that has made me this excited in forever.

Lilah: She says hey back and hopes she can see you soon, maybe not in court next time.

Jax: Really? Tell her we'll have to plan something soon. I'll text her.

Lilah: That sounds great. TTYL guys.

"So, are you going to tell me what you were talking to them about?"

"Nope. Nothing important." I feign innocence.

"Lilah. I hope you didn't say anything to Jax about me. I have zero interest in dating him. He's a total player. And, he isn't even that hot." Who is the girl fooling? That man is so objectively good looking, most of the female population would agree. Oh, and she just blushed again and probably didn't even know it. Lexi doesn't do that for just anyone. I guess she forgets how well I know her.

"Whatever you say. Turn Friends back on."

She peers at me while unpausing the show. As the episode starts up again, her cell phone vibrates. She looks at the phone then at me. "Lilah? *What* did you do?"

I press my lips, but I can't help the small laugh that escapes. She shakes her head, part amusement and part agitation fight for real estate on her face. Oops, I guess Jax couldn't wait to schedule that date.

Lilah

THIRTY-ONE

I don't know how much more makeup I can smear on my face to cover up these ugly purple-yellow bruises. At least my nose looks okay. The doctor told me I'm healing wonderfully but that the bruises will take a while to go away.

I rub more foundation on them in hopes I look somewhat human for the meeting today. This will be the first time in five days Damian and I'll see each other, so I want to look pretty. The last time I laid eyes on him was during his arraignment.

Every day I miss him more. Is this what our lives will be like? Constantly craving to be together but somehow always falling short? I guess so. But I'll wait as long as it takes because there's no one else for me. It's as simple as that.

People have relationships while one is in prison all the time. We can do this. I wonder if they'll allow conjugal visits. Oh no, what if he's transferred somewhere far? I want to believe everything will work out, but there's a deep doubt building within me, one I can't quite shake.

I rub my temples as I stare into the full-length mirror. Feeling as though I should look professional, I put my hair up in a high ponytail and slip into a navy pencil skirt and a white blouse.

My attorney called yesterday letting me know that the forensics are back, so Damian and I, along with our lawyers, were asked to come in today to discuss the findings. I glance at myself one last time, hoping I don't look as terrible as I think I do, and head out the door.

I get into my car, turning on the engine and a song that always reminds me of Damian begins to play. I grip the wheel tightly and close my eyes hoping the ache in my throat goes away. But as the words wash over me, words about finding love when never expecting it, I lay my head down and sob.

It's not the pretty kind, it's messy and raw. It's the kind that shatters every piece of you. The kind that has your body shaking with the fury of your tears. The kind that hurts so much you don't know if you'll ever recover, but eventually you do. You pick up the pieces and you go forward because staying behind isn't an option.

After a failed attempt at making myself look like I didn't just spend the last fifteen minutes crying, I arrive at the courthouse and spot my attorney in the front. As we walk in together, she asks, "How are you holding up? I know none of this has been easy for you."

I shrug. "Some days are a little better than others. And sometimes I wake up thinking I've imagined it all, and then I see my bruises and come crashing back to reality. I just hope he can come home soon."

She nods, furrowing her brows. "I hope so too."

We near the room where the meeting's going to take place and as we're about to enter, panic scratches inside me. I stop short, placing my hands on my knees, breathing in and out rapidly.

"Are you all right?" Ms. Silverman asks. "If you need a few minutes, take them. There's no rush. We're early anyway."

My pulse quickens within my temples just as my body breaks out into a sweat. I grab onto the nearby wall and pull air into my lungs. This is too hard. I can't shake the fear that something bad is about to happen. I just know it.

"Here, take this." She holds up a paper cup filled with water. I hadn't even noticed her leaving. I take small sips, and each time cold liquid flows down my throat, my heartbeats slow.

I finish the drink and toss it into a trashcan. I take another deep breath and release it slowly. "Okay, I'm ready." She opens the door as we walk inside.

Damian's attorney and Mrs. Thompson are there, but Damian isn't. We say hello and I take my seat next to my lawyer. "We're waiting on Mr. Prescott then we will get started," Mrs. Thompson informs us. She's her usual pleasant self, riffling through paperwork, not making any eye contact.

There's an awkward silence in the room as everyone waits for Damian to arrive. I fidget with my hands in my lap, a nervous excitement humming through my system. *Come on, where is he?* And then my question is answered as the door swings open. A court officer walks in with a handcuffed Damian. *I love you*, I mouth.

"I love you more," he says, loudly, and my heart skips a beat, before a smile spreads across my face. Doubt he was supposed to do that, but I don't care. Those words meant everything. I hadn't realized how much I needed to hear them until he said them.

"Okay, enough of that, have a seat Mr. Prescott," Mrs. Thompson scolds. I inwardly roll my eyes.

"Yes, ma'am." As he sits, I catch a small smirk and bite the inside of my cheek covering up a laugh. He always finds ways to make me feel at ease, even when he isn't trying.

"Let me cut to the chase so I don't waste anyone's time. The forensics have confirmed Ms. McDaniels' version of events. The way the knife entered the deceased showed that it was done at an angle consistent with someone stabbing him from behind. Therefore, based on all the evidence along with Ms. McDaniels' confession, I am dropping the involuntary manslaughter charge against you, Mr. Prescott."

"Oh my God this—" But her narrowed gaze makes my blood run cold, interrupting me.

"I'm not done." Of course she isn't, why did I think otherwise? I sink into the chair, gripping the sides.

"As I was saying, the District Attorney's office has no intention of pursuing manslaughter charges against either one of you." I clasp my hands tighter around the arms of the chair. *Please, just stop talking. Don't say anything else.*

"However," *no don't finish that sentence,* "because of the nature of the case and your interference in a murder investigation, my office will be charging you with Obstruction of Justice, Mr. Prescott."

"What!" I push my chair back and stand. "You have got to be kidding me! How could you do this, huh? Don't you have a heart?"

"Sit down, Ms. McDaniels," she reprimands sternly.

"No! I will absolutely *not* sit down." Placing my palms on the desk, I stare into her cold eyes and lean in closer. "Don't you think we've been through enough? A prisoner escaped on *your* watch, broke into my home and held me at knifepoint. And now you want to dig the knife a little deeper? How dare you!"

"Lilah, please sit down," Ms. Silverman urges me.

"Baby, it's gonna be okay." *No, it isn't!*

I ignore them all. The anger brewing within me has found its prey. This vile woman who claims to mete out justice, does nothing of the sort.

"You'll be removed if you can't contain yourself," she adds. *Fuck you, you bitch.*

My breathing grows heavy, and a panic attack mounts in my chest. But I don't let it take over, I continue to glare at her, not blinking once.

She clears her throat, eyes downcast for a second before they meet mine. "I'm just doing my job. If you two had been up front from the beginning and not wasted my office's time, nor the time of the police, we wouldn't be here." How dare she judge us? *I hate her.*

I narrow my eyes. "Have you ever been mentally and physically abused, Mrs. Thompson? Have you?"

"This isn't about—" But this time I interrupt *her.*

"Did you watch as your mother was beaten for years by your father? Did you listen to her pleas for help before he killed her, all the while not realizing those would be the very last words you'd ever hear her say? Have you lived *every day* in fear of what your boyfriend would do to you next? Have you ever wondered whether today would be the day he kills you? Have you prayed for his strikes or his punches not to hurt as badly as they did yesterday?"

I catch a brief tightening of her jaw. "And then when you finally think he's killed you, you find out you're alive, only to come face to face with him again because the justice system failed to keep you safe. Because people like *you* failed to keep me safe! The only person who's ever tried to protect me is Damian, and now you're punishing him for that. You didn't have to do this to us. You *chose* to. I hope you sleep well at night, but I can't imagine how." I push the chair away and walk out the door.

Damian

Hearing those words pour out of her destroyed me a little bit at a time. I wanted to break free from these damn handcuffs so I could hold her close and tell her that we'll be okay. This is good news. A year in prison is nothing compared to what I was previously facing. A year gives us a future, a life we can carve out for ourselves. This is just a small bump in the road and if it's the worst thing we go through, then I'll happily accept. Knowing Ash is dead and no longer a threat to her, fills me with an overwhelming sense of relief. I can do a year knowing she's finally safe.

I lift up my gaze to Mrs. Thompson, who's scanning her files. I don't know if Lilah's statement made a difference, but it doesn't matter. I'm damn proud of her regardless. She never got to tell her story in court, he took that from her too. I hope this somehow made up for it.

"Well, your girlfriend certainly had a lot to say," she says, finally looking up. I bite my tongue instead of letting her know exactly what I think of her. It's best for everyone I keep my mouth shut.

"My client is rightfully upset, considering she's been victimized from all avenues," her attorney says, arching a brow.

"I'm not heartless. That's why I didn't charge her. But there was wrongdoing involved and it's my job to see that through. Now, if you'll excuse me. I think we're done here." She rises to her feet, taking her briefcase with her, and exits.

The court officer returns to take me back to hell. As I walk out, disappointment drowns me at not seeing Lilah out here. Fuck, I hope she's okay. While I'm being dragged away, I turn around and call to Lilah's attorney. "Tell her I love her and that it'll be okay. This isn't the end of our story."

She nods as I turn back around, a step closer to the shithole they call a cell, but every moment is a step closer to her.

Lilah

THIRTY-TWO

When returning home from court two days ago, I felt nothing but resentment. The high that was coursing through me after telling that woman off had melted away, leaving me hopeless and broken. Lexi had heard about what happened from the guys, who I guess heard it from Damian's attorney. She called and left messages asking if I'm okay, threatening to come over if I didn't reply, so I did. I told her I needed to be alone. I still do, content with my own solitude and misery.

I meant every word I said to that woman. No regrets. Instead of showing compassion, she threw another wrench in our life. My only regret was that I left Damian without a goodbye. I didn't even look at him as I walked out. But I needed to leave. I was close to breaking apart and there's no way I'd ever cry in front of her.

I roll onto my stomach and hug the pillow, inhaling the whiff of his woodsy cologne, the one I sprayed last night. The scent of it that was once all over his clothes is nothing but a whisper now. I find myself spraying it on the pillowcase whenever it disappears. It's the only part of him I have left.

I hope he isn't angry with me for using his childhood in my tirade, but everything just came pouring out of me and I couldn't close the dam. I needed that woman to know how much we've both been through.

My attorney called this morning, telling me what Damian said to her before they took him away. I rushed off the phone before the tears began. He's right. This isn't the end of our story. I guess knowing Damian only faces one year in prison should make me grateful somehow, but I feel nothing but anger.

This isn't how our life was supposed to go. I was supposed to break up with Ash, giving Damian and I a real chance at a future. But now, he's going away for something he didn't do. How the hell am I supposed to feel grateful for that?

A light knock on Damian's door cuts off my train of thought. Who could that be? I know it's not Lexi because she's at work. I'm kind of jealous she's there while I'm stuck here. At least at my job I could hide behind my cases instead of focusing on how awful my life is. But my boss had insisted I take another week, encouraging me to fully heal before jumping back into a busy schedule. Maybe I should've insisted.

Whoever it is knocks again. I was kind of hoping they left after I failed to let them in. I grunt, slipping out of bed, and head for the door. "Honey, it's Mom. Open up." *Ugh, damn it, Lexi!* Under normal circumstances, I'd want my mom, but not today. Today, I don't want anyone's pity or their kind words telling me that everything will be okay. I'm so sick of hearing that.

I pause in front of the door, looking up at the ceiling. "I know you're in there, Lilah." I roll my eyes and flip the lock open and turn the knob.

"Finally! You had me worried, honey." She pushes past me and walks inside, looking way more put together than I do in her jeans and floral blue top. I'm going for tragic, hobo chic in my loose pajama pants and messy high bun.

"Hey Mom, what are you doing here?"

"Well I called you a few times yesterday, but you never called back, so I called Lexi and she told me what happened." I hadn't even seen her missed calls.

I shake my head. "Are you sure she's not your daughter instead?"

"Well maybe you should return my calls, young lady, so I wouldn't have to call her." She walks over to the couch and drops her black handbag on the floor.

"Come on, go get dressed. I'm taking you out to lunch. I'm not going home until tonight. So we'll have a girls' day."

I grunt and cover my face with my hands. "Be serious Mom. Do you think I want to go and have fun while he's rotting in jail? No, thank you. I was doing pretty well here before you showed up, so if you'll excuse me, I'm going to return back to my bed."

She captures my wrist gently in her palm. "Oh baby, I'm sorry you're hurting." Yep, there's that pity. "But do you think that amazing man would want you moping around here alone? I don't think so. Let's go, honey. You got a half hour to get ready or I'll drag you out as you are."

I glare, lips in a tight line. "Fine."

Well, she won. I'm at some outdoor restaurant among all these people I have very little desire to be around. The girl next to us is complaining to her friend about a bad manicure and how she's going to post all these bad reviews. I'm close to turning around and telling her to shut the hell up because some of us have real problems. But I don't. I try to tune her out instead.

At least I could wear my sunglasses and avoid eye contact with everyone. I kept my high bun and just threw on a black tunic dress and grey flats. My outfit represents my mood quite nicely.

"I don't understand. How is that possible?" Mom asks after just learning Damian is the same boy she once knew long ago. "You know, the day you were in the hospital the doctor mentioned his last name and for a second I thought what if he's the same boy. I never knew his first name or any of their first names. If it wasn't for their mailbox, I probably wouldn't know their last name either."

"Believe me, I was just as shocked as you are." I sip on my iced tea, while stabbing at the Caesar salad with my fork, like it's my enemy.

"Wow. I can't believe he's the same person. That little boy was so hard, so beaten down by life. But the man I met is nothing like that." She's right, he isn't, but she didn't know the boy like I did. She didn't see the boy who simply wanted a friend; the one who tried to hide his pain away; the one who wanted someone to help, but no one ever did.

She lets out a deep sigh. "That poor boy...everything he went through as a child." She shakes her head at the memory. "His father was a horrible man. I don't know how much you remember, but God he was vicious to that woman. We were all afraid of him. One day, Johnny, the neighbor on our floor, heard Damian's mother screaming for help and called the police. Damian was only maybe four then. But before the police arrived, Johnny went to intervene and ended up with a broken arm. After that, most of us minded our own business. I wanted to do something, but your father had told me to stay out of it."

My heart races at the mention of my father. I hadn't heard her speak of him in a long time. When I was young, I didn't understand why he left. I thought I had done something to send him away. But Mom told me it wasn't my fault. She said sometimes adults make poor choices and that my father's choice wasn't caused by anything I did.

I loved my father and I thought he loved us too, so it was difficult to understand how he could just leave and never look back.

When I was fifteen, I asked my mom to tell me the truth about what happened, and she did. I'm glad she didn't hold anything back. I needed closure.

I recall how we sat down together, my hands in hers while she told me how my father met another woman and had gotten her pregnant. Once Mom found out, she kicked him out and he felt it was easier if he cut all ties with us. I think he just wanted to erase the family he created and start from scratch. I rub at my throat, still feeling the loss.

My mother is oblivious to my internal torment as she continues on. "I always felt sorry for Damian and his mother. When I heard what his father did, I couldn't stop thinking about him. I'm glad to see he turned out as well as he did."

If she only knew what kind of man he really is, how much he sacrificed to protect me, to see I don't suffer anymore. "Mom, I have to tell you something."

She lifts up her fork, stopping it mid-air. "What is it, honey?"

"You don't know everything."

She gently sets her fork down. "What are you talking about?"

"Damian he— he took the blame. For me," I whisper. "I'm the

one who killed Ash." She covers her mouth with her hand, and I tell her everything without missing a detail.

"Oh baby, I wish I could make all of this better for you both."

"Nothing can make any of this better. Nothing. I just want him. I want us. That's all. But I'll wait for him. He's worth it."

"He is honey, he is."

For once today I'm grateful, grateful for the sunglasses that hide the tears brimming in my eyes. *I love you* I whisper, hoping my words are strong enough to travel the distance and reach inside his heart.

Damian

"With good behavior you'll probably be out in six to ten months. But one thing at a time, Damian. There's no indictment yet." My attorney shuffles around inside his briefcase, stuffing a manila folder back inside as he sits across from me in the meeting room.

"She's out for blood, my blood, so you know she'll find a way to convince the grand jury I'm guilty. When will that hearing be anyway?" I ask.

"It can take a few weeks or a few months. I'll let you know as soon as I find out." *Months? Fuck!* "You've been dealt a shitty hand but try to hang in there." *Tell me something I don't know.* He stands, pushing the chair back and waves. An officer returns to take me back to my cell.

I wish they'd sentence me already, that way Lilah can visit. How am I supposed to survive not seeing her for months while the District Attorney's office figures their shit out?

Laying my head down on the dirty pillow, I close my eyes, recalling the night that we first met and how much I wanted her. The image is so vivid, so I reach out and touch her even though I know she isn't real.

You're everything I need, she whispers, the same way she did that day we sat on my sofa, that day before everything went to shit. I've held on to those words since she said them. I pray like hell she still feels that way. I hope I'm still enough even when I can't be there. But I have to believe this isn't the end, it's only the beginning.

Lilah

THIRTY-THREE

A week passes, or should I say drags. Every day is slower than the last and every day my heart aches to be with him. I haven't received any updates on his case, but that's to be expected. These things take a long time and I have no choice but to be patient even when I don't want to be.

On Tuesday, I called my boss and told him I'm coming back sooner than he wanted me to and returned the next day. I can't spend another minute cooped up in Damian's home with all of his things, thinking about every painful experience of the past few weeks. I needed a distraction. Work is the perfect one.

"So, we're going out tonight," Lexi announces, as she struts into my office.

"Maybe *you* are, but I'm going home." It's one thing to go back to work but a whole other ballgame to go and enjoy myself while he suffers. Not happening.

"Please! Think of it as an early birthday present for me." She pouts. "I'm your best friend."

"Your birthday isn't for another month." I roll my eyes. "Try again."

"Fine. Jax and Gabe are coming too. They asked me to invite you. Come on, please Lilah. I *need* you there."

I squint, glaring at her. "Why do you need me to come?"

She sits on my desk and scratches her nose. "I can't be alone with Jax. He makes me want to scream. I need you as my buffer."

"Oh please, can you go fuck him already? I know you two like each other, so just do it."

She swallows, looking down. "Well...."

My eyes go wide. "Wait. What? Oh. My. God. You didn't?"

"Twice. Don't look at me like that! You just told me to do it!"

"I'm just shocked right now. Wow. Wait, are you dating? I think it'd be great if you guys did."

"Date Jax?" She laughs. "It was just sex that one day. That's it. Neither one of us wants anything more." My mouth flies open. I hadn't anticipated that. "I was sad when you were in the hospital so we... ya know."

"What?! When? Where?"

"In his car...while you were in surgery." She bites her thumbnail. "He's got a really nice... car."

"Oh my God, Lexi!" I don't even know what to think.

"I do mean his car, but I also meant other things..."

"Um, so how was it?" I probably shouldn't ask.

"Ugh. I wish it wasn't good," she runs her hand through her blond hair, "but man he can fuck. Best I ever had kind of good." She closes her eyes, as though reliving it as we speak.

"Yep, that's enough information. Thanks."

"Hey, you asked. But I'm nervous. I can't be around him."

"Can't be around him without wanting to jump him you mean?" After her fiancé cheated a year ago, it took months just to get her out of the slump. *Bastard.* Maybe Jax could make her happy.

"Shut up!" She laughs, smacking me on the arm. "So please, will you come? It's just dinner."

"Fine! But I'm not staying long."

"Yay! Thanks."

Wow, Jax and Lexi. I wonder if Damian knows. When I had wanted them together, I never imagined it'd just be a random hookup. That could spell trouble. What if they have a falling out? Damian and I'll be stuck in the middle. Oh Lexi, what am I going to do with you?

I get home from work and reluctantly get ready for tonight. If I didn't love that girl there's no way I'd ever be doing this. I throw on a pair of tight fitted jeans and a flowy burgundy top. My cell vibrates with an incoming text and I don't even have to look to know who it is.

Lexi: Make sure you dress up. Jax said it's a fancy place.

Lilah: I'm wearing jeans.

Lexi: Oh, come on! You know that's not what I meant.

Lilah: Do you want me to come or…

Lexi: Fine! Wear your jeans. I'm wearing a dress.

Lilah: Do you want a medal?

Lexi: Haha. You're not funny. See ya soon. XO.

This is as dressed up as I'm getting. She's lucky I'm even wearing heels. I'd much rather stay home in bed and think about Damian, like I do every morning and every night. There's a constant ache inside me. It's deafening. Not that I ever want the twinge of pain to stop. I want to feel the hurt, I want to swim in it until I'm covered in agony, and when I close my eyes and dream, I want it filled with us.

Lilah: I'm heading out now.

Lexi: Me too.

Lexi: Jax offered to give me a ride…

Lilah: Oh, I bet he did.

Lexi: Shut up! I do kind of wish it was that kind of ride though.

Lexi: OK, never mind, I take that back.

Lilah: You're so going to screw him again.

Lexi: Shhh, stop sending out the bad juju.

Lilah: Bye! See you soon. Try to keep your legs closed on the ride over.

Lexi: I hate you!

Lilah: I love you more.

How am I supposed to look at Jax knowing he's banged my best friend? *Ugh.* Can't wait to see how this plays out.

I park my car at a garage and walk the block over to the restaurant. I enter Le Amour and by the looks of it it's very classy and very French. I glance around the busy dining area and the women are dressed in slacks or dresses. No jeans in sight. Well, I'm definitely a tad underdressed, and the old Lilah would care, but the miserable Lilah doesn't. At. All.

The hostess leads me to our table where everyone's already waiting for me. Jax spots me first. "There she is!" He stands up, giving me a quick hug and pulls out my chair.

"Thanks."

"I'm glad you came, Lilah," Gabe says. "We wanted to make sure you're doing okay. Damian would want that." He picks up his glass of white wine, pulling in a sip.

I take in the large, dimly lit room with its high ceilings and wall to floor windows then look back at him. "Well this place is a bit fancy just to check in on me. I would've been fine with something less um, expensive."

"Don't worry about it. It's our treat," he replies. "Also, Jax here won't stop talking about your friend Lexi over there and was a little shy about asking her out, so here we all are."

"Shut up, jackass. Don't believe a word he says. I've never been shy around women, they all run to me, Lexi included. Isn't that right, Lex?" He wags his brows and her lips curl in a snarl.

"First of all, don't call me Lex. Only my friends call me that, and you and I aren't friends. And second, you wish I'd run to you. It's more like flying away from you as fast as I can."

"I love a woman who plays hard to get." He grins arrogantly.

She pretends to vomit. "You're disgusting."

"But you love it. Should I tell them how much you love it, Lex?"

"It depends."

"On what, baby?" he asks, leaning back cockily in his chair.

"How badly do you want to die?"

He breaks off into a laugh just as the waiter comes over, clearly hearing Lexi's last statement based on the suspicious look in his eyes. He takes my drink order and scurries away probably thinking we're a bunch of freaks who don't belong in such a nice establishment. He's not wrong. We pick up our menus and I glance at the choices, but I'm not hungry.

"So Lilah, how are you doing?" Gabe asks, placing his menu back on the table. "Have you found a way to get a hold of Damian?" The waiter returns and places my drink on the table.

"No. My lawyer told me there's no way for me to see him right now and that it could be a while until the case makes it to trial. I mean that bitch hasn't even sent the case to the grand jury yet. It feels as though she's taking longer because she wants to hurt us."

I pick up my glass of water and take a big sip, needing to swallow the painful lump of emotion clogging up my throat. He nods in understanding. "At this point, I won't see him for a long time."

"It may be sooner than you think," says a voice behind me, a voice that sounds too much like Damian's. I hate when that happens. I sometimes daydream about him and it's so unfair because it feels too real, such as right now. I glance around the table and they're all staring at me with smiles on their faces.

"Turn around, baby." An icy chill slides down the length of my body. It can't be him. I'm afraid to move. I'm afraid this is one of my dreams and I don't want to wake up. My hands tremble, and I shake my head choking back tears. No. He isn't here. This isn't real.

"Turn around, Lilah." I close my eyes, silently letting the tears slip down my face. Turning slowly, eyes still shut, I pause, taking a deep breath. My heart beats like mad when I fully face that voice and open my eyes.

"Damian?! Wha—how?" I leap out of my chair and jump at him. My vision is clouded by the tears now falling free. I wrap my legs around his hips and hold on for dear life, never wanting to let go.

I reach out and cup his face, my eyes roaming every inch of it. "How are you here?" A sexy grin flashes across his lips and my heart almost beats out of my chest, clearly missing him as much as I did.

I kiss him, never giving him a chance to answer. We kiss hungrily while the world just melts away. Our mouths devour one another, making up for lost time. He growls as I slide my hands into his hair, nails scraping along his scalp.

"Hey Lex, would you welcome me home like that if *I* went away to prison?"

"Ha, you wish soldier boy. I'd ask why they didn't keep you longer."

Oh Jax, way to ruin the moment. Our mouths separate reluctantly, but I'm still in his arms. "I really don't want to let you go," he whispers against my neck, kissing up to the curve of my ear.

"So don't."

"I think this place will probably frown upon that."

"Eh, who cares?" I smile against his cheek. "We've already put on quite a show. Who decided on this place anyway?" My hands caress his back and his corded muscles twitch beneath his button-down shirt, the ones I missed so much, the ones I want to feel on top of me. Right now.

"Jax did."

I roll my eyes. "Of course."

He places me down as the waiter brings us another chair, looking at the two of us as though we've just created a travesty, and takes our dinner order. *Whatever*.

Crossing my legs, I look at everyone. "So you guys all knew and planned this whole thing?"

"I'm sorry, Lilah. I wanted to tell you *so* badly but they all would've hated me," Lexi says, her forehead creasing.

"Don't be sorry. This is the best surprise ever!" Damian scoots my chair closer to him, and for a split second, my brain takes me back to the night with Ash, the night that changed everything. I sip on my water, swallowing the memory away.

I take Damian's hand in mine, squeezing it as though still not believing he's here. "But I don't understand. How are you here right now? Why would she let you out?" I ask.

"I don't know what happened exactly, but my lawyer came to see me two days ago and told me the charges were being dropped. I got released this morning. Everything you said to her, I bet it made a difference. You got through to her even though she pretended you didn't. You set me free, Lilah. It was all you. I really believe that." I push back the tears swimming in my eyes and smile, and for once in what feels like ages, I'm truly happy.

"Our boy is out the joint! We need to celebrate!" Jax announces.

Damian shakes his head. "Nah, not today."

"Tomorrow then. The whole crew will want in. Come on, man.

I can rent a place in the city. We'll make a thing of it. You guys deserve a party." Jax looks like an excited little puppy. He's kind of sweet. And if I have to admit it, he's kind of growing on me. Lexi is staring at him, twirling her hair, and she doesn't even know it. They'd make some cute babies.

"Just say yes, Damian," Gabe mutters. "You know he won't stop hounding your ass until you agree."

He looks over at me. "What do you think, baby? It's your call." Way to put me on the spot there, handsome.

I grab his face and kiss him, just a touch of our lips and my body ignites again as I stare deep into his eyes. "I say let's do it." We hold each other's gaze as Jax hollers, "Hell yeah!" But we ignore him, too busy stuck in our own world.

Damian leans over, his mouth against the shell of my ear. "I've missed you so much, beautiful."

"I missed you more," I whisper back, while the waiter places our food on the table. "Do you think they'd mind if we left now?"

"Do you care?" he asks.

"Not even a little." I ravish his neck with tiny kisses as his pulse races wildly under my lips.

"Good, let's get out of here," he says, and my excitement grows. *Finally.* "Hey guys, Lilah and I are out of here. You stay and enjoy yourselves." He pulls my chair out and as I rise up, he entwines our hands, his long fingers rubbing against my skin. My body grows hot, a wave of pleasure coursing through me.

"I guess I should say we hope *you* two enjoy yourselves," Jax says, grinning like a teenager.

"Oh God, you're such a pig!" Lexi berates. A pig she wants to bang. She stands and hugs me tight, whispering in my ear, "I'm so happy for you. You deserve it."

"So do you, Lex, so do you. Be careful getting home. No drinking and driving for that one." I point at Jax.

"I'd take his keys before that ever happens." She steals a glance at him. "He's annoying, isn't he?"

"Annoyingly obsessed with you maybe."

"Stop talking about me, Lex. How about you come sit on my lap and tell me all about it."

"Ugh! See what I mean!" she grunts out loud, invoking a deep laugh from Jax.

Getting up, Gabe hugs me and pounds Damian on the shoulder. "No more trouble from you two, okay? I'm not bailing either one of you out of jail. Got it?"

"Yeah, our crime spree is over," I giggle. "Promise." We wave goodbye to them and walk out of the restaurant hand in hand.

Being with him right here in this moment feels surreal. I inhale the night air and whisper a thank you to whoever's listening.

"I'm kind of glad you wore jeans," he says, tugging me away from my thoughts with his lopsided grin.

"Why's that?"

"Because now I can do this," he picks me up while I yelp, placing me on top of his shoulders, "without worrying about you flashing that pretty ass."

I laugh, half afraid. "Put me down Damian! I'm gonna fall!" I tighten my grip around his neck while he holds my thighs, ignoring the look of the passerby getting out of a taxi.

"I'd never let you fall, not without catching you first." And with that, I lean my head against his, completely content, knowing that in his arms, I'm always safe.

Damian

THIRTY-FOUR

The ride over was excruciatingly hard, pun intended. All I wanted was to rip her out of those damn clothes and fuck her in the car, just let her ride my cock right there on the front seat. I flex my jaw while she tries to open the door, her hand trembling as the keys finally enter. As soon as the door closes, I grab the back of her head and pull her mouth hard against mine. I kiss her like I'm starved for the air she breathes, like I've never kissed her before, like I never want to stop. It's unapologetically gritty, but from the way she moans into my mouth, I know she likes it.

Our fingers claw at each other's clothes, and a button flies past as she rips open the top of my shirt kissing my chest. I grow rigid, groaning at the feel of her tongue.

"I need to taste you, Damian. Everywhere." She doesn't give me a chance to reply. Instead, she sinks onto the floor, undoing my belt without taking her eyes off of mine. I swallow the hard lump in my throat, balls aching to feel her mouth. *Fuck, I've missed her.*

There goes my zipper, then my pants and boxers are around my ankles and my cock's in her hands. She works me hard, fisting the head tightly within her grasp. "Damn baby, you keep that up and I'll come before I get to be inside you. Oh shit—" Her tongue glides up the underside of my dick and she takes the tip into her mouth, squeezing it between her lips at the same time as her tongue swirls around it.

She withdraws, looking up, and I thread my fingers into her hair. "That mouth, fuck baby." A wicked grin appears on her lips as she goes back down sucking harder this time, her mouth taking me deeper as she gags a little. She's a relentless little thing as she works me faster until the pleasure builds. *Oh damn, this feels so good.* Our eyes connect once more, and I could come just from the way she looks at me. She's loving this. But what I need more than anything is to fuck her, hard and deep. I want her to feel what she does to me.

I pull her head back gently by her hair and my dick falls out of her warm mouth, making us both groan at the loss. "Stand up, beautiful." She does, rising to her feet, those sexy heels still on. I grab her by the back of the head and bring her in for a searing kiss, loving the taste of me on her tongue.

"Where did you learn how to use that mouth so well, hmm?" I lick my way up her neck, nipping the flesh in between my lips. She moans, her nails digging into my shoulder.

"I want to do it again," she rasps, "I loved feeling you get harder in my mouth." I growl, gripping the hem of her shirt and ease it off her body. I pop open the button of her jeans and slide the zipper slowly.

"Are you wet for me, Lilah?" She nods, her mouth parting as her breaths turn heavy. "We'll see about that." I slip down her jeans until they hit her thighs, and without giving her a second to think, I shift her panties to the side and plunge two fingers inside her. She cries, clinging to my shirt for stability. My thumb circles her clit, while I continue to fuck her, loving the way she cries out my name. Her thighs begin to tremble as she clenches around my fingers, almost there. A few more thrusts and—"Damian... yes!"

My voice rumbles with deep satisfaction. Geez, she's dripping and I'm not even done. I pull off her panties and take the jeans with them, tossing both over my shoulder. I unclasp her bra and growl in her ear, "I need you bent over that couch." She whimpers. I pull her in close by her hips and flick her clit. "Now, baby." Biting her lip, she grips my wrist, her pussy still sensitive.

She makes her way over and I fist my cock watching her ass jiggle behind her. I step out of my pants just as she bends over the couch, turning her face to the side, waiting for me.

I descend upon her with greedy steps, and as I near, my hand skirts up the length of her back, loving the goosebumps that rise under my touch. I lower myself on top of her, my dick flinching at the feel of her bare flesh.

"I can't go slow, baby. I want you too much."

She nods. "I don't want it slow. I want to get fucked. I want all of you. I've waited long enough."

Shit. "I have a condom. Do I need one?"

"No." I was hoping she'd say that. I want her bare.

Reaching down with my free hand, I grip my dick and position it against her wet, hot entrance. I ease the tip inside her, once, twice, and hit home, making us both cry out from the sheer magnitude of the feeling.

I pump in and out with commanding thrusts, tugging at her ass cheeks as I take her deep. Her fingers splay against the sofa, curling every time I impale her. She screams loudly, my thrusts turning brutal. And when she tightens around me, I know she's close as I near the peak with her. "Damian...oh yesss!" she gasps as she explodes, barely able to hold on to the sofa.

"Fuck, baby I'm coming too." A few deep thrusts and I'm there. She's so perfect and all mine. I angle forward, over her body, circling my arms around her stomach. "You're amazing, baby girl," I say, nipping at her shoulder.

"Mmm, I can't move, Damian." I grin against the side of her neck. "I hope you're not too tired because I'll be ready for round two very soon."

"Not sure you can top that."

"Oh, you have *no* idea." I flip her around and lay her back on the sofa. Legs spread, I dive in between her thighs and make her scream my name for the third time tonight.

Lilah

The morning sun shines brightly, a perfect day for doing something awful, yet necessary. "Are you sure about this?" Damian asks.

I tie my shoelaces as I look up at him, standing before me. "I'm sure. I think I have to do this for myself."

"You don't have to rush. I just want to make sure you'll be all right." Am I? I genuinely don't know. It's a question filled with so many answers, none of which I want to think about.

I had a nightmare last night and it scared him. When I became a little calmer, we talked, and I told him what I thought I had to do to get rid of these horrors that infest my mind, and I wanted to do it today.

After Ash hurt me, I started having these terrible dreams where he killed me. They weren't there every night, but when they did come, they rocked me, sending me into a panic driven hell. Damian was there to hold me together more than once.

When Ash died, the nightmares still continued, except this time they were from the day he broke in. He'd pry the knife out of his neck, very much alive, turning it on Damian, killing him instantly, and then coming for me. I'd wake up drenched in sweat, breathing like I've ran twenty miles to escape him.

I don't think my brain has caught up to the fact that he's gone and he's never coming back. This man has been my tormentor and my warden for so long, it may be a while until I realize the cage is open, I can fly.

We drive silently as he holds my hand, stroking his thumb against my skin in a soothing manner. Looking out the window, I'm deep in thought. Am I really doing this? I won't lie and pretend I'm not nervous. I'm terrified. I run through the things I'll say, things I never got to say to anyone. But now is my chance, even though there'll be no one to hear the words.

We park in front of the cemetery and get out. Damian holds my hand and we walk up together, my pulse racing as we get closer and closer. Maybe I shouldn't do this. He's right, I should've waited. But will I ever be ready? I have to start healing, and this is one way I can try to do just that. As we arrive in front of Ash's plot, I reluctantly untangle myself from Damian. "Do you mind if I do this alone?"

He kisses my forehead. "Of course not. I'll go visit my mom. She's right over there." He points to the left.

I grab his hand, holding tight. "Would it be okay if I meet her after I'm done here?"

His eyes shine with emotion and he pulls me close. "I'd love nothing more," he says, and his voice breaks just a little. "Thank you for wanting to. I love you, baby."

"I love you more." I kiss his chest. "I'll be done in a few minutes, then I'll join you."

As he walks away, I turn to face the man who even in death finds a way to haunt me. Taking a deep breath, I try to find the right words.

"When I met you, I never dreamed we'd be here. You made me happy. At first. But slowly you turned into someone I barely recognized. I guess that's who you always were, only showing me the real you once I became most vulnerable. I know none of this is my fault, the blame is all on you. But some days are hard, some days I blame myself for everything. I guess the many years you spent criticizing me for everything wrong in our relationship still lives in me. And maybe I could say I forgive you. I could lie. But I won't. I'm done lying. Maybe someday I'll get there, to a place where the pain you've caused me no longer matters as much, and maybe that's the day I forgive you, but today isn't that day. Today I let the hurt win. Today I remember. Remember each time you hit me, each time you told me I was worthless, each time you held me down and took everything, destroying me in the process. But I found someone so much better than you, and through him I'll heal all the fragile scars you've left behind. Maybe in death you'll finally find the peace you never found while alive. And if you don't, I don't care. You're no longer my problem."

I take a final look at his gravestone and walk away, feeling more at peace than I've ever felt, and I realize I'm smiling. I guess sometimes just letting the words out into the world is enough.

I near Damian, his lips move while his gaze is fixed on his mother's grave. He looks up once he hears me approach. "Are you okay?"

I cup his face and kiss his lips. "I've never been better. Now introduce me to the woman who made such an incredible man."

"Well Ma, this is her. I guess you knew what you were doing when you sent her to me because I have no doubt it was you." My heart squeezes as a full avalanche of emotions permeates within.

I glance up at the man who's been there for me from the moment I met him, then I look down at the place holding his mother's memory and my tears drift down my face. I cry for her suffering, I cry for the days she never got to watch him become someone she'd be proud of, and I cry for him, for all the years he never got with her.

I wrap an arm around his middle as we both stare at her gravestone. "Thank you for giving me someone so incredible. My heart's finally whole."

"She would've loved you, baby."

I lean my head against him and sigh. "I know I would've loved her too." We spend the next few minutes catching her up on the good and the bad that's been our life, and as we stroll away hand in hand, I know she's smiling down upon us, telling us everything's all right now, we can finally breathe.

Jax wasn't kidding when he said he'd take care of everything for this party. I don't know how he managed it so quickly, but the Chelsea rooftop lounge he rented is incredible, offering guests the most spectacular views of the city. Waiters stroll around with trays of tiny food, while music plays in the background, blending with the chatter of people. I've absolutely no idea who any of these men and women are but there's a good fifty people up here.

As we near the table where our friends have gathered, I find someone there I didn't expect. "Mom?" I cry out, running toward her. "What are you doing here?! You told me you couldn't come!"

"Surprise!" She brings me in for one of her tight hugs and I sag against her. "I'm so happy this is finally over," she says loudly over the booming music.

"Me too, Mom." When she notices Damian behind me, we separate and she comes over to him.

She takes his hand in hers, peering down onto the floor for the briefest of seconds before looking up into his eyes. "I just want to thank you for what you did for my girl. She told me everything. I'm so thrilled she has you."

"You don't have to thank me for anything. I'd do it all over again." She pinches her lips together and nods.

"Also," she continues, "I need you to know I'm sorry. I'm sorry I didn't do more for you and your mother when you were just a boy. I—"

"It's okay." He places his hand over hers. "I swear, there's nothing you could've done. He'd never stop."

Wiping her eyes with her free hand, she says, "Thank you for saying that." He brings her in for a warm embrace, and as I stand and watch, I can't help the tug of emotion burning in my throat.

Grabbing some food and drinks, we make our way back to the table. While our loved ones are deep in conversation, Damian catches my eye and smiles. Not just any smile, one that sends butterflies deep into my belly and brightens up the whole room, taking my heart with it. And as I smile back, we share more in that look than some people say in a lifetime.

Jax stands and whistles, causing the music to stop. "Guys and girls, this day is dedicated to our man, Damian, right here and the beautiful, Lilah. Cheer for them will ya?" The place erupts in claps and whistles, and my cheeks feel warm from the attention.

Gabe rises next. "These two have been through a lot, so we wanted to do something for them. It's also not every day one of your best friends lands in the big house." Everyone bursts into laughter and I can't help but join them. It's nice to be able to joke about this now.

"Get up, say a few words," Jax urges Damian, who scratches his head, getting up hesitantly. The room gets quiet as he begins to speak. "The last few weeks have been trying, to say the least, and without this woman right here," pointing to me, "I'd be nothing. Come here, baby." I take a sip of my wine, needing liquid courage. I hate being in front of a large group of people.

He reaches for my hand and links them together, squeezing tight. "She's not just beautiful, but she's strong and courageous too." He faces me while I try not to cry. "When I was a boy, you showed me what it means to have a friend, and as a woman you've shown me what it means to love, and I'll forever be grateful. Not all of us get lucky in life, but I'm so lucky you decided to love me. I'll never take that gift for granted." And here come the tears tracking down my face.

He lets go of my hand and gazes at me with deep devotion. And before I realize what's happening, he lowers himself to the ground on bended knee and whispers *I love you*. My fingers jump to my lips and every inch of me shudders with both shock and anticipation. *Oh my God. No, he isn't.* He fishes through his pocket and reveals a red box, opening it, just as my heart somersaults. *Yes, he is!*

"I love you so much, baby. It may be too soon but when you know, you know, and I know that with you I have a family and a home. So, would you make me even happier by starting a life with me? Will you be my wife?"

As I stare into the eyes I've loved since I was seven, I give him the only answer there is to give. "Yes! So much yes. I'll marry the hell out of you." He chuckles, slipping the dazzling round solitaire on my trembling hand, before lifting me up off the floor. And as we kiss passionately, taking our time, feeling the love pouring out from our mouths, I know our forever can finally begin.

Damian
20 YEARS LATER

EPILOGUE

O ur love was like a fire, growing stronger, bolder with time. After I proposed, it took a month-long engagement to make us realize we didn't need to live by anyone else's standard of love. Yeah, we barely knew each other but we knew the important things, and at the end of the day, the things that make us who we are inside are what really matter.

We said I do exactly six months after I slipped the ring on her finger. She was the most beautiful bride I'd ever seen in my entire life and she was pledging to be mine.

I'd like to think my mother was there that day, sitting among our friends and family, smiling one of her beautiful smiles, the ones I'll hold in my heart for as long as I live.

It didn't take long for us to start a family. Well, I kinda knocked her up on our wedding day, or so I'd like to think, because our son, Caden, was born around nine and a half months later, and our daughter, Quinn, came along three years after that.

To say I'm happy is an understatement. I'm the happiest man I'd ever imagine being. If someone had told that little boy one day he'd have all this, he would've called them a liar. She gave me a life I never dreamed I'd have, and children I never thought I deserved.

After she got pregnant, I worried about turning into my father. For months, I agonized and feared that the stress of day-to-day life and being responsible for a family would destroy me, and I'd become angry like him, but that's all in the past now. Once I saw my son's face for the first time, that fear melted away.

My children and this woman by my side give me strength and purpose I never would've had without them. I'll spend my life protecting my family, not destroying them like my father did. I'll cherish every day because the days we have are gifts, ones I'd never take for granted.

She says I healed her too, that my love repaired the cracks created long ago. There's always a light in her eyes now, the fear she used to carry there is ancient history.

"Daddy, where are we going?" Quinn asks as we near our destination, her brown curls flowing over her shoulders.

"You'll see, my impatient little princess." She squints her eyes at me and pursues her lips. My daughter is one sassy four-year-old. I don't know where she gets it from but boy are we in some trouble. I think she came out of the womb with an attitude.

As we near the animal shelter, I pull the car into a parking spot directly in front. "Ooooh, Dad, are we getting another dog?" Caden asks excitedly.

"Not exactly."

"Ah man!" He folds his arms across his tiny chest, looking all too unhappy.

I glance over at Lilah, her belly only just starting to show as she grows our third child. Damn, does she have to be so sexy? I don't think my need for her will ever die and thank fuck for that. She grabs my hand and kisses my knuckles, while my other's on the steering wheel.

"Come on Dad, wouldn't it be great if Rex had a friend?"

"He has you and Quinn. I think he's maxed out on friends at the moment." One dog is plenty for us, especially with a new baby. Potty training a pup and changing diapers round the clock doesn't seem like a fun way to live.

"Are you feeling okay, baby?" I ask Lilah.

She smiles, her blue eyes bright. "I'm fine. Stop worrying, will you?"

She knows me well enough by now to know I'd never stop worrying. This pregnancy has knocked her down. She's been really sick, so the doctor put her on medication. I told her to stay home and rest, but she insisted on sharing this moment with us. My woman. "I love you, you know that wife?"

"Can we go, Dad?!" Quinn says impatiently. "Yeah, what are we waiting for?" Caden adds. We both laugh at the interruption. Those cock blockers. They're lucky we like them.

Her mouth lifts in a small grin. "I love you more, husband." We're one of those couples that make others around us sick with our affection, expressing it every chance we get, not caring who hears or sees. We kiss and cuddle in front of our children, not only because these things come naturally, but because we want them to see what real love is like, to be surrounded by affection not anger.

We hope this teaches them to never settle for anything less than what they deserve. Yeah, Lilah and I may argue as all couples do from time to time, but our disagreements are just that, disagreements. No one yells or says an unkind word, it's not our way. Plus, the makeup sex is worth a little heated squabble.

Exiting the car, I take Quinn out of her car seat while Caden unlocks his booster and steps out. We enter the shelter as I make my way to Rodney, the manager, whom I met with just days ago.

He waves as he sees me. "You guys came. That's great. I really appreciate it. Come with me."

"Are you going to tell us what we're doing here, Dad?" Caden asks, looking at all the dogs with a scowl on his face as we're led to the back.

"Nope." I drape my arm over his shoulder, pulling him into me. "Just wait and see, but I promise you'll love it."

"Fiiiine." If I can be patient waiting for him to clean his damn room every day, he can be patient for me.

We proceed into a large room with cages all around. "So here are the kittens that you'll be feeding today, kids," Rodney says. "They're about two weeks old so you'll be using small bottles. Do you think you guys can handle that?"

"We can, we can! Oh my God, we're feeding little kitties!" Quinn squeals. "Thank you, Daddy. I love you." She runs over and squeezes my leg tightly. I pick her up, planting a kiss on her forehead before setting her back down.

"They're so small, Mom, look at them," Caden remarks, petting one who's pawing the cage.

"I can see that, sweetheart, they're so precious."

"You kids can make yourselves comfortable on this rug right here," Rodney says, "and I'll take two of them out and show you how to do it."

I wrap an arm around Lilah as he helps my kids fulfill a dream I had since the moment they were born. It may not seem like much to some, but it means everything to me to share in the tradition my mom had created long ago.

"They're so happy, Damian. You're such a great father. Your mother would be so proud."

And as I look upward, closing my eyes, I whisper, "I hope so, baby, I really do."

The End

THANK YOU
FOR READING!

If you can spare an honest review, I'd appreciate it. They help a
lot!

PLAYLIST

- "Can I Be Him" – James Arthur
- "Let It Go" – James Bay
- "Praying" – Kesha
- "Landfill" – Daughter
- "Falling Like the Stars" – James Arthur
- "Chances" – Backstreet Boys
- "Battlefield" – Lea Michele
- "No Saint" – Lauren Jenkins
- "Power Over Me" – Dermot Kennedy
- "I Get to Love You" – Ruelle
- "One Drink" – Picture This
- "Loved You Before" – Natalie Taylor
- "In My Blood" – Shawn Mendes
- "I Belong to You" – Jacob Lee
- "Where You Belong" – The Weeknd
- "For You" – Liam Payne & Rita Ora
- "How Can I Forget" – MKTO
- "Better Than Today" – Rhys Lewis

ALSO BY LILIAN HARRIS

Fragile Hearts SERIES

1. *Fragile Scars* (Damian & Lilah)
2. *Fragile Lies* (Jax & Lexi Book 1)
3. *Fragile Truths* (Jax & Lexi Book 2)
4. *Fragile Pieces* (Gabe & Mia)

ACKNOWLEDGEMENTS

To my readers, thank you for taking a chance on me! This story means so much for many reasons, so I hope you enjoy reading it as much as I've enjoyed writing it.

There are so many other people to thank, but the first and most important person is my mother. I've been lucky enough to have a very supportive one. She's supported me not just simply with her words, but with actions too. Thank you, Mom, for always helping me reach the stars. It means the world.

I owe a special thank you to Melanie Harlow and Jenn Watson. Without your guidance and support, I wouldn't have these brand-new book covers for the series.

To Corrine, Kristen, and Alexis, thank you a million times over! You've made me confident in my storytelling, more than I could've ever been without you. Thank you for all the hours you've spent reading, helping me with my cover, and so much more. You ladies are amazing!

Tammy, I owe you so much gratitude for assisting me with your legal expertise! I appreciate you taking the time to help. This book and I owe you!

Lastly, to my husband and my kids, thanks for putting up with my hours on the laptop. Hopefully I make you proud.

Within every heartbeat there's a story

For Lilian, a love of writing began with a love of books. From Goosebumps to romance novels with sexy men on the cover, she loved them all. It's no surprise that at the age of eight she started writing poetry and lyrics and hasn't stopped writing since.

She was born in Azerbaijan, and currently resides in Long Island, N.Y. with her husband, three kids, and a dog named Gatorade. Even though she has a law degree, she isn't currently practicing. When she isn't writing or reading, Lilian is baking or cooking up a storm. And once the kids are in bed, there's usually a glass of red in her hand. Can't just survive on coffee alone! Lilian would love to connect with you!

Email: lilanharrisauthor@gmail.com
Website: www.lilanharris.com
Newsletter: https://bit.ly/LilianHarrisNews
Signed Paperbacks: https://bit.ly/LHSignedPB
Facebook: www.facebook.com/LilianHarrisBooks
Reader Group: www.facebook.com/groups/lilianslovlies
Instagram: www.instagram.com/lilianharrisauthor
TikTok: www.tiktok.com/@lilianharrisauthor
Twitter: www.twitter.com/authorlilian
Goodreads: https://bit.ly/LilianHarrisGR
Amazon: www.amazon.com/author/lilianharris

11713640R00152